NORTHERN LIGHTS

DEBRA DUNBAR

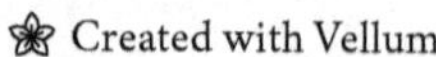 Created with Vellum

PROLOGUE

Long ago, when our ancestors had just begun to fish the waters and hunt the land, the Sun came to walk among the humans. He was tasked by the Creator to ease the lives of men, to fight back the darkness that threatened to engulf the world each night. The Sun warmed the waters and touched the ground. Where he walked, green grass grew to feed the animals. Where he swam, fish thrived.

The Sun was lonely. He missed his brothers and sisters in the sky. One evening as he strode toward the sea, he happened to look behind him and saw the most beautiful of sights. It was Moon, walking in all her silver glory. Hers was the only light in a spreading night, white and pure, but cold and harsh. She was the enemy, the bringer of the darkness, but sometimes there is love between those who should only have hate toward each other.

Their love was forbidden, two beings of the sky, each destined to remain forever apart. At dusk, the Sun would turn his face to see her along the horizon. At dawn she would do the same to watch him. His heart yearned to be closer to her, but he could not disobey the Creator's orders.

The Moon was not so obedient. She began to walk faster, leaving the night behind and entering the day, where her light weakened. She didn't care. All she wanted was to catch the Sun and hold him in her embrace. The Sun watched her approach, happy as she made her way closer to him each night.

And one day they met. The Moon enveloped the Sun, plunging the world into darkness. The Sun knew it could not last, but savored every moment that he and the Moon were together. Too soon the Moon needed to continue on. She was of the dark, and he was of the light. Their love could only last a brief moment in time, for if they were together forever, the world would freeze and die.

But the Moon loved the Sun so much she gave him the gift of a child before she journeyed back into the night. It was *their* child, a baby of both lightness and dark. The Sun felt his heart nearly burst at the gift, but he knew he could not keep this child of their love, for such was forbidden.

With sorrow in his heart, the Sun came to a wise man among the humans. "Can you take care of my daughter for me? Can you raise her to be strong and kind? Can you protect her from both the darkness and the light, keeping her safe for all eternity? She is the perfect image of love between the Sun and Moon, and her life is more precious to me than any other."

The wise man took the baby and agreed to raise her as his own. He and all of his descendants would cherish and protect the girl until that day came when the Sun and Moon could embrace once more, and a child of darkness and light would be welcome in the heavens.

CHAPTER 1

AHIA

"That guy stole a shot glass."

Jess rolled her eyes, her thumbs still lightning fast on her cell phone. "Who cares? They're ninety-nine cents. Free, if they've got one of those cruise ship coupons."

I cared. There were rules that were made to be broken, and those that were to be followed. Stealing food, medicine, a warm blanket were all okay in my book. But a shot glass? Who the hell needed to steal a shot glass? This was just some punk-ass kid looking for a thrill or thumbing his nose at "the man."

I should know. I'd been watching punk-ass kids grow up for five thousand years. I'm sure at one point I'd been a punk-ass kid. Heck, I probably wasn't too far from one now.

"We're supposed to care. That's why they pay us the big bucks."

Jess snorted. "Then you go take care of it. I'm one text away from the end of my shift."

I watched the guy, boy actually, as he ran his fingers across a stack of postcards and meandered with excessive casualness toward the door.

"Hey!"

The guy blinked as I suddenly appeared before him. Jess wouldn't have looked up from her phone for anything, and none of the tourists in the store were paying the slightest bit of attention to me.

"I saw you take that shot glass." I extended a hand toward the guy for the stolen item.

He smirked. "I put it back."

"No. You didn't."

The smirk grew into a full-on grin. "This shot glass?" He brought his hand to the front and bounced the item a few times on his palm before shoving it down the front of his pants. "Come and get it, baby."

Just to make sure I got the creepy sexual innuendo, the guy jiggled his pants. They were tight enough that I could see the bulge of the shot glass right against the bulge of his manhood. Lovely. Just lovely.

Any other employee would have let him walk. Heck, any other employee would have done like Jess and just ignored the whole thing. But I hated when people broke the rules—especially stupid, cocky, slimeballs like this.

He wanted me to come and get it? Fine. I reached out and grabbed the guy's crotch. His grin froze in place, his eyes widening. Then I sent a small surge of energy right into his pants. That's all it took. The glass shattered. He shrieked soprano. And it was my turn to grin. "Know what? I think I'm gonna let you keep that shot glass."

He scurried out the door and my moment of satisfaction quickly faded. My temper always seemed to get the best of me. Like Jess had said, it was a ninety-nine cent shot glass that the owners gave away free to get cruise-ship tourists into their store—a store filled with imported crap that had pictures of bears and moose, every last item emblazoned with 'Alaska' in bold letters.

It wasn't just that I'd employed excessive violence in the punishment of what wouldn't have amounted to even a misdemeanor that bothered me, it was my increasing impatience with humans. As well as werewolves, if I were to be perfectly honest.

The door chimed and I looked up to see four brawny men enter the shop, one a wall of muscle, dark hair escaping from a knit cap, a neatly trimmed beard lining his jaw. "Emasculate another one, Ahia? What did this one do, ask you out for dinner?"

I couldn't help the smile curling up the edges of my mouth as I walked over. These were my guys, part of my pack, and I felt understandable feelings of affection and protection whenever they were near. The fact that one of them was the Alpha didn't change that. "He stole a shot glass, Brent."

"Whoa, that's a hanging offence where I come from."

"Surprised you didn't kill him for that one."

"You gonna hunt him down later and slit his throat?"

Tough talk from the peanut gallery. I'd known all of them since they were in diapers. I'd known their parents and grandparents and great grandparents since *they* were in diapers, but for now, at this point in our life, we all seemed somewhat close in age. Peers. Friends. Mine. Mine to care for, although according to pack law they were the ones who were supposed to protect and care for me—for all of eternity.

"Seriously, Ahia. He was clutching his junk. I smelled blood. You can't do that," Brent scolded.

It was strange getting a lecture from a man I'd seen poop his pants and eat strained peas what felt like yesterday. It always seemed strange. But he was right. I couldn't keep doing things like this. And I *was* embarrassed by my display of temper and extreme measure of justice, although I wasn't about to let these werewolves know that.

"He'll think twice before he shoplifts again." And he probably won't be enjoying sexual relations, either with his hand or another person for a few weeks at least. "I didn't do any permanent damage. Just a few little cuts, that's all."

"Now all he has is a broken shot glass in his pants and a bloody cock, which sounds very British." Zeph grinned and my mood took a more positive turn. Of all the werewolves, Zeph was the most likely to approve of my hijinks.

Brent sighed and draped an arm around my shoulder, improving my mood further. He might be the Alpha, but we were still best friends. Once, when he was younger, I'd thought we could be more. Over the ages, I'd taken lovers only to watch them grow old and die in the blink of an eye. It was easier to keep things casual, but with Brent I'd let my fantasies of a lifetime mate, of children, fill my thoughts. Nephilim were supposed to be especially fertile, and although thousands of years of lovers had never once ended in pregnancy, I still had hopes.

Foolish, stupid hopes born of loneliness. It wouldn't have been fair to Brent to tie him to my peculiar brand of crazy, to have a mate that wouldn't age with him, that might never give him the children he so wanted. Our affair had been brief, the transition to best friends easier than it should have been. He went on to see other women, where I'd vowed to keep my legs together for a few centuries at least.

"There's a problem up north. It's out of our territory, in the area claimed by the Swift River Pack. They asked for you."

His words filtered through the miasma of affection, regret, and, I'll admit it, lust. Hey, he was a good looking guy, barely into his mid-forties. A girl could still admire, even if that ship had long since sailed.

"What is it this time?" Lately rifts had been opening around the state, swallowing up humans and spitting forth monsters. I was the only being who could see the rifts, and to my frustration I was unable to do anything about them. The monsters I could do something about. All three Alaska packs had jumped in to help eliminate these trespassers, partnering with humans to get the job done, but sometimes there was a monster beyond a werewolf's ability to kill. That's when I stepped in.

I was a Nephilim. Which meant I had special powers and was damned near indestructible. Plus, I had this irrational sense of protectiveness that encompassed the humans, the werewolves, the flora and fauna, the rock and dirt and ice of the land itself. They were my responsibility, and drop bears, manticores and chimeras weren't going to take or damage one hair on their chinny-chin-chins. That protectiveness made me dangerous, it made me fight with a berserker fury. I was their last line of defense, and nothing defeated me. Well, sometimes things defeated me, but I just reassembled all my limbs, rose from the dead and went back at it until I eventually won.

"We've got a hydra. It killed two of the Swift River Pack and disabled one—possibly permanently. It's taken out two boats of fishermen, as well as Old Man Bufont who was out in his canoe."

I tamped down the blinding anger roaring through me. Werewolves dead. Humans dead. Old Man Bufont, who I'd known since he was a squalling baby, dead. Fucking hydra. Damned motherfucker. Not in my Alaska. This thing was so going down.

"Hope they didn't cut off any of the heads," I said, trying to keep my voice calm. I was evidently unsuccessful because there was a spark of unease in Brent's eyes, quickly hidden. His arm dropped from around my shoulder.

They were afraid of me when I was like this. I was their greatest weapon, their best defense, their Nephilim, but

Brent had once explained that when I was angry I lost anything that was human in me. Angry, I became other-worldly, more angel than human.

"No, they did their research. It's got three heads, and venom, and has taken up residence in Martin Lake."

Pretty far north, but it would have to be for the Swift River Pack to be involved. No matter. I could fly, and I didn't mean by shapeshifting into a hawk. I could do that too, but I was faster just using the wings that had unexpectedly appeared from my back a few millennia ago, wings that I was able to hide and summon at will.

"Tell them I'll take care of it. Let me just grab my purse."

I gathered my stuff and clocked out while Brent and Drew looked over the T-shirts and Alaska-themed boxer shorts. Zeph and Nick were busy flirting with Jess who had abandoned her text conversation to lean over the counter, giving the werewolves a nice view down the neck of her shirt. The guys were such hoes'. Not that I had any room to talk. Relationships with humans were common here where the locals knew about the werewolves and lived in harmony with the pack. I'd done my fair share of fraternizing with the humans myself. I'd done my fair share of booty-calls with the werewolves too.

"See you Tuesday," Jess called to me, leaning farther over the counter.

I was so busy paying attention to them that I almost missed the crack in the six-foot-wide space between the cabinet full of antler jewelry and leather pouches. It was a jagged lightning-shaped slash that sparkled like it had been doused with glitter.

Oh no. Not another one, and right here in the store too. I froze, my eyes fixed on the rift, poised to attack anything that came through and defend my co-worker and pack members.

Nothing came through — yet. I cast a quick glance around the store to make sure no one was watching, then edged closer to the slash of light. It was big enough to walk through, if I'd been suicidal enough to entertain such a thought.

Well aware that I probably looked like a candidate for the insane asylum to anyone watching, I walked up to the rift and touched it. This one was different from the tiny jagged tears that decorated the state like glittering strands of tinsel. It was different than the others that took humans and left monsters in their place. This one felt hot and sharp, like lava with a charge of electricity. A discordant note hit my ears, one that only I could hear. Red. Orange. Augmented fourth.

I took a few steps backward, tensing as it pulsed, yellow light forcing its way through the rift. And then it was gone. I stuck a finger into the air where it once was and felt nothing.

These rifts were getting worse, and now one had opened up right in the store where I'd worked. I was only one Nephilim. If hundreds of these opened across Alaska, I wouldn't be able to kill the monsters fast enough. I wouldn't be able to protect those that called this area home.

I'd swallowed my pride a few weeks back and asked for help. As much as I feared what that help would be and what it might mean for my continued existence, I knew when I was in over my head. And my life meant nothing compared to the humans and werewolves that lived here. If I died, so be it. As long as the humans and the werewolves continued on, loved and protected, I'd gladly sacrifice my life.

CHAPTER 2

RAPHAEL

"Alaska? You can't be serious."

I stood beside my eldest brother, the Ancient Revered Archangel Michael, next to the gateway to Hel in the ruins of what had once been a mall in Columbia, Maryland. Technically I was Ancient and Revered as well. Technically. Angels rarely attached those prefixes to *my* name.

"When have I *not* been serious? Yes, Alaska."

Micha seemed to have found his sense of humor over the last two years, after an imp had stolen his heart. He was still the perfect straight man, though. Not as stick-up-the-ass as Gabe, but pretty darned close. At least, compared to me.

"Why? These rifts are opening up everywhere. Alaska is in the middle of nowhere. Hundreds of them could open up and it wouldn't matter. Why is Alaska a priority over, say Paris? Or Amsterdam? Or a nude beach in Cannes?"

Micha shot me a puzzled frown. "I have not heard of any rifts opening at a nude beach in Cannes."

Neither had I, but I'd rather go there than some mountaintop in Alaska.

"Normally I would assign this a lower priority," Micha

continued, "but the guardian angel there was quite insistent. I originally told him he'd need to wait, but when he said a rift had opened up dangerously close to the gateway to Hel, I reconsidered."

I sucked in a breath, equally alarmed at the idea. We archangels had created seven major gateways to Hel, spread throughout the world. They were stable, able to withstand just about anything that humans or nature could throw at them. Well, except a nuclear bomb, that is. After the humans had inadvertently destroyed one of our gateways decades ago with their testing we'd relocated it to a more remote area — on top of a mountain in Alaska. An interdimensional rift colliding with a gateway would have the same disastrous effect as a nuclear bomb. Probably worse. It would be horribly embarrassing if one of our gateways exploded and took out the upper third of the continent. Very embarrassing.

"Why me? Send Gabe. Or some other angel. Closing rifts isn't really my strength."

"I know. Trust me, I wouldn't send you if anyone else was available."

That was pretty darned insulting, but I was used to it. It wasn't that Micha doubted my abilities even though I was the least powerful compared to my three remaining siblings. Micha, as well as the others, doubted my dedication, my ability to focus on the task at hand, my ability to take anything seriously.

I cared. I really did care. It's just that my brothers always seemed to assign me the most boring tasks, and there was always something more interesting going on nearby. Absolutely not my fault.

And he was right. I probably *would* muck this up. "Send Chialiel. He's looking to advance. He'll jump at the chance to do this."

Sycophant. If that angel got any more up Micha's ass, he'd need to do penance for sodomy.

"I can't send Chialiel. I need an archangel in case that rift opens too close to the gateway. I need someone with the skill to stabilize it and make sure it doesn't detonate. That's you."

There were other archangels, but Gabe was struggling to hold Aaru in the face of rebellion, Micha had his hands full leading the Grigori, and Uriel was on a pilgrimage and basically off the grid. It seemed I was the only one left.

"Fine. I'll go to Alaska, close these rifts and make sure the gateway doesn't go boom."

Micha gave me a stern look. "No getting the guardian drunk, or running off to hunt polar bears with the werewolves, or rappelling naked down the side of a mountain. I mean it, Raphael."

He did mean it if he was calling me by my formal name. I held back the eyeroll and gave him my most serious expression. "Yes. All business. I promise."

My brother eyed me then sighed in resignation. "You'll need a demon to partner with."

I hid a grin. "Sam? Can I have Sam?"

There was a very intentional change in my vibration pattern — a change angels got when they were thinking very naughty thoughts. I had no plans to lure my brother's imp of a lover out of his arms and into mine, but I enjoyed teasing him. Micha didn't have a jealous bone in his manifested body except when it came to her friendship with me. Sam and I were buddies, but I got the feeling Micha often wished me as far away from her as possible. Which probably had something to do with this assignment in Alaska.

"No, you cannot have my Cockroach," Micha scowled. "The pair of you are like a flame and dry tinder. With the two of you together I don't need to fear a rift exploding the gateway, you'd do it on your own."

"Fine." His fears were not unfounded. Sam was chaos incarnate and an imp, and I was…well I was probably the least angelic angel in Aaru. I still hadn't grown used to an imp on the Ruling Council, or of demons who had diplomatic immunity and were free to walk among us. After so long apart, it seemed we were finally coming together.

I reached out and touched the gateway in front of me, one of the seven that led to Hel — the land of the demons, the land where nearly three million years ago we'd banished half our angels after a bloody war. Recently there had been a battle between a demon and two angels that had demolished the mall, but thankfully left this gateway undamaged.

"So are you keeping this one here?" I asked Micah. "It seems like an odd place, in the middle of the shopping mall. I figured you'd take the opportunity to move it somewhere more remote."

"I have been overruled. It seems the consensus is that a shopping mall *is* the perfect place for a gate to Hel," Micha drawled. "I put forward the idea of relocating it only to be informed that the only acceptable options would be the Prime Outlets in Hagerstown or the casino in Anne Arundel County."

I stifled a laugh. "You are so whipped."

"No, I have not yet been whipped." He kicked a piece of concrete with his toe. "Not for lack of her trying, though. I've been offered that delightful experience numerous times but have so far managed to decline."

"I expect I'll be seeing you with whip marks sometime this month?"

"Yes, probably so." He shrugged, shooting me a sheepish grin. "She does tend to talk me into things."

Totally whipped. It made me jealous. Not that I really wanted someone whipping me, though that did sound like a fun experience. I was jealous of the closeness Micha and Sam had. I was jealous of the bond they had, that they'd each found their match, their perfect other, the one who complimented and completed them. Micah was six billion years old. He was double my age. Would I need to wait another 3 billion years to find what he had? Would I ever find what he had? There were times when I felt I was destined to always be alone — the crazy angel, the one who wasn't fully an Angel of Order, but not quite an Angel of Chaos either.

"I'll leave this afternoon. I'm assuming you'll send some decently skilled demon to assist me?"

Otherwise there wasn't much use in my going. I could close the rifts, I just couldn't see them. These projects required two — a demon to locate the rifts, and an angel to close them. If Micha didn't have an available demon to send with me, I'd need to wander around the state, hoping to stumble blindly into one of the rifts. Alaska was a big state. That could take decades. And from what he said, we didn't have decades.

The glance my brother sent my way wasn't reassuring. "I'll get you one. Who, I don't know. Maybe that information demon. She's proven useful. She's a little odd, but I think you would get along with her."

Why did that sound like Micha was setting me up on a blind date? "Whatever. Just make sure one shows up tonight, otherwise I might have to occupy myself with body-shots, skinny dipping in the glacier lakes and wrestling walruses."

That got a laugh out of my normally staid brother. "Times like this I wonder how you ever were designated an Angel of Order, Rafi."

It was something everyone else, myself included, wondered as well.

CHAPTER 3

AHIA

A chill spring breeze tore through the mountain passes, riffling my feathers and nearly knocking me off the rocky ledge. It was gorgeous up here. April meant there was still snow among the trees and patches of brownish-green grass below. There was ice rimming the edges of lakes and rivers, along with a glorious bite in the crisp air. But spring was marching across the north, causing hardy flowers to bloom like splashes of color in the snow, and gifting the trees with golden-green buds.

Martin Lake was a mile away as the crow— —or in my case Nephilim— —flies. It was huge, a dark greenish gray with a surface that reflected light like sea-glass in the afternoon sun. Even at this distance I could clearly see the hydra prowling close to the shore, and the twisted hull of a fishing boat floating nearby. Wings weren't the only perk of being a half-angel, but super-sight wasn't really necessary when a big, multi-headed monster bobbed above the water.

My pack helped to control the chimeras that were crossing through into Chichagof Island, but I'd told them as well as the Alpha of the Swift River Pack that killing this hydra had now become my sole responsibility. Two of them were already dead and one quite possibly lame for the rest of her life — and werewolves were legendary for their ability to quickly heal any wound. Luckily I was built of sturdier stuff. The werewolves might be descended from Nephilim, but I was first generation and thus harder to injure. And based on all the things that had happened to me in the last five thousand years, I had a strong hunch that I was immortal.

There. The hydra was finally in a position where it wouldn't see me coming. I'd need to fly fast and be ready so I dropped the pack from my back and dug out my supplies, wishing that being a Nephilim meant additional limbs. I could really use a few extra hands right now.

Stepping off the cliff I fell, holding my wings tight to gain speed. About fifty feet from the ground I spread them outward, feeling muscles strain as I transferred my downward momentum into lateral. By the time I hit the hydra I was ten feet from the water and moving at roughly forty miles per hour. I plowed into the creature, snapping my wings backward before hiding them safely in the ether. I'd learned the hard way that they were my most vulnerable spot. A bite there would disable the wing for weeks and probably end with me drowning.

I wouldn't die, but it would be most unpleasant as well as embarrassing. The werewolves would never let me hear the end of it. I'd drowned, I'd crashed into the side of a mountain, and one time I'd fallen three hundred feet into a crevasse. I'd been mauled by a grizzly — which seemed to happen at least once a year. Grizzlies didn't like me. They didn't like werewolves either, but I seemed to be on the top of their shit list.

It took the hydra seconds to recover. After slamming into the side of the creature, I'd quickly wrapped my arms around one of the heads, holding tight to my supplies. It thrashed and bucked like a rodeo bull nearly giving me whiplash. Somehow I managed to hold on, container of Morton iodized salt in one hand, obsidian knife in the other. This better work. The textbook way to kill a hydra was to have one person cut off a head, then the other cauterize the wound before it sprouted two more. Rinse and repeat. There was a problem with that method. I didn't have either Hercules or another Nephilim to help me and I wasn't about to risk a werewolf life. I thought once more about the assistance I'd requested. Of course, whoever they sent would be just as likely to kill me as this hydra.

The creature realized it wasn't going to dislodge me and dropped the head I was riding down low, snapping at me with the other two. I'd read somewhere that hydra have nine heads. This one thankfully had three. I wasn't sure if my resource was in error, or if that meant this was younger than others. All I knew was that I was grateful. Having two heads trying to take a chunk out of my flesh was two more than I really wanted to deal with, eight would have made this task impossible.

This was the moment when I needed more than two hands. I gripped the thing with my legs, slashed with the knife and frantically tried to get the metal spout on the salt container open without dropping the darned thing. Finally, I gave up and opened it with my teeth, making it all the more difficult to defend myself against two snapping heads.

It bit me. It hurt. Then I didn't feel anything at the wound. Before my whole arm went numb and the salt fell from my hand, I managed to pour half the container into the gaping hole where a hydra head had once been. It screamed, then bit me a few more times while I tried to hold on with one arm, the other numb and useless.

Right before my eyes three heads grew from the salted neck. Damn it all, this wasn't going to work. I let go and tried to hold on with my legs, using my one working arm to stab the thing with the knife. The three brand-spanking-new heads twisted around to latch onto my shoulders and waist, sending venom through my body. My heart stopped. My lungs seized. The hydra shook me like a rag doll and threw me onto the shore where I bounced across boulder-sized rocks and crashed into the trunk of a pine tree.

My last thought before my brain shut down was that I needed help. I seriously needed help. And I needed the help of someone with more skills and power than a werewolf.

* * *

"I NEED HELP. As in right now, not next month, not next week. Now."

Nisroc eyed me in astonishment. His light brown wings expanding as he walked over and stuck a finger against my cheek. "What in all of creation happened to you?"

"Hydra." I was having to articulate carefully because my whole body, including my mouth, was swollen. I'm sure I looked like an over-inflated parade balloon. Evidently hydra venom isn't as easy to metabolize as rattlesnake.

Nisroc nodded, as if my answer clarified everything. "I asked for help. They'll send someone either today or tomorrow, probably a minor angel along with a demon. Evidently closing these rifts is a team activity."

Nisroc was a minor angel, a gate guardian. I know he lacked the skill to close the gateways because he was the first one I'd turned to for assistance. Whatever minor angel they were sending, he or she had to be of a higher level than Nisroc.

The gate guardian had become somewhat of an honorary pack member after a rocky introduction to the area. The heavenly host had decided in their infinite wisdom to put a gateway to Hel on top of Devil's Paw, the nose-bleed high mountain peak of the range separating this section of Alaska from Canada. Used to having autonomy and independence from the angels that few packs enjoyed, the werewolves bristled at the arrival of an intruder. Eventually we'd all come to an understanding—and part of that understanding was that Nisroc kept my secret. It was a task he'd taken on with surprising enthusiasm, becoming a sort of affectionate, over-protective uncle.

Well, *I* thought of him as an uncle. It had become clear within seconds of meeting him that the gate guardian had other feelings for me. He'd never openly declared anything but friendship, and hadn't made any moves on me, but from the way he looked at me, the way he occasionally brushed against my wings with his shoulder, I knew he wanted more than friendship. It was weird. My whole life I'd been told angels would kill me on sight and the first one I meet in five thousand years had a schoolboy crush on me. It made me wonder if the danger was greatly exaggerated. Maybe there never had been a cause for me to fear angels. Maybe things had changed in five thousand years and up here in Alaska we hadn't gotten the memo. Either way, it was clear I had nothing to fear from Nisroc beyond some sappy looks and the occasional bossiness.

"You do realize this means you'll have to go into hiding. No tourist-shop job. No drinking with the werewolves at the Fjord. No leaving your house. In fact, I think you should stay in the basement of your home for a few months, just to be safe. I can bring you food."

Did I mention bossiness? Nisroc seemed about as dangerous as a kitten. I wasn't convinced another angel would rip me apart even if he *did* somehow discover my presence. Still, it would be wise to lay low, just in case.

Although I wasn't about to cloister myself to the degree this angel was mandating.

"I'm not losing my job, Nisroc. And I'm not hiding in my basement. I'll stay out of the way. I won't fly around the glaciers, I won't visit you up here, but I'm going to live my life."

The angel scowled. "No shape-shifting. Or using any energy at all. I don't know who they're sending but some angels are very good at sensing that sort of thing. He can't know you're here. I still think it would be best to stay in your basement. I'll check on you to bring you food. I'll make sure you're safe. I'll protect you."

I rolled my eyes. Whoever the Ruling Council sent would be busy running around closing rifts, and hopefully killing that hydra. Plus, if they were bringing a demon, they'd have their hands full. I'd never met a demon, but I heard they broke a lot of rules. I wasn't big on rule-breakers, and I was pretty sure angels felt the same. I could break the rules, but I really didn't like it when others did. Actually the thought of a demon in my Alaska gave me far more anxiety than the thought of an angel here. Someone better keep a tight leash on that thing, or I would have to come out of my hidey-hole in the basement and open up a whole can of whoop-ass on its leathery wings.

"I mean it, Ahia." Nisroc shook a finger at me. 'Lay low. I'll be very upset if you're found out."

I knew he'd most likely lose his life if he had to defend me, and defend me he would. I knew that, and it made me more sympathetic toward his excessive paranoia. "Fine. I'll stay in Juneau and remain in human form. But I'm working, and I'm still hanging with the werewolves. And I'm still going to drink beer at the Fjord."

He grunted in reluctant agreement. "I'll need for you to give me a map of where the rifts are, plus the location of the creatures, and I'll make sure I pass it along to whoever the Ruling Council sends."

It was a good idea. Nisroc had assured me that the angel-demon duo would be able to find the rifts, but this would be quicker. Alaska was huge, and I didn't want them to accidently miss any and have to come back. And I wanted to make sure they killed that hydra.

Actually, *I* wanted to kill the hydra. I owed that thing, not just for my wounds but for the deaths of two werewolves and over a dozen humans. I'm sure an angel would be able to take care of something so minor as a hydra without breaking a sweat, but I still wanted a piece of the action.

Oh well. Can't always get what you want.

"Will do. I'll put together a map and a list. Meet me at my house tomorrow morning and I'll give it to you."

Nisroc nodded, then grabbed me into a hug, his wings closing around me like a second set of arms. For a second the hug seemed to cross the line, then the angel stepped back, still holding my hands and giving me a quick, chaste kiss on the forehead.

"Please be careful, Ahia. Be careful until this angel leaves. I...I don't know what I'd do if something happened to you. You make this whole ghastly assignment bearable. You are the moonlight in a dark night. This angel can't know you are here."

He'd always been over-protective, but this came uncomfortably close to a declaration of love. The only time I'd heard him this worried was when an archangel and some demon had come through town a few years ago and I'd had to leave to hide up in Fairbanks. "I thought you said the Ruling Council was sending a minor angel? I know I'm no match for one, but surely I'll be safe from detection by a minor angel."

Nisroc gave my hands a squeeze then let go. "I just have a

bad feeling about the angel they're sending. I worry he might take you from me."

I smiled at him. Silly old fool. "Take me where? Alaska is my home. And if this angel does somehow manage to discover me, I'll win him over with my incredible charm, just as I've done with you."

The angel shook his head. "That's what I'm afraid of," he muttered.

CHAPTER 4

RAPHAEL

There were worse things in the universe than being sent to Alaska. Ruling Council meetings. Guarding the gateways to Hel. Chasing down demons. Dealing with the stupid pig-headed rebels in Aaru. I kept trying to tell myself that as I stood up on top of this isolated, snow and ice encrusted mountaintop, trying to keep myself from being blown into Canada by the powerful wind gusts. Why couldn't this have been going down at a nude beach in Cannes? Why?

Although it *was* breathtakingly beautiful up here in Alaska. Cold — even in April with spring flowers breaking through the remaining patches of snow, but beautiful. The best thing about this area was that the vast expanse of uninhabited land meant I could fly without freaking out the humans. That wasn't something I could do on a nude beach in Cannes. See? Always looking on the bright side, that was me.

Actually I didn't mind freaking out the humans by flying around in front of them, but then word would get back to Micha and Gabe and they'd chew me out, subjecting me to some mind-numbing lectures about responsibility and positive evolution or some crap like that. Here…I got the feeling that Alaska was a place that kept her secrets, that if I flew through downtown Juneau, or dive-bombed a cruise ship with spitballs, the locals wouldn't say a word. Okay, yeah, the place had its appeal. Add in nude sunbathing on a glacier and a beer bong and I'd be completely sold.

"Where is the demon?" The gate guardian asked me, breaking me out of my plans to liven things up here a bit. Nisroc. That was his name. Guardians might be at the very bottom of the rung in the angelic hierarchy, but watching one of the seven major gates to Hel was a critical job. It was also a tedious and boring job that no angel wanted to do. The humans had built cities around some of the gates, providing those guardians with some form of entertainment beyond killing the occasional demon trespasser, but this particular guy had the worst of a bad assignment.

Devil's Paw. Only Gabriel would think it a good idea to locate an angelic gate at the top of a remote mountain that separated Alaska and Canada. Aesthetics were paramount to my brother, even if the poor guardian that spent a century watching the gate got to see nothing but swirling snowstorms and jagged white-capped rocks.

No wonder this guy snuck off to go to town. I didn't blame him one bit. I'd have done the same, probably abandoning my post with far more regularity than this Nisroc did. And nobody would have said a word, either. Well, except for Micha and Gabe, but only if they found out. It was good to be an archangel.

Sometimes.

"I don't have a demon yet. Micha wasn't able to get the one he had in mind and there don't seem to be any others available right now. I tried six that were hanging out at the Iblis' house and none of them could sense the rifts. The one

Low who can is dealing with a unicorn issue. There just aren't enough demons to go around."

It was a funny dilemma. Five years ago we'd slaughtered every demon that came through the gateways, but now we needed them. Hopefully we needed them enough to help soften the hatred and animosity still simmering almost three million years after the war fractured the angelic host in two.

"No demon? But how are you going to find the rifts to close them?"

I gave the guardian my best knowing look. Either I wasn't very good, or he was clueless. I was assuming the former.

"You sent for me. You told the Grigori that there were rifts opening up at an alarming rate across Alaska, that one was dangerously close to the gateway. Clearly you have a demon here who saw these rifts and told you about them. I'll just use him."

The gate guardian shook his head, gold curls bouncing from side to side. "There is no demon here. None. I can't sense the rifts, but there are chimeras, drop bears, yeti, a hydra — all appearing within the last few weeks. It doesn't take a demon to connect the dots."

I watched Nisroc intently, pushing through the words into the tangle of thoughts and emotions behind them. He wasn't lying that I could tell, although admittedly sensing falsehood wasn't my strength. Perhaps I'd been wrong. And if that was the case, we were both screwed. I had no demon. I probably wouldn't be able to get one for months. All I could do in the meantime was fly around the state, killing creatures that came through the rifts and hoping I was lucky enough to stumble upon one on my own.

"Humans are missing," Nisroc continued, as though I needed further convincing. "Just 'poof' missing. A hunting party of twenty vanished last Monday. If the appearance of chimera and a hydra doesn't prove we have a problem, then these disappearances do."

This wasn't Nisroc's job, and he'd been far away from his post if he'd been checking on missing humans, but I wasn't about to report him. There were rules to bend and rules to follow. This whole gate guardian job was one giant rule to bend as far as I was concerned. Although Nisroc would probably never realize how lucky he was that the Ruling Council had sent me here instead of one of my brothers. Gabe would have had a fit that Nisroc had wandered more than five feet from the gate to Hel.

But the whole speech gave me a weird feeling. He wasn't lying, but I'd spent billions of years in Ruling Council meetings, and I knew how easy it was to skirt around an answer with half-truths. Maybe if I pushed this guy a bit, he'd reveal more.

"Are you sure?" My head turned to follow the guardian as he walked back and forth across the frozen snow. "Humans go missing all the time. Maybe they fell into a crevasse, or got lost, or a bear ate them. Maybe these chimera came from some other location and migrated here. I don't want to waste time blindly wandering around Alaska looking for rifts that are halfway across Canada or down in Washington State."

Nisroc snorted. "You're joking. Twenty humans went missing in that hunting party. That many aren't going to fall into a crevasse, and any bear who can eat that many humans in one sitting isn't a being native to this realm. They're gone. And the rifts are here, not over in Canada or down in the lower forty-eight."

Honestly, twenty humans was a pretty big meal for a bear. But the part of Nisroc's speech that got my attention was that he was positive the rifts were here. And then there was one other part of this tale that made me wonder.

"I was told there was a rift that opened close to the gateway. Where is it?"

The angel fidgeted, his gaze sliding off to the side. "It's closed. It was only open for a few hours, but I was concerned. Because, you know, a rift opening near the gateway might blow the whole state up."

It closed. How very convenient. "Were the monsters that came through a threat to the gateway? Did they damage it at all?"

He eyed the gateway, obviously knowing that I could check its structure and tell that no one but possibly a demon had used it in the last fifty years.

"No monsters came through that one," he admitted.

Bingo. "How did you know the rift was here? You can't see them, and there were no monsters appearing from nowhere to clue you in. How did you know?"

"I heard…saw…humans vanished right in front of my eyes. I was sitting here, guarding the gateway, and a whole group of rock climbers vanished."

Such a lie. And I got the impression the lie wasn't actually about who pointed out the rift to him. There never had been a rift near the gateway. He'd lied to get an angel here sooner rather than later, *and* he had to have lied about not having a demon in the neighborhood. It was time for *me* to do some lying of my own.

"I wish I could help you, but without a demon to assist, I'd be wasting my time." I stretched my wings, as though I was getting ready to leave. "If you figure out exactly where the rifts are, let me know. Otherwise I'll be back in a few months with a demon."

"No!" The angel twisted his hands together. "What about the hydra? It's in Martin Lake. At least take out the hydra for me. And if…if I get maps with exact coordinates for the rifts, can you close them without a demon?"

I sighed dramatically. "The hydra is a two-angel job. And

the coordinates have to be exact. I'm not walking around a twenty square foot area, feeling the air like some idiotic mime. If you've got exact coordinates, then I'll stay. Otherwise, I'll see you in a few months."

"We don't have a few months."

The gate guardian was clearly distraught. Poor guy. I had no intention of leaving a hydra or abandoning these humans. Besides, looking like an idiotic mime and trying to take out a hydra single-handedly was better than dealing with the shit-storm in Aaru right now or how much grief Micha would give me if I came back without finishing the job. I also got the feeling Nisroc was covering for this demon due to some romantic feelings on his part. I'm a sucker for romance. If the gate guardian wanted to impress his demon lover by showing him how quickly the Ruling Council responded to his call for help, I'd play along. But first I had to get the dunderhead to actually admit he had a demon tucked away somewhere.

"I'll get the coordinates," Nisroc added. "Tomorrow morning, I'll have them. They'll be accurate within a few feet, I promise."

I created a watch on my wrist, just so I could look at it. "That's too late. I need to *start* tomorrow morning. If you don't have the maps in the next few hours, I'm outta here."

Nisroc shot me a panicked look. "I will. I'll do that. I'll get them. Meet me here in two hours, and I swear by the Creator I'll have the maps for you."

I frowned, as if contemplating whether or not that fit into my amazingly busy schedule. "I can do that. I'll see you in two hours." Actually I planned on seeing him before that. Nisroc was obviously getting these coordinates from someone who could see the rifts — a demon, *his* demon. And whether he knew it or not, this demon was about to be mine on loan for the duration of this project.

CHAPTER 5

AHIA

"I need the maps now. Right now. Detailed coordinates."

I'd never seen Nisroc so anxious. He'd appeared unannounced in the middle of my living room, nearly giving me a heart attack and making me spill my glass of wine.

"What happened to tomorrow morning? And how detailed?"

"The Ruling Council sent an angel, but they didn't have a demon available. He was going to leave and come back in a few months. I convinced him to stay and try to close the rifts by himself, but he needs locations within a foot or two, and he needs them now. I'm meeting him in two hours, and if I don't have the maps, he'll leave!"

Crap. My locations consisted of "A mile north of Elfin Cove and a few yards past the glacier tip," which should have been enough if the angel had a demon that could sense and see the gateways. But GPS locations down to a few feet, and within a few hours? Impossible. Impossible, but I'd somehow have to make it happen. I couldn't wait two months for this dickhead angel to find a demon and mosey his way back to Alaska.

"I've got it." No, I didn't have it, but I'd fake it. I'd get as close as I could on three or four of them, then get the rest to Nisroc tomorrow once I had the time to pull it all together. There was no way this angel could close four rifts by tomorrow afternoon. And if I worked all night, I could get the rest done before lunch.

Eyeing the puddle of merlot on my floor, I grabbed a notepad and fired up the computer, zooming in on a map of Alaska. If I used satellite view to recognize the spot, then did an overlay with a GPS map, I should be able to get coordinates close enough to satisfy this angel.

Nisroc paced while I typed and wrote in the notebook. "Hurry. Can't you go faster than this? I thought you knew where these gateways were?"

"I do know where they are. I can fly you right to them. I just don't know coordinates." Duh. As if I used coordinates to fly anywhere. Like the birds, I used landscape markers and a nifty magnetic sense even most werewolves didn't have.

"Well, maybe you need to start taking note of these things," Nisroc snapped.

Not many beings had the guts to chasten me, but in spite of knowing this angel only fifty years, he commanded the same respect as the werewolf Alpha and the local tribal elders. Part of it came from the fact that he was the only thing beyond the mountains and sea that was older than me. Way older. The angel might look young with his gold ringlets and soft features, but I could tell his creation was somewhere close to the birth of multi-celled organisms.

"I'm sorry," he said in a more modulated tone. Then he paused and came over to me, putting his hands on my shoulders. "It's just that I wanted to do this for you. I wanted to show you that I care, that I take your wishes and desires to heart. I know how important this is to you."

"It's okay." I turned to smile up at him. "I really appreciate that you went out on a limb for me. I can't imagine how difficult it was to get your request heard by the Ruling Council, let alone convince them of its importance. Thank you."

He beamed and I felt something odd, like a warmth against me even though he was only touching my shoulders. It wasn't unpleasant but I didn't particularly want it to continue. The angel looked at me intently, a shadow of longing in his eyes. The warmth increased, as if it were trying to become a part of me.

"Is it hot in here?" I asked. "Do I have the heat up too far or something?"

Nisroc sighed and took his hands from my shoulders. The weird feeling of warmth went away. "Hot in here. Creator grant me patience," he mumbled. Then he shook his head and took a few steps away from my chair. "Can you get this done in time?"

"I've written down two so far. I figure by the time he's done with three or four, I'll have the rest done and you can swing by to pick them up."

He started to pace again. "I'm worried if the angel leaves, we won't ever get him to come back, not even in a few months."

I blinked in surprise. "Is he such an asshole that he'd go off in a huff and refuse to come back? It's not our fault he can't manage to score himself a demon. What a dickhead."

Nisroc nodded in agreement. "I wish they'd have sent someone else. This one...he can do it. He's capable, it's just that he isn't very serious about anything. He'll be likely to close one rift, then spend the rest of the afternoon bowling with drop bear heads or doing free-falls from the mountain cliffs."

Sounded like my kind of guy. "So? Encourage him to do some drop bear bowling tomorrow morning and by the time he's done I'll have all the coordinates for the rifts."

The angel stopped again by my chair. "No, I won't encourage such frivolous and unseemly behavior. For an angel of his status, he should have a much higher vibration pattern. He should be concerned with the enforcement of rules. He should fill his time with his considerable duties and responsibilities as well as striving to obtain a centered state."

Ugh, that sounded horrible. "I don't concern myself with those things, Nisroc. Do you think so poorly of me too?" I was partially teasing, but this angel did have an annoying habit of trying to improve me. Not that he was succeeding.

"No, not at all," he hastily reassured me. "You're young. In time you'll come to realize the importance of these things. With the proper guidance from someone who only wants what's best for you, you'll be able to bring your vibration pattern into a higher state."

Over my dead body. That was so not going to happen. If Nisroc saw himself in the role of my tutor/lover, he needed to take an icy bath in a glacier lake. But before I could argue, the angel tilted his head, a look of dismay coming over his face. Then he picked me up right out of my chair and threw me into my coat closet. I landed in a heap on top of shoes and boots, a cascade of jackets coming off their hangers to fall onto my head. The angel tried to close the door on me, but it jammed against the top of a snow boot.

Through the two inches of open door I saw a flash of light. Shrugging off the parka that had fallen on my head, I leaned close to peek through the opening and saw a second angel in my house, right in front of Nisroc.

CHAPTER 6

My heart thudded with a weird combination of fear and excitement. I'd gotten used to Nisroc and had begun to believe that maybe there wasn't any threat from angels. But old habits die hard and thousands of years of ingrained caution kept me firmly in the closet, hoping that this guy left without discovering my presence.

I'd also become a bit cocky about my abilities and strength over the years. Seeing this angel brought home to me how much of a big-fish-tiny-pond world I lived in. The energy rolling off him was unlike anything I'd ever felt in my life. It reminded me of films of nuclear bombs, where the trees were bent sideways and stripped with the force of the blast. Every hair on my body raised, every cell vibrated. I was acutely aware that this was a being that could kill me with a snap of his fingers. That turned me on as much as it scared me, because yes, I'm that crazy.

Was *this* the angel that the Ruling Council sent? The *minor* angel who was capable, but irreverent and easily distracted? If this was a minor angel, then I didn't want to know what an archangel was like. Against all common sense, I pressed as close to the opening in the door as possible. I couldn't see the angel's wings right now since he'd hidden them. Actually, I kind of *could* see his wings. They were like tracings of gold from his back — there but not there.

As I got a good look at him, I realized something. Wings or no wings, this guy was gorgeous. He had the kind of face that graced advertisements in all the high-fashion magazines. Dark, shoulder-length wavy hair, high cheekbones, angular jaw, defined chin, eyelashes I'd give my right arm for. And his eyes were an odd purple-blue, almost violet. His shoulders, arms, even his chest stretched the fabric of his shirt, and his faded, low-slung jeans did nothing to hide the strength in his thighs and hips. In spite of the very muscular physique that I could clearly make out under the clothing, his face was almost too beautiful. He had to be gay. No guy that stunning could possibly be straight.

Were angels gay? I'd never really thought about it before. Nisroc looked rather asexual in appearance, even though he clearly had some sort of thing for me. But this guy…there was all that power, the gorgeous face, the rockin bod, and something in the curve of his lips that hinted at a playful sort of sexy. Maybe I was wrong, or maybe he *was* batting for the other team. Either way, I wasn't going to find out, because I'd been told my whole life that angels killed Nephilim on sight. That right there ruled out any of the lurid fantasies that were running through my brain at the moment. Even if everyone was wrong and he was no threat to me, he'd hardly want to go frolic in the fields with a Nephilim. No angel with that much power would be interested in little ole me, even if I wasn't half human.

Instead of greeting Nisroc, Pretty-boy looked around as if he were an interior decorator and found my house completely lacking in aesthetics. "Well, that certainly looks like the sort of thing a demon would have in their house."

He was pointing at the line of stuffed heads on my wall and his drawling tone made me puff up with indignation. This was Alaska. Everyone had deer and bear heads on their wall. Mine just included chimera and a manticore. And hopefully would soon include a hydra and some drop bears. Hopefully.

To Nisroc's credit, he didn't even side-eye the closet where I was hidden. "Taxidermy is an acceptable accent in human room décor, especially in this state. It's not been two hours yet. It hasn't even been an hour yet. You said I'd have two hours to get the map."

The angel strolled over to my computer and looked first at the map, then down at the scrawled notes I'd made.

"Yes, I know. Don't worry, you still have two hours. Is this it? I never thought we angels were much in the way of human tech, so your demon must be the one with computer skills."

"I told you, there isn't a demon in Alaska. I don't have a demon anywhere let alone in this house. Now, if you'll excuse me, I need to get back to work. I'll meet you by the gateway at our agreed-upon time."

No, he didn't have a demon in this house, he had a Nephilim. I narrowed my eyes, glaring at the pretty-boy angel. I *wasn't* a demon. The very thought of someone calling me a demon made me want to get my rifle.

In spite of the clear dismissal, the angel didn't leave. "You have someone who is giving you these coordinates — someone I would like to meet. If not a demon, then what? A witch? A sorcerer? An unusually skilled werewolf? This place feels like werewolves and by the way, that watercolor of bears in the river is dreadful."

Fuck him. I'd painted that. And it wasn't bears, it was beavers. Not that he probably would recognize a beaver if it was right in front of his face. And yes, I meant every bit of the sexual innuendo in that.

"Yes, yes. This house belongs to one of the local werewolves. I try to have a good relationship with them. And now, if you'll excuse me…"

Pretty-boy raised an eyebrow. "This project is important enough to you that you begged me to stay, that you're away from your assigned post to work with *someone* getting these coordinates. Demon, talented werewolf, psychic human, whatever. I'll need to borrow him if you want me to close the rifts right now as opposed to in a few months."

I edged away from the closet door, my palms sweating. He couldn't "borrow" me. I wasn't a demon, a werewolf, or a psychic human, I was a Nephilim, the product of angelic sin. As hot as this angel was, as harmless as Nisroc was, I was still a bit worried that an angel would do me harm if he found me out. If Pretty-boy would just go away and let me finish writing down the rift locations, this would all be fine. And by fine, I meant rifts closed and me not dead.

Nisroc looked like a deer in headlights. "There is no demon, werewolf, or psychic human. Please, just let me finish and meet you in an hour. Please."

Pretty-boy folded his arms across his magnificent chest. Biceps bulged. I drooled. It was a testament to my level of crazy that I wanted to crawl all over this angel. Angel. Scary, otherworldly being that might or might not kill me on sight. And I wanted to run my hands, and more, over his naked body.

"Come on, Nisroc, you know as well as I do that you didn't sense those wild gates. You didn't. The werewolves didn't. The humans sure as heck didn't. It has to be a demon. I don't fault you for letting one sweet-talk his way through the gate from Hel and into staying here. I'm hardly the angel to be enforcing the letter of the law. You've got a crisis. I don't feel like flying all over this enormous state with a map, trying to figure out where these rifts are. I need a demon that can see them. You obviously know a demon residing locally that can do so. Stop with the lies and bring him out of the closet. I can promise immunity if the demon assists in the project."

I nearly shit my pants when he said the thing about the closet, but clearly that was a metaphor and not some angelic ESP that there was a Nephilim, as opposed to a demon, in the closet.

Nisroc looked terrified, as if he were having the same fears about angel ESP that I was. "I can't. I don't have a demon in the closet."

The pole holding the coats in said closet chose that moment to fall, raining the rest of the jackets, hats and gloves, as well as hangers down upon me with a crash and whacking me in the head. The door yanked open and I looked up into Pretty-boy's amazing violet-colored eyes, peeking out at him from under a mountain of clothing.

Those dark eyebrows rose. "Thought so. Come out of there."

"You said I'd get asylum or immunity or something. I heard you say that and as far as I'm concerned, that's a contract. We have a contract and if I come out of this closet you won't kill me."

He rolled his eyes. "I said if a demon worked with me to close the rifts, he'd get immunity. Coming out of the closet is the first step in that process, but that action alone doesn't grant you any sort of exception to the rules."

Such an angel. It's not like I had much of a choice though. Maybe it would work in my favor if I did exactly what he said. Beyond that, I wasn't about to face my possible death crouched down on a closet floor with five layers of clothes on top of me. So I pushed them off and stood.

The smug, you-are-so-busted look on Pretty-boy's face became something else. He looked as if he were on the verge of passing out, or maybe he was suffering a catastrophic cardiac event.

"Ack."

That's what the angel said. It was a choking noise which reminded me of the time Sabrina had gotten a chicken bone lodged in her throat. Was something wrong with him? Was 'ack' something in that weird angel language? Was that what angels said before they killed Nephilim?

I looked at Nisroc. Would he defend me? Would we both die?

"I'm not…you…where…?" Pretty-boy was now speaking, which ruled out choking. I eyed his chest, wondering if I dared push him to the floor, jump on him, and rip his shirt off to do CPR. It would totally be worth my death to get my hands on this guy's naked chest and plant my lips on his. Totally worth it.

"I saw her first. I have first suit. You can work with her, but you have to stand aside and let me have my chance."

What the fuck was Nisroc talking about?

Pretty-boy recovered his composure and scowled. "You knew. You knew and you told nobody. You knew and you hid her from the rest of us. Just because you were the first angel to lay eyes on her doesn't give you the right to claim first suit."

And what the fuck was *he* talking about? If they wanted a suit, I knew of a decent rental place in Juneau, but what did I have to do with that? Did closing the rifts require formal attire?

"I'll file a complaint," Nisroc shot back.

Pretty-boy shimmered, glowing a bright white. The energy he exuded increased to the point that I found it hard to stand. Suddenly he was no longer powerful-sexy-playful angel, he was just powerful. And dangerous. Forget Nisroc defending me, would I defend him? I'm embarrassed to admit I wasn't sure.

"A gate guardian, one who is tasked with enforcing the rules of the treaty and delivering punishment to those who break the treaty, will file a complaint that *I'm* not following protocol?"

Nisroc winced. "Please don't. Please don't throw her into Hel. Please don't kill her," he pleaded. "It's not her fault. She doesn't even know."

Yes, don't kill me. And didn't know what?

Pretty-boy shook his head, those violet eyes narrowing. He was still glowing. "You and I will speak about this later," he told the other angel.

I tensed as he swung his head around to face me, unsure if this was the end.

CHAPTER 7

RAPHAEL

I'd expected a demon to come crawling out of that closet. I hadn't in all my wildest dreams ever expected an angel.

An angel. And she was beautiful. Curvy in all the right places with hips that begged for a pair of hands to grip them. She had golden-brown skin and long black hair, dark, almond-shaped eyes and a round, button nose. And she was beautiful beyond the pretty native form she'd assumed. Her spirit-self beneath it all was unique. She didn't have the lofty vibration pattern that Angels of Order aspired to, nor the deep tones of a demon. This angel was dead center, clear and clean as a church bell, enticing as wind chimes in a spring breeze.

And she was watching me with uncertainty in her eyes, tensed and ready, like a dog who expected to fight for its life. It pissed me off, but it pissed me off more that Nisroc had hidden her existence from the Ruling Council. I knew why he'd done it. He wanted her for himself. He said she didn't know what she was. Well, *he* did, and he was keeping silent in hopes of winning her affection before competition moved in.

First suit my ass. He was free to woo her, but he had no right to request first suit. He wouldn't get it either, because from the moment I saw her step out of the closet, I wanted her too.

Three billion years I'd lived. I'd had my fun. I'd enjoyed intimate encounters with both Angels of Chaos and Angels of Order, yet never had I experienced that punched-in-the-gut sensation I'd felt when this angel rose to her feet before me. This Angel of Chaos was not like the ones I'd known before the war had separated our kind. She was so close to the dividing line, almost an Angel of Order. She was that rare angel that straddled both worlds, one that held traits of each. She was just like me, but where I'd been a little bit further on the side of Order, she was clearly a bit further on the side of Chaos.

I could barely wrap my head around it. An Angel of Chaos, right here in Alaska. They'd been banished following the war. They'd gone to Hel to live and interbreed, producing the demons, while Angels of Order stayed in Aaru and became even more entrenched in their rules and restrictive existence. Angels of Order couldn't create without an Angel of Chaos, so there hadn't been an angel birth in almost three million years.

She wasn't that old. She was probably around five or six thousand judging by the tracings of her hidden wings and the energy that flowed from her. Her existence meant an Angel of Order had been having illegal contact with a demon — more than illegal contact. And somehow the naughty angel that sired her had managed to hide her away. For thousands of years an Angel of Chaos had been calling this section of the human world her home, and she didn't even know what she was. That was wrong. That was so very wrong. And it was a wrong I intended to right, no matter how hard Nisroc begged.

"How long have you known she was here?" I glared at

him. He'd lied by omission, helped conceal her. I was barely an Angel of Order, and even *I* felt the gate guardian had committed an unpardonable offence. I should remove him from his post, send him to the head of his choir to atone, but this gateway to Hel was a difficult assignment, and I wasn't *that* much on the side of Order.

Nisroc stepped sideways, trying to angle his body between me and the woman. "About fifty years. When I came here the werewolves were sheltering her. Don't blame them. They don't know either."

Fifty years? "She's got to be at least five thousand years old. Where was she before the werewolves came to Alaska?"

The woman's dark brown eyes sparked, her body shimmering as she straightened her shoulders. "Don't talk about me as if I'm not here. I've been with the werewolves for almost two hundred years. Before that I was with the Tlingit. And before that the Inuit. And before that a group of humans from across the ice. And before that some humans farther south."

The humans had been hiding her too. Did *they* know? Not that it mattered. I looked over at Nisroc, saw his aggressive stance, the flash of silver in his eyes. I needed to talk to this Chaos angel, and talk to her alone, but it was clear the gate guardian wasn't going to leave without a fight. I'd always enjoyed a good fight, but now wasn't the time, especially in front of the other angel.

"Go on back to Devil's Paw and the gate. I'll speak with you later tonight."

He glared. "I'm not leaving you alone with her."

Seriously? Did he *want* me to knock him on his backside? "I won't hurt her. And I'm not asking you to leave, I'm ordering you."

"Don't tell her."

That wasn't a promise I was going to make. Whatever she

thought she was, she had a right to know the truth. I could understand the humans and werewolves not recognizing a young angel when they saw one, but Nisroc knew and he hadn't told her.

"Now. I won't say it again."

"I'm not leaving. I claim first suit. I—"

I turned around to face the gate guardian and flung out a hand. Nisroc vanished, forcibly transported.

I barely had time to take a breath before I felt her jump onto my back. I fell forward, my face smashing into the oak flooring. She gripped my hair, twisting it tight. "Where is he? Where's Nisroc? You better not have hurt him."

Each word was punctuated by my head being yanked up by the hair and my face smashed into the ground. I stifled the urge to laugh. Sassy didn't begin to describe her. Who was this angel and why hadn't she appeared in my life two billion years ago? She was more fun than a basket full of rats.

With a flash of light, I vanished, appearing just behind her.

She spun around, long black hair flying as she jumped to her feet. With an outstretched hand her eyes glowed silver, and I knew what was coming. I grabbed her hand, cycling the electricity in a loop back into her own body.

She yelped, raising the other hand to do the same. This time when I grabbed it, she held back the surge of energy. There was a brief tussle with me holding both her hands tight and dancing out of the way of her kicking feet. I'll admit the whole thing was really starting to turn me on.

"What did you do to Nisroc?" she snarled, giving up on the physical attack.

I shook my head, struggling to restrain myself from reaching beyond her skin to touch her spirit-being. "He's fine. I returned him to the gate before he hit me and wound up being sent back to Aaru in disgrace."

The angel stopped trying to pull her hands from mine and bit her lip. It was oh so sexy. "But *I* hit you."

"I can hit you back. Maybe straddle you and smack your face into the floor a few times, just so we're even."

It was so wrong of me to tease her like that, but I couldn't help it. She was beautiful, and one of the few angels in the last few centuries who'd had the daring to attack me.

"Like hell you will," she snarled.

She was just as sexy angry as when she was biting her lip. I held her gaze, raising an eyebrow. Minutes passed before she dropped her eyes from mine.

"Just don't punish Nisroc. He was only protecting me."

Fierce. Loyal. They were admirable traits, but I couldn't keep from teasing her further. "He's hardly innocent, he's been hiding your existence and leaving his post to come into town. I'm betting he's even been ordering take-out Chinese food."

She winced. "You all dumped him here, away from any other angels, to serve out a hundred-year sentence watching that stupid gateway to Hel at the top of a mountain. The local pack befriended him. When he found out there was a Nephilim in the pack, he chose to keep our secret— my secret. For the last fifty years my pack and I have been more a family to Nisroc than any of you were."

Did she...could she possibly have feelings for that angel? He'd had fifty years to woo her, was it possible he'd won her affections? I felt a stab of panic at the thought. The first angel that had ever stirred my heart and she could possibly have given hers to another. I might be fighting a losing battle, but I was still going to give it my all. The virtues weren't normally my thing, but I was persistent, and confident no matter how slim my chances.

"I won't hurt Nisroc," I promised. Much. I wouldn't hurt him much.

"Or me? If I help you do I get that immunity you promised?"

"Full immunity. And I won't hurt you, either. Unless you're into that sort of thing, then I am completely willing. Whips. Chains. You first, then me. I'll even let you throw me off a cliff. Does that sound fun?"

There was a hint of a smile on her lush, full lips. She tugged to free her hands, and I reluctantly let them go.

"I'm not into the whips and chains thing, although I might take you up on the offer to throw you off a cliff. You're kind of silly."

"I get told that a lot."

There was a moment between us, a second that seemed to last an eternity as we looked into each other's eyes to the spirit-self beneath the flesh. I saw her begin to glow white, the aura of her true self revealed. Then she shook her head and broke the spell.

"When do we start?" she asked.

Start what? My first thought was that she wanted to know when we would begin what I was hoping would be a series of torrid physical encounters, then I realized she meant closing the rifts. Not nearly as much fun. Although, I could make this project fun. That was my special skill — turning boring assignments into exciting adventures. "First thing in the morning. I'll stay here with you, and we can set out at dawn."

Her eyebrows shot up. "Nice of you to invite yourself for a sleepover. Don't they teach you angels any manners up in Aaru?"

I smiled, putting every bit of sexy into it. "For convenience sake, can I please stay at your house?"

Her breathing quickened and she looked abruptly away. "The couch folds out into a bed. You can sleep there. And don't expect me to cook anything special. If I'm making mac and cheese, you'll eat mac and cheese or order yourself a pizza. And pay for it yourself. Got it?"

She was so sexy, I couldn't help smiling at her sass. "Got it. What's your name, hot-stuff?"

She squirmed and blushed. And something else sparked in those dark eyes. By all that was holy, did she…was she *physically* attracted to me? Maybe she didn't have feelings for Nisroc. Maybe I did have a chance. And maybe this was the very angel who would be on board with all those interesting things I'd been eager to try.

"Ahia."

A pretty name. "I'm Raphael." I wasn't about to list all my titles or brag about my position on the Ruling Council. For once it would be nice if an angel actually wanted *me*, instead of using me for a favorable ruling on some matter or to climb a few rungs up the angelic hierarchy.

"So, Pretty-boy, does immunity mean you're not gonna kill me after this is all over, or throw me through the gateway into Hel? Because if you are, I'm definitely not sharing my mac and cheese with you."

Like I'd *ever* kill her or throw her into Hel. Of all the angels in Aaru, I was the one least likely to rat out an Angel of Chaos here in violation of the treaty, let alone do one harm. Others would have immediately thrown her through the gates to Hel, and no angel would have batted an eye if they'd killed her. Angels of Chaos had been banished to Hel, and for one to be here…well, it was a death sentence.

But things were changing. And even if they weren't, I tried to follow the rules as little as possible.

I grinned. "Well then, for the sake of mac and cheese, I vow that I will not kill you or send you to Hel either before, during, or after our project. Does that suffice, Hot-stuff?"

She grinned back, making me feel as if I were on the

verge of something wonderful. Or possibly catastrophic. Often, the two were one in the same.

"Sure does, Pretty-boy."

"So what should we do first? Mac and cheese? Plan our course of attack for tomorrow? Or you give me a tour that ends in you showing me exactly how comfortable this fold-out couch is?"

Again there was that spark of attraction in her eyes — the eyes that did a slow tour of my body before rising to meet mine. "Let's plan out tomorrow. That's why you're here. Might as well get down to work."

Disappointing, but what did I expect? I'd been too fast. Like always I'd pushed things along at breakneck speed and now it was all about business. For now. This project would take some time to complete, and I'd have plenty of time to regroup and try again.

CHAPTER 8

AHIA

I was alone with an angel whose power and looks made me weak in the knees. He didn't regard me as an abomination. He didn't have any intention of harming me. In fact, I was pretty sure his intentions were quite the opposite judging from how he was flirting with me. And yes, he was flirting with me. Five thousand years and I certainly knew flirting when I saw it. Two angels, both interested in me, but where Nisroc made me think of a kindly uncle, Pretty-boy elicited far different feelings.

And down that road lay danger. Normally I'd be running full-speed straight into danger, but for once in my life I hesitated. Yes, I was a weird combination of awed and turned on, but I wasn't going to let this angel get to me. I wasn't going to jump him right here in my living room, ravish the heck out of him, and spend days or weeks working beside him in awkward silence. If hot, sweaty sex with this angel happened, then it happened — eventually, after a reasonable progression of time. I'd only known him five minutes. That was inappropriately soon. Twenty-four hours would be a suitable time to wait. Or maybe two hours. Yes, I'd wait two hours, then do him.

But for now, work. So I straightened my shoulders, walked over to the computer and picked up my notebook. "There are quite a few of these rifts. Do you need particular conditions in order to close them? Noon? Full moon? Is there a priority you assign to these or do you want me to let you know which are the most dangerous to residents?"

I was yammering away like an idiot. Part of me was still awed. Part of me wanted to drag him off to my bedroom. For once, the first part was getting the upper hand. I'd never in all my five-thousand-odd years met anyone who made me this nervous, even the first time I'd met Nisroc.

"Why bears? I mean, I understand the symbolism of the stream. Landscapes evoke a feeling of eternity. They're an unchanging background to a tumultuous existence. And water is meditative, calm and soothing. I prefer the skies, the rush of flying, but I get it. Well, I get everything except the bears."

My brain did one of the vinyl record screech noises. What the heck was he talking about? What had rifts and monsters to do with bears?

"The colors are pleasing. It's an amateurish attempt, but the work clearly has meaning to you if you framed it and hung it on your wall in such a prominent place. A friend painted it? Someone close to you?"

Sweet stars above, he was talking about my painting, standing in front of it as if he were at an art gallery. He had one hand on his hip, the other stroking his chin, his head tilted to the side as he examined the artwork.

"I painted it. I never made any claim to be a professional artist. I did it at one of those drink-and-paint events. And it's not bears, it's beavers."

The look on his face was priceless — a mixture of chagrin and horror. I realized that he'd been trying in some weird, charmingly goofy way to compliment my painting. He'd totally hosed it and was well aware of the fact. I was intrigued to find out how he was going to rebound from this one.

A struggle of emotions ran across his face. "Those are *not* beavers. I mean, seriously? Who in their right mind would think that was a beaver?"

Huh. Artistic sensibility won over polite flattery. "They're beavers. In a stream. I wouldn't expect you to recognize them, given that you've probably never seen a beaver before in your life."

His head snapped around. Those violet eyes had a wicked glint as they met mine. I hadn't expected him to get the innuendo, but he clearly did.

"Oh, I know full well what a beaver looks like." He pointed at the painting, his eyes never leaving mine. "Those, Hot-stuff, are not beavers."

I opened my mouth, one breath from offering to show him my beaver for comparison, then snapped it shut.

"Can we get back to the project at hand?" I went back over to the computer and sat down, fanning my face with the notepad. "We should probably start with the rift near Hoonah on Chichagof Island."

I heard him walk over to me, singing softly. It was that Kenny Rogers song *Islands in the Stream*, only he'd changed it to *Beavers in The Stream*. I was shocked at the bawdy lyrics. Well, not exactly shocked, but I wasn't expecting that sort of thing from an angel. I bit my lip hard to keep from smirking and tried to appear uninterested. Gorgeous. Charming in a goofy, fun way. He was like a naughty little boy — a very powerful naughty little boy. And the attraction was irresistible. Would he really bowl with drop bear heads? Because

I was starting to think Nisroc's accusation wasn't that far off base.

"We've killed three chimeras in the last week," I continued once he'd finished the tune. "The werewolves and I can't keep running over there and tracking them down, not with the growing yeti population in Denali to manage, the hydra in the Martin Lake, and the stupid fucking drop bears near the Bering River. Do you have any idea how much a pain in the ass drop bears are? And I'm still puffy from the hydra bites. That thing almost drowned me."

He was silent for a moment, and I got the feeling he was trying to decide whether to continue ribbing me about my painting or go along with my change of topic.

"Hydra are a two-angel job," he informed me, putting a hand on the back of my chair and leaning over me to peer at the map on the computer screen. He smelled like the crisp, clean air of a mountaintop in spring, and beyond his hand on the back of my chair, I had the odd sensation that he was touching me — that warmth like I'd felt with Nisroc, only unlike with Nisroc, this sent a surge of electricity right up my spine.

"Tell me about it. I tried to cut off a head and pour salt into it, but I lost my salt and then three heads grew back and it threw me into the woods." I turned toward him as I spoke and found his face temptingly close to mine, his mouth turned up, a dimple creasing his cheek. Of course he had a dimple. Of course. Why couldn't they have sent an ugly angel to do this job?

"Maybe we should tackle that first, then the drop bears you seem to be having such an issue with. After that, we'll go to Chicago Island and the chimera."

The urge to touch that dimple, to run my thumb along his lower lip was almost overwhelming. "Chichagof. And the drop bears are just as much of an issue as the hydra. We've already told Fish and Wildlife to put out a warning for the Martin Lake area as well as warned the locals, but these drop bears have to go. They're trapping mink out of season, and they don't even have a license. You have to have a license to trap. All the humans have a license or they get fined, maybe even go to jail. I can't put the drop bears in jail, so I just kill them. Is that okay?"

The dimple got deeper, as did the odd electric feeling of warmth. "I have no personal objection to you killing drop bears. Especially those who are trapping mink without a license."

"Good. They come through the gate faster than I can kill them, though. They're going to affect accessibility of a major tourist hunting spot this year if we don't get rid of them. That's not fair. Human livelihoods often depend on these hunting tours. It's wrong for these drop bears to screw them. Wrong." I had no idea what I was saying at this point. All I could think about was the warmth of him, the weird sensation of every cell in my body coming alive, that damned adorable dimple.

"We will definitely take care of these poaching drop bears and ensure the rift is closed. Highest priority. Drop bears. Then hydra. Then chimera, which, by the way, you have a lovely example of on your wall here. Did you say you killed three? Because you only have the one head mounted. Were the other two mangled beyond the skills of human taxidermy?"

He was making fun of me. And I liked it. His teasing reminded me of the guys in the werewolf pack. It made me feel less nervous. It made me think that perhaps there was a chance of me getting laid in the very near future. Sex with an angel. Did they even have sex? They must. I was living proof of that. And this angel…I got the feeling that sex with him would rock my world.

Chimera. That's what he'd asked me about. "No, Brent has the other two. He delivered the killing blows, so it was only right for him to take the trophy." I couldn't help the pride in my words. Brent was fearless and strong. He was an amazing Alpha. I'd spent generations with the werewolves and he was the best that I'd seen.

"Brent."

I was suddenly cold, like he'd pulled away from me. There was nothing untoward in his voice, but I got a feeling of unease from him. Why? Did he not like werewolves? How could anyone *not* like werewolves?

"He's the Alpha. Our previous one died in a boating accident. As powerful as werewolves are, they're not all that great out at sea. Brent took over younger than most Alphas do, but he's done a great job so far. He's got charisma, is a strong fighter and a good leader. He was amazing to watch with the chimera." Not so much with the drop bears, but it didn't feel right to nit-pick, or to point out the werewolf's failings to an angel I'd just met.

Raphael walked over to the chimera head and stared at it a moment. "Is he your toy? Your lover?"

"The chimera? Ew. Not in this lifetime."

The tension dropped down a notch. "No, Hot-stuff. I mean the werewolf. This Brad guy."

"Brent. We used to be lovers, but not anymore." And now the tension was through the roof. "We're best friends. He's a great guy."

None of that seemed to help. The angel scowled at the chimera head, and for a second I thought he was going to rip if off the wall and punch it.

"I'm sure he is. And Brad goes hunting chimera with you? And drop bears and the hydra too? What else do you do together?"

"Brent." He was jealous. It was adorable. He was jealous of

Brent, even though our brief affair had been over twenty years ago. "He's hunted chimera and drop bears with me, but not the hydra. That one is too much for a werewolf to handle. Other werewolves in my pack were there at the chimera hunt. They all hunt. I change into a wolf and go with them, although I tend to get distracted and wander off if we're trying to track elk or something boring."

He walked back over to me, his violet eyes stormy as he put his hand on my chair once more. "Good. I changed my mind. I want to do the hydra first. Are there any other rifts we need to close, or just the three?"

Just the three. As if that were no big deal. "There are ones here and here," I pointed to the map on the screen. "Nothing has come through those that I'm aware of, but this one took a hunting party of twenty a few days ago. We've marked it with caution tape, but there's always a chance some idiot will go through anyway. Oh, and the one the yeti came through. We definitely need to close that one before the yeti outnumber the humans in the state." Should I mention the rift earlier today in the tourist shop? It closed on its own, so I guess that one wasn't important.

"Then after we take care of the first four, we'll close the others and kill the yeti."

Was he insane? "No! The yeti are cool. They play by the rules, so we leave them alone. They make a nice fish stew too. They're gracious with excellent hospitality. The ones already here are welcome to stay. But the drop bears, the hydra and the chimera have to go. I think we should probably tackle the drop bears first, then close the rifts in that area before heading to Martin Lake and the hydra."

Raphael nodded. "So, first thing in the morning we go kill drop bears, then close a bunch of rifts, then kill a hydra. Then close more rifts, and not kill the yeti. I'm guessing three to four days, then we should do a sweep of the state just to make sure we haven't missed anything. Count on a few weeks at a minimum, more if these rifts keep springing up."

He sounded oddly pleased at the idea of roaming around Alaska, finding and closing rifts for the next few weeks to months. In all honesty, I was pleased too. This had been an annoyance, a worry, but suddenly the whole thing seemed like an exciting adventure. I envisioned us lopping the heads off hydra, having lunch with the yeti, bowling with drop bear heads — all the sorts of things I enjoyed doing that none of the werewolves or humans seemed particularly interested in.

"I've got a few shifts at work that I can't get out of, but other than that, I'm all yours."

That warm, electric feeling was back, and so was the dimple. "And I, Hot-stuff, am all yours."

Holy cow. And he meant it too. What would the fallout be if I actually did have sex with this angel? Several times. Many, many times.

He leaned closer. "Anything else? Or are we free to make mac and cheese. And I definitely need a demonstration of the fold-out couch bed."

The couch bed. My bed. The backseat of my car. Out in the woods. But before we got to that, there was something else. I closed my eyes for a second, gearing up to ask something that had been worrying me since these rifts began opening. "Before you close the rifts, I want to go through and see if I can find the humans that fell in. I want to bring them back."

When I opened my eyes I saw sympathy in Raphael's face. "They're dead, Ahia. Most of these rifts lead to places incompatible with human life."

"How do you know that?" I argued. "If these places support chimera and hydra that seem to adapt to life here just fine, then who's to say humans couldn't do the same in *their* home-world?"

He shook his head. "Even if that's so, they'd have starved, or died of exposure, or been killed by any number of creatures. There's no sense in risking yourself to find dead bodies — even if you *could* manage to find bodies."

Now he was making me angry. Brent had used the same argument. The only reason I hadn't already gone through the rifts was that I knew he and half of my pack would follow. I'd risk my life to bring back human survivors, but I couldn't risk theirs.

"Humans aren't the helpless weaklings that you think. These people that went missing are hunters and hikers, mountain climbers and back-country skiers. They are used to surviving in adverse conditions. They're used to thinking on their feet and coming up with creative solutions to problems. I've seen lost hikers manage for days before someone found them, building shelter from rocks under a ledge and eating berries and starting fires with two sticks. These humans would have rifles, survival packs, hunting knives. They're fit, savvy. They have a chance. And I can't just sit here and give up on them when they could be fighting for their lives, praying that someone would come to save them."

He sighed. "I get it, really I do, but the chance that these humans would have survived is very slim. While you and I are gallivanting around somewhere with twice the gravity and temperatures in the negative triple digits, more rifts will be taking more humans and spitting out more monsters. The best use of our time, the course that will ultimately save and protect the most humans as well as werewolves, would be to close the rifts, kill the monsters and pray those who fell through didn't suffer."

I hated this. Hated it. It was that whole "sacrifice a few for the good of many" argument. He was right and I hated it. The thought of closing the rifts and potentially trapping humans on the other side made me sick, but it seemed a new rift opened every day. Did we really have time to take a few days per rift to try a rescue operation? Would we come back empty handed to find dozens of humans had vanished or been killed while we were trying to save five hikers?

His eyes were intent on my face. "Let's close the ones that haven't taken anyone, but we can take a quick peek through the others. If there's any chance at all that a human could survive there, we'll…I don't know, take a day or two and go look."

"You'd do that?" Brent had forbidden me, and we'd ended up having a huge fight that still rankled, yet this angel I'd just met compromised. And I got the feeling he was doing it not just for me, but for the benefit of human lives too.

He grinned, turning his pretty-boy sexy back into naughty-little-boy sexy. "Well, I'm hardly going to let you go by yourself. And yes, I'll brave high levels of radiation, pits of lava, temperatures that solidify nitrogen, just so that you can sleep at night knowing you did all you could to save your people."

He got me. He really got me. I leaned back in my chair, against his hand, and broke our gaze to look back at the computer screen. He had a sense of humor. He was powerful, but he was capable of levity, of being silly and goofy, of being playful. He was gorgeous. He'd promised not to kill me. He actually cared about humans. I could work with that.

I could fall in love with that. And unlike all the humans I'd cared about in the past, this angel wouldn't age and die right before my eyes. Yes, I could fall in love with him. And I'd no doubt suffer heartache. He flirted with me. I got the feeling he wanted me. But I wasn't fooling myself that an angel would want any more than a fling with a Nephilim. I wanted more than a fling. I wanted so much more than a fling. But sometimes a half-angel had to take whatever the universe offered.

"Thank you. I owe you one."

Again I had that odd sensation of more warmth touching me. Something electric filled the air and from the naughty smirk on his face, I got the impression he was thinking of all sorts of things he could request in redeeming this favor.

"And now it's time for that mac and cheese." I stood and walked past him to the kitchen, feeling overwhelmed by the speed at which things seemed to be moving. I had an angel in my house. He was flirting with me — at least it seemed like he was. How in the world was I going to be able to get any sleep knowing he was out here on my couch, probably naked? Oh, God. Naked. And now as I put a pot of water on to boil and got out a box of mac and cheese, I was envisioning me naked on the couch with him.

"I see you weren't kidding about your choice of food. Mac and cheese. Canned soup. You've got more box dinners than a doomsday prepper in these cabinets."

He'd followed me. I didn't have to look, or even hear his comment to know. I could feel him, sense where he was in my house. It was as if there was a non-physical part of me acutely aware of this angel.

"Nope. I never kid about instant dinners. Tomorrow you can pick from my selection of canned soups, but tonight it's mac and cheese. And if you're lucky, I'll throw some bacon in there."

He came closer, and once again I felt as if he were touching me, sparking every nerve ending, even though he was at least four feet away. "Am I lucky?"

Wow, that question was loaded. Dare I go there? *Why yes, I think I will.*

"Absolutely. Keep going and you won't be sleeping on the couch."

What was I doing? I was so going to go to hell. Angels

probably didn't have normal sex. They probably didn't even have cocks. I'll bet all this flirting was leading up to us playing harps and singing Hallelujah. I was going to go to bed horribly frustrated. Although he had been joking with me about beavers earlier, and there *were* those incredibly lewd lyrics to that song.

"Really? Am I to sleep on the porch then? On the floor? Is there a dog house outside that I'm now supposed to crawl into? Where do you propose that I sleep?"

Oh, that deep, teasing voice of his. I'll bet if I looked at him right now he'd be smiling that wicked little boy smile with that dimple in his cheek. But I wasn't going to look. No looking. Otherwise I would lose the little bit of control I had. Instead I dumped the noodles into the boiling water and swished them around so they wouldn't stick together. Then I dug my colander out from a cabinet. It all gave me time to think, time to slow down my raging libido.

"It depends. Where you bed down for the night depends upon my mood at the time."

"And what do I need to do to ensure you are in an optimal mood?"

Get naked. Do the dishes, preferably while naked. Tell me my painting of beavers in the stream is so amazing it belongs in a museum.

"You're not gay, are you? And does sex involve stringed instruments with you guys? I mean, I'm assuming you're not gay, but you're really pretty, like really-really pretty. And how do you feel about harp music?" That's what came out of my mouth instead.

I heard the rumble of his laugh. "Not a big fan of harps. And gay as in happy, or gay as in homosexual?"

"The latter. Although I'm thinking it might be nice if you were happy."

He was silent a moment, while I stared at the noodles churning in the boiling water.

"Angels are beings of spirit, and we do not have genders. I can appear in a male or female form, but in our spirit-self we are neither."

Okay. Weird, but okay. Still didn't quite answer my question, though. "You look male right now. If you were going to have physical sex with a human, would you choose a guy or a girl?"

"Angels of Order should not lower their vibration levels to indulge in sins of the flesh. Beyond that we're forbidden from having sex with humans, so I wouldn't choose either a guy or a girl."

What a crock of shit. "You might be forbidden, but clearly it happens. I doubt I'm the only Nephilim to be born in the last five thousand years. So if you were going to break the rules and send your vibration levels, whatever they are, into the gutter, would you go for male or female?"

"Neither. And you're not a Nephilim."

I turned to stare at him wide-eyed. "Raphael, I *am* Nephilim. I've been told my whole life that the angels would kill me if they found me. I now wonder how true that is after meeting Nisroc and you, but the humans and werewolves honestly believed it. And my father, who gave me to the humans for safekeeping, clearly believed it too."

The angel ran a hand through his dark hair. "Call me Rafi. And your sire gave you to the humans for safekeeping because knew he would suffer punishment, and quite possibly death, for his sin. Yes, some angels would have killed you, still might kill you, if they find you. Most would have sent you to Hel." He leaned closer. "But not because you're a Nephilim, Ahia. Because you're an angel. You're a full angel. And because you're an Angel of Chaos, you're not supposed to be in Aaru or here among the humans. Hel or death are your choices. Those are the fates your sire feared you'd face. And honestly, he probably feared for his own life just as much as he feared for yours."

It couldn't be. It just couldn't be. I shook my head. "No, I'm a Nephilim. If I were a full angel, someone would have known. Someone would have told me."

"Nisroc knew. You'll have to ask him why he didn't tell you. You're an angel and he definitely knew. Nephilim don't have wings. Nephilim can't see the rifts and wild gateways. Nephilim can't do this."

I felt that warmth, that zing that ran through every cell of my body. And this time I felt something more. It was like he was caressing me, stroking my skin without even touching me. I felt something deep within myself leap to the surface, eager for his touch.

And then I pulled away, backing myself against the edge of the stove. "What is that? How do you do that?"

He tilted his head, his smile uncertain. "You're a being of spirit. Angels manifest physical form here among the humans, but it's not how we truly are. That was my spirit-self touching your spirit-self. Angels and demons are the only beings who can do this."

I spun around to face the stove and think. This was too much. An angel. I couldn't be an angel. If I were, then my parents had abandoned me. They'd made me, then tossed me to the humans to take care of. What the hell did they intend? Was I supposed to go to Hel and live with my...mother, or whatever my demon parent was? She'd ditched me with 'dad'"." And he'd handed me off to the humans. For over five thousand years I'd seen so many generations born and die that I truly felt adrift, as if I were without a family. I'd had some fantasy of my father's grief when my mother died, or that they'd both died and that's why no one had come for me. But no, they made an angel that wouldn't be welcome anywhere and dropped me off on the humans' doorstep like an unwanted puppy at the pound.

"That's not what happened, Ahia." I felt his hands on my shoulders, the heat from him against my back, felt his breath at the side of my head. "I know what you're thinking and it's not true. Five thousand years is nothing to an angel. I'm three billion years old. Your maker couldn't take you to Hel, it would have been too dangerous there for a young Angel of Chaos, and your sire couldn't take you to Aaru. But things are changing. I'm sure they both meant to come back for you."

"Are you? Because I'm not." I should have gone to get the bacon out of the fridge, but I didn't want to walk away from his comforting warmth, his hands on my shoulders.

His thumbs began doing little circles on my shoulder. "Yes, I'm sure. Never feel alone, Ahia. The humans and were-wolves may not live as long as we do, but their affection is deep and sincere. You are precious to them, otherwise they wouldn't have welcomed you into their homes, as a member of their family. And someday, you will be reunited with your sire. Someday soon you will have a family, a choir of angels that love you. Nisroc cares for you. And…others will too."

I got the feeling he had been one syllable from saying he cared too. I just met this angel. Literally just met him a few hours ago. But it was more than only lust between us. Something about him felt so right. His sense of humor, his kindness, his perceptiveness, his hands on my shoulders.

"Are you an Angel of Chaos or an Angel of Order?" I knew there were two types of angels, but didn't know much about them or exactly what had happened in that war so many millions of years ago.

Raphael's thumbs stopped the circles on my shoulder and his hand moved up next to my neck. "I'm an Angel of Order. Sort of. It's a long story."

One that I wanted to hear, after we'd known each other longer than all of a few hours. "And do you have sex? I mean, you said you'd–"" Ugh, what was I saying? I blamed hormones. I hadn't had sex since Brent and I called it quits over two decades ago, and this angel had stirred me up from the moment he'd appeared in my living room.

He chuckled. It was a low throaty sound that shot heat right down between my legs. "Some of the more sinful and naughty among us have physical sexual intercourse. Demons definitely have physical sexual intercourse. All angels do something similar to sex that involves our spirit-beings. Some really kinky angels like to do both."

I caught my breath. Oh wow. I loved kinky.

"We're non-gendered, but some Angels of Order are attracted to their own kind, while others prefer Angels of Chaos or demons, and vice versa."

His fingers caressed the side of my neck. I stared intently at the macaroni noodles, wondering how mushy they would be if we ran to my bedroom for quick sex right now. Five minutes. Or maybe thirty. Or maybe I should just turn the stove off and forget about dinner.

"So do *you* like Angels of Order or Angels of Chaos?" He was beautiful, too perfectly beautiful. And I wanted him like I'd never wanted anyone before in my long life.

"I have always preferred Angels of Chaos." His hands brushed my hair aside and I felt him put his lips against the side of my neck. "And yes, I am very, very kinky."

Forget the macaroni, I was ready to melt into this guy. He was gorgeous, and built. He radiated power that drew me in just as much as his looks. And he was kissing my neck. I leaned back against him and closed my eyes, tilting my head to give him better access. Maybe this was just a fling for him — a quickie. Would I be okay with that? Me, the love-them-

and-leave-them queen? How would it feel to be on the other side of that equation?

I was too far gone to back out now. His mouth sliding kisses down my neck, his hands dropping from my shoulders to my hips, pulling me tight against him. That weird feeling of coming alive inside my skin, of touching-but-not-touching increased. Something deep inside me rose to the surface, to merge with him. Kinky was an incredible understatement for this experience. Was this the something extra that angels brought into the equation? Spirit dick? Whatever it was, I wanted more, pushing both my body and that other part of me against him, reveling in the burn of his energy on my skin. I was so going to fuck this guy. Well, more like he was going to fuck me. And I was going to enjoy every second of it.

My front door slammed open. "Ahia! Got a problem up in Yakutat!"

Brent. Raphael jumped away from me. For a moment I thought it was because he didn't want the werewolf to see him in a compromising position with me, but as he strode from the kitchen I realized he was contemplating tearing Brent to shreds for the interruption.

Oh how funny. An angel cock-blocked by a werewolf. I had every intention of having Raphael naked and in my bed, but I was crazy enough to want some fun first. Making an angel jealous. Yep, certifiably crazy.

I raced out and beat the angel to Brent, who scowled when he saw who — and what — my companion was.

"You okay, Ahia?"

The werewolf puffed up his chest, ready to defend me. I was pack. He was the Alpha. My safety was his responsibility, even if he did get smashed to a pulp by an angel. I understood his motivations. Raphael clearly did not. The angel's wings burst into view, the power rolling off him making it hard to breathe.

He was peacocking. And that was an absolutely accurate term for his amazing wings. They were the lightest lavender at the top, the purple shade darkening in a gradient to near black at the flight feathers. Fucking gorgeous. Just like the rest of this angel.

"Yes, she's okay. Who are you?"

There was so going to be a cockfight. And bad me was practically salivating at the prospect. Poor Brent didn't stand a chance, and I was a horrible, horrible pack-mate and best friend to want an epic battle between the two.

"Brent. And who are you?"

They were no more than two feet apart, almost within the danger zone of personal space when it came to werewolf etiquette.

The wings spread out. "Raphael," the angel snarled. "You're the Alpha? The one who helped kill the chimera?"

"Yeah. What's it to you?"

Fight, fight, fight!

"You've been hiding her." Raphael pointed to me. "That's a violation of your existence contract. I'm sure that's the tip of the iceberg as far as your and your pack's violations."

He was trying to scare Brent, to intimidate him into either backing down or revealing a weakness. I didn't know about werewolves elsewhere, but in Alaska, wolves didn't back down. And they never sacrificed a pack member, even if it was the only way to protect the rest of the group. If I were truly in danger, the entire pack would come to my defense, and nothing Raphael could say would convince them to abandon me.

It's one of the things I loved about this furry group that I considered mine.

"Cut it out, Pretty-boy." I reached out to grab the top of the angel's left wing, steering him to the side and away from Brent. I knew how sensitive these things were, and doubted he'd try to pull away from me and risk bending, or bruising, the wing.

What I didn't expect was the way it felt in my hand. The feathers were silky soft. Something warm hummed through them, something that traveled up my hand and into my very soul. Something that stirred a feeling — lust and more.

The angel turned his head, tilting the wing forward and increasing the pressure of my hand on the feathers. Violet eyes met mine, and reflected that same spark. I caught my breath, wanting nothing more than to fall into Raphael's arms, even with Brent right there in my living room.

"Ahia?"

Shit. "Yeah. Yep. This is Raphael. He is the one the Ruling Council sent to help close the rifts. It's a two-person job, so I'm helping him. He's promised me immunity in return. He won't kill me."

I was hoping he'd do other things to me. Like right now. Like as soon as Brent left.

Brent turned his scowl on me. "You called in an *angel* to help? Ahia, what were you thinking? He could have just as easily killed you as work with you. We've got the chimera under control. We don't need him."

"Yes we do need him," I argued. I still had my hand on Raphael's wing, oddly reluctant to let go of the soft feathers. "We need to close the rifts. We can't keep killing chimera every few days, and that hydra isn't going down easy. Plus, the drop bears — remember the drop bears? If these things open up all across Alaska and start spilling out monsters, the three packs and the humans aren't going to be able to keep up. And what if something comes through that's worse than the hydra? Like a dragon, or something like that? We need to close the rifts, and we need someone around or on call who can make closing new ones a priority."

My speech seemed to reduce the testosterone level in the room — at least the portion coming from the angel. Brent still glared, now at me as well as Raphael.

"I came here to tell you that some winged-things came through near Skagway. A group of hunters shot them, but they grabbed two and went back through the rift at nightfall."

"Grabbed two what?" Raphael asked. "Humans? Elk? Polar bears?"

"Humans, you idiot. As if we'd care if they grabbed elk or polar bears."

I caught my breath, eyeing Raphael in alarm. As much enthusiasm as I had for a fistfight, I really didn't want to see the angel smite the werewolf for disrespect.

"*I* care about elk and polar bears," I interjected before blows, or worse, were exchanged. "Do you think we should go there now, or wait until morning?"

"It would be nice to close the rift now before those things come back, but I only have some vague landmarks as location markers. It would be easier to pinpoint during the day."

Brent had a point. I had many talents, and my night vision was damned good, but Alaska nights could be dark, especially in the forest away from any light pollution. It was cloudy. It was spring. It was already dark out.

"Okay, at dawn then." I walked over to my computer where the satellite view of Alaska was still up. "Show me where and give me the landmarks. I've been up to Skagway enough that I might recognize them."

I plopped down and Brent came over, his hands on the chair arms caging me in and putting him right up against my shoulder. "I need to talk to you," he murmured in my ear.

Great. Raphael already looked like he was trying to decide whether to rip Brent's limbs off, or just stomp out in a huff never to return again. So much for that sexy kitchen interlude. And so much for my great make-the-angel-jealous idea.

"I'll go check on the noodles," Raphael told me. His voice was steady and low, in a tone that signified mass murder might occur later. He'd heard Brent. Of course he'd heard Brent. Werewolves had amazing hearing. I'd expect an angel's would be even better.

The angel turned around and headed for the kitchen. I watched him go, waiting for him to be out of sight, although I was pretty sure he still would be able to hear us.

"What?" I snapped at the werewolf. This had to be the weirdest night of my whole life. Stuffed in a closet. Partnered with an angel who promised he wouldn't harm me in return for my help. Enough sexual tension to burn half the state to ash. And now this. Whatever this was, I doubted it would end in sexy-times. I'd be lucky if it didn't end with blood on the floor.

"What are you doing?" he hissed. "An angel. Ahia, this is going to end badly. You seem confident that he's not going to kill you, but what if he tells other angels you're here? You'll need to leave, go hide with one of the other packs. If they're anything like that guy, we can't protect you. I'm not even sure the entire pack working together could do more than ruffle that guy's feathers."

His words were a cold splash of reality. Was my libido getting the best of me? Blinding me to the pitfalls? If he was going to rat me out to the Ruling Council, there was nothing I could do about that now. I'd need to leave once this project was over — for the pack's safety as well as my own. Alaska had been my home for thousands of years. I didn't want to live anywhere else. This land was mine. The humans here were mine. These werewolves were mine. Damn it all. I didn't want to leave.

"And don't think I didn't notice what was going on between you two either," Brent continued. "He's already acting like he's staked a claim on you. How do you think that's going to work out? A quick fling with an angel isn't going to be like a human pick-up or hooking up with one of the pack. He's going to rip your heart apart, then leave you without a second thought."

I thought of the chemistry between the angel and me, the way his lips felt on my neck, that odd sensation of touching-not-touching. I was so out of my league — and that hadn't ever happened before. I knew with him I'd be vulnerable. He'd strip my emotions bare. I'd give everything to him. And then what? He was a thousand times more powerful than me, he was billions of years older than me. I was probably quick entertainment, a perk of a project in the middle of nowhere, someone to use up then toss aside without a thought once it was time to go back to Aaru and the other angels.

I was such an idiot. And I still wanted him, in spite of the absolute train-wreck my future would be if I slept with him. Crazy. That was me all right.

"Can I ask you something?" I twisted in the chair to look up at him. "How did you all know I was a Nephilim? I mean, your great, great, great grandparents. When they found me living with the humans here in Alaska, how did they know I was part angel?"

Brent looked at me as if I'd suddenly gone crazy. "You heal in a blink. You shapeshift in a flash of light. You're like a werewolf only hundreds of times more powerful. Why wouldn't we think you're a Nephilim? Plus, there's an energy you give off, a kind of angel energy. A shaman or magic user wouldn't have that energy."

"He thinks I'm an angel — a full-angel angel." I nodded my head toward the kitchen.

Brent opened his mouth then shut it, tilting his head in thought. "I...I don't know. I mean, you don't have the level of energy output that he does or even Nisroc, but Nephilim are half-angels. Of course you seem like an angel."

"But could you tell the difference?" I pressed. "If you met a young angel and a Nephilim, could you tell the difference?"

He stared at me a moment. "You're more powerful than the Nephilim in West Virginia, or the ones sheltered by other packs. They all have different strengths and abilities, though. We just assumed you were particularly gifted, that you'd gotten more than your fair share of angel."

I believed Rafi. And Brent's words confirmed it. It made sense. It made perfect sense. And Rafi would have no reason I could think of to lie.

"Maybe he's just saying that to flatter you, to get in your pants," Brent said, glaring toward the kitchen.

I snorted. As if the angel needed to flatter me to get in my pants. "Like telling me my eyes are the color of onyx, or my hair is softer than mink?"

The glare turned my way. "Hey, that's not fair."

I bit back a smile. Brent had said those things to me long ago when *he'd* wanted to get in my pants.

"I don't trust him," the werewolf said. "I want you to promise me you won't sleep with him."

I turned back to face the computer screen. "Tell me where this rift is. And describe the winged-things."

I wasn't going to discuss the conflicted nature of my thoughts and emotions with Brent. He was the Alpha. It was his job to protect me. But we had history together, and there was no way in hell I was going to confess to the werewolf how very much I wanted to go screw that angel in the kitchen. I might be crazy, but I wasn't cruel.

Brent sighed, putting a hand on my shoulder and giving it a quick squeeze. "North about five miles out of town. East of 98."

"Here? In the mountains?" That was going to be a nightmare. Yes, we could fly, but the rifts were hard to spot with aerial reconnaissance, and trying to cover that ground on foot would take forever.

"Closer to Goat Lake, near that ridge, from what the hunters said."

It looked to be seven miles or so out of Skagway as the crow, or angel, flies. There had to be something else I could look for. "You said the winged-things took two hunters? Would there be remains? A trail of blood leading back to the rift?"

He shrugged. "Unless it rains or snows or wildlife cleans it up there should be some blood. The hunters shot them full of holes, so the blood wouldn't just be human. And there should be feathers too."

"What did they look like?"

"The wings looked like eagle wings, only partially plucked. And they had bird-like upper bodies with beaks."

"Hippogriff? Gryphon?"

"I don't know. All these weird creatures are starting to run together. Half this, half-that. I can't keep them straight."

"Back end of a horse or a lion?"

"Snake? Maybe?"

Crap. "Cockatrice or possibly a wyvern." *Don't let it be a wyvern.* Even with angelic back-up I didn't want to have to face a dragon-light.

"Well, whatever it is, I'm hoping you can close this rift before they come back through." Brent gave my shoulder another squeeze and stepped back from my chair. "I'll meet you guys up there at sunup."

Like hell he would. "We've got this. There's no sense in you or any of the pack risking yourselves. If it's a wyvern, it's got a venomous bite. If it's a cockatrice, it might have poisoned breath."

Brent snorted. "Like you in the morning, before you brush your teeth?"

I threw a dry erase marker at him, but smiled. Yes, he'd experienced my morning breath up close and personal. And it was awesome that we could joke like this without feeling awkward or weird.

"There's another reason I want to be there," Brent added, shooting a significant glance toward the kitchen.

"He won't kill me," I countered. "I told you, he promised and evidently that's a pretty serious thing with angels."

"It's not him killing you I'm worried about."

I rolled my eyes. "We're hardly likely to have a romantic encounter while fighting off venomous bird-thingies and trying to close a gateway. Stay like a good doggie, and I'll bring you by a bone when I return."

He threw the dry erase marker back at me and walked toward the door. "Make that a steak and you can call me 'doggie' all you want."

I watched him walk out, a fondness warming my heart. I'd known him as a baby. I'd known him intimately. I'd watched him as he took control of the pack. And in the future I'd continue to watch him as he married and had kids, as he aged and died. And through it all, I hoped Brent would always continue to be my friend.

CHAPTER 11

RAPHAEL

What in all of creation was I doing? Two hours after meeting this angel and I was all over her like butter on toast, then practically coming to blows with her werewolf friend.

Except he had been more than a friend once, and I wondered if they still were. There was a warm affection in their interactions clearly built on a shared history that included more than hot sweaty sex. *That's* what I wanted. Well, yeah I wanted the hot sweaty sex too. It had been millions of years — the longest dry spell ever. Angels of Order weren't into the sort of things that I was, and most of them weren't attracted to me anyway. Here was an angel that *was* attracted to me, that I got the feeling would be open to all sorts of fun. Of course I wanted to rush into sex like some teenage human with his first girlfriend. Of course I'd be all over her right after we met. It wasn't just that spark of attraction, though. There might be something more there, but I didn't really *know* her yet. And I wanted to.

Okay, either way I'd still want to have her, but if this could be something more I didn't want to ruin it by rushing into physical and other types of intimacy. There would be plenty of time. I was three billion years old. I certainly could take a few months to woo an angel. Or days. Or perhaps hours if I found myself unable to hold back.

Patience was not my virtue. In fact, for an Angel of Order, I had very little to do with virtue and I liked it that way. But I needed to win this angel's heart. She'd lived her whole life among humans and werewolves. How did they woo their females? Flowers. Chocolates. Shoulder massage. Oral sex. No, I think the oral sex was supposed to come *after* the wooing was done, which was a real shame. Flowers, chocolate and oral sex sounded like a successful way to win the affections of another.

I could hear them in the other room as clearly as if I were standing right next to them. I could tell that werewolf had his hands on her. The macaroni noodles were almost done, so I tried to ignore them and pulled the pack of squeeze-cheese out of the box and looked in the fridge for bacon.

Wait. I knew what I wanted to do. It never would have worked on an Angel of Order, but I had a skill that should push the odds in my favor if she was at all the angel I thought she was. Turning off the stove I teleported myself, popping back in less than two minutes. Yes, the grocery store had been closed. Yes, I'd lifted a few things. They'd never know and I wasn't about to beat myself up over it.

By the time I heard the door close and felt Ahia walk into the kitchen I was done.

"How's dinner coming?"

There was a teasing note in her voice. She put a hand on my back, making me wish I hadn't hidden my wings. The way she'd taken hold of them in the other room, gentle and firm, her fingers caressing the feathers as she talked, had nearly undone me. I'd wanted to turn and take her there, even with that cursed werewolf watching.

"I think I've managed to put together reasonably edible mac and cheese." I couldn't help feeling smug as I dished the food into two bowls.

"Bacon? Sausage? Or plain?" She leaned against me and I couldn't keep from reaching out to touch her with my spirit-self. It had been far too long, and she was so near. If I didn't get some distance, this whole woo-first/sex-later plan was going right out the window.

"Bacon. I already added it." I handed her the bowl and a fork, picking up my own. She stared down at the contents, a puzzled frown on her face.

"It's not yellow. Did I buy the box with the white cheese instead?"

"I did something different. I hope you like it."

Still standing in front of me, she scooped a bunch onto her fork and popped it in her mouth, long strands of cheese trailing from her lips to the bowl.

"Holy crap," she muttered with her mouth full. "What did you put in this? It's amazing."

"Manchego and a few other cheeses."

She swiped the strands into her mouth. "I don't have Manchego. Where did you get it? Do you fly around with wheels of cheese in your pockets or something?"

"At the grocery store. I didn't like any of their bacon, so I used yours. There's an incredible farm in Virginia that raises heritage breeds and has their own smokehouse. I didn't feel right popping in there at this hour and raiding his storehouse, but next time I'll get some for you. You'll love it."

She took another bite. "You're a foodie. Huh. And although you didn't feel right raiding a Virginia farm in what is probably the wee hours of the morning there, you didn't have a problem going to a closed grocery store and grabbing cheese?"

"No." I held my breath, waiting for the lecture on how this

sort of thing negatively affected my vibration levels, or that stealing was a sin, or that angels shouldn't be indulging in sensory pleasures.

"Works for me." She went over and plopped down at the little kitchen table, stuffing macaroni and cheese into her mouth like she hadn't eaten in days. I could fall in love with this woman. Anyone who enjoyed food like this, food *I'd* prepared, was halfway to winning my heart

After dinner we cleaned the dishes the human way with me washing and her drying. She'd insisted on tying some frilly apron thing around me, and as we worked, we talked. She preferred her men commando over boxers or briefs, but for herself stated that a pair of bikini-style underwear were vital to keeping the seams of jeans from chafing important areas. She hated thongs, claiming that if she wanted something up her butt, it wasn't going to be a narrow strip of lace. We lamented over how we had to recreate our shirts every time we revealed our wings, how we either had to modify the clothing to stay secure around our feathered appendages or fly around with bits of fabric flapping in the breeze, chest exposed. We discussed how best to hover, argued over who could dive deeper when plunging into water from thirty feet in the air. She described flying at top speed through the narrow canyons of mountains, the feeling of sitting on top of a glacier, looking down into the sea, how incredibly ugly eagle babies were up close and how sharp a mama eagle's talons were when an angel got a bit too close.

I told her about Aaru, about diving off the top of Angel Falls, about flying so high that you could see the curve of the earth right below you, about helping the Iblis set loose a bunch of rabid durfts into Aaru, and the ensuing chaos, about Infernal Mates and my hopes that someday angels and demons could live together once more, that Aaru would once again be graced with creation, with offspring — both Angels of Order and Angels of Chaos.

Our dish duty was finished far too soon, and we stood for a moment in the kitchen staring at each other, clearly waiting for the other to say or do something.

"Should we plan for tomorrow? We should plan for tomorrow then go to bed," She babbled, turning around and practically running for the living room. I smiled as I walked after her, because I knew she was flustered, that she was feeling the same things as me, but unlike me hadn't realized how incredibly right this was between us.

"So, here are our priorities." Ahia picked up a notepad and shoved it at me.

Bird things. Two nearby rifts. Fucking drop bears. Chimera rift. Hydra. Other shit.

I couldn't help but smile at the "fucking drop bears."

"I'm all yours. You set the schedule. You lead the way. Show me where these bird things are and point out the rift and I'll close it."

She licked her bottom lip. I watched intently, gritting my teeth to keep from launching myself at her.

"We'll need to do a sweep in case any of the bird things came through before we head off to the other rifts and the drop bears. And what's our plan with the hydra? I chop heads and you cauterize, or vice versa?"

This was going to be so much fun, all of it — bird things, drop bears, hydra, and every other moment I was with her. "I'll cauterize. Between the bird things, the two rifts, and the drop bears, I'm not sure we'll get to anything else tomorrow. In fact, I'm not sure I can manage more than two or three rifts per day. We'll have to be a bit flexible on the schedule."

She nodded, a gleam in her eyes making me wonder if she wasn't trying to drag this whole thing out as much as I was. "We should probably be rested up for the hydra, so maybe do it the following day, and the chimera rift. I can ask the pack to come help track down any stray chimera. They tend to wander far from the rift."

I didn't like the idea of the werewolves helping. Actually I didn't like the idea of one particular werewolf helping. "How many drop bears are we talking about, by the way?"

She shrugged. "Twenty? They swarm you and it's kinda hard to count."

"Sounds like fun."

She grinned. "It will be. I can't wait to kick some drop bear butt. They chewed me up last time, but this time I'll be ready for them." Then she glanced over at the couch, then back to me. "Guess I should go to bed and get some sleep. Do you sleep? I'll get you some sheets and blankets."

I heard the unspoken question in her voice, and I wanted to follow her into her bed and ensure that neither of us got any sleep, but I didn't want to rush this any more than I already had. Besides, I had a gate guardian I needed to have a word with, and I wanted to do that before Ahia and I headed out in the morning.

"No need for a blanket, I'll be good on the couch." I almost changed my mind at her disappointed expression. "For tonight. Tomorrow maybe I'll get lucky and score better sleeping arrangements."

Those beautiful lips curved up once more. "Keep cooking for me and washing dishes, and you'll definitely get lucky."

CHAPTER 12

*N*isroc looked like he was ready to punch me as I landed beside him at the gateway to Hel.

"How dare you forcibly transport me like that," he snarled. "I'm not in your choir, and I am temporarily assigned to the head of the Grigori. I'm not your lackey to order away. You were sent here to help with the rifts, not interfere with my work or spend your time trying to seduce a young angel to your less-than-pure ways."

Micha would have used his immense power to pummel this guardian for his insubordination. Gabe would have demanded the respect due his high vibration pattern. Uriel would have shamed him with blistering words. But I was different. I was far more tolerant of disrespect, of contrary viewpoints. But this angel's disrespect came from less than pure motives.

"She's an angel." I let that sink in a moment so he'd know exactly what the topic of our conversation would be. "How long have you known she was here? And why didn't you tell her? She's running around with a bunch of werewolves thinking she's a Nephilim. Keeping such a thing from the angelic host is understandable, but keeping her true nature from her is a deplorable act."

Nisroc smoothed his snowy robes and brushed a fleck of dirt from them. "I thought it for the best. After a somewhat rocky start here in Alaska, I befriended the werewolves. They confessed to me that they had a Nephilim among them. I gave them my vow that I would protect her. I was just as surprised as you were when I saw what she was. I'd promised the werewolves I'd keep their secret, so I did."

That was complete and utter bull hooey. "You promised them you'd keep the secret of a Nephilim from the Ruling Council. That promise in no way excused your continuing to let her believe she was a Nephilim for *fifty* years."

"What difference would it have made?" Nisroc shot back. "What possible benefit would it have been to tell her that she was an angel? She can't go to Aaru. She would be killed the moment she crossed to Hel. The werewolves and humans wouldn't care — for them a half-angel is pretty much the same as a full one. It wouldn't have made one difference in her life whatsoever."

"You kept it from her in the hope that you could woo her, that you'd be her chosen. A Nephilim might be flattered at the attention of a gate guardian, but an angel of her potential would be out of your reach. You lied to give yourself time to make her yours. Well, let me tell you buddy, if you haven't sealed the deal with fifty years of effort, then it's not gonna happen."

She could have her pick of any number of open-minded angels in Aaru who were willing to turn a blind eye to the treaty. And experience had shown me that angels didn't always choose based on power or status. We were capricious beings, attracted to whomever we wanted, and determined to get what we wanted, too. I wanted her. My blood danced with the thought that I might have a chance, that she might want me in return.

Nisroc glared at me. "I'm taking my time. I'm treating her with respect and recognizing her potential. I'm not swooping in from Aaru, making a huge show of my power and status and trying to dazzle her with false importance."

I folded my arms across my chest. "You've had fifty years. Give me three days, and if I can't win her affections by then, I'll leave and not return."

The guardian narrowed his eyes. "Joining doesn't count as a win. She needs to commit to you or it's just a young angel experimenting with her spirit-self."

I winced. Ahia was attracted to me. I had no doubt I could join and more with her in the next three days, but would it just be a fling? Could I convince her to give me her heart in such a short time? I'd need to try, give it my all, because I was already half in love with this angel and to walk away in three days might be the hardest thing I'd ever done.

"I vow that if I do not win Ahia's heart in the next three days, I will leave and not return. I will keep her presence a secret from the other angels, and I will allow you the time you need to present your suit."

Nisroc nodded. "I vow that I will allow you three days without interference to make an effort to win Ahia's heart. Although if she comes to see me or requests my presence, then I'm not to be held responsible for any efforts I make to further my suit."

Three days. I tamped down the panic that I had such a short amount of time to make a favorable impression. I'd made some headway tonight, but so much of our attraction was lust. I needed it to be more. And I needed to know how far Nisroc had gotten in his suit.

"Have you offered for her yet?" Offered for her. I was the naughty one of Aaru and I couldn't come out and ask if he'd joined with her. Part of me didn't want to know. Part of me wanted to rip this guy's wings off at the idea.

"No." The angel scowled. "She's young and pure. It would be unseemly of me. And I'd hardly offer for her after only fifty years."

I hid a smile. Good. She clearly wasn't going to wait fifty years with me from the way she'd responded in the kitchen. Now I just had to make sure the werewolves, especially that Brent, stayed out of my way.

"Do not sully her with your deplorable vibration level. You might be an archangel by birth, but you're hardly one when it comes to purity. You're barely an Angel of Order." Nisroc's voice was tight with anger as he looked up at me with narrowed eyes.

I felt a wave of fury at his words. Nisroc might be speaking out of bitterness because I had the advantage when it came to trying to win this angel, but there was truth in his words. We archangels seemed to be falling into the sin of anger, as well as the sin of lust, envy, and pride. Especially pride. Well, except for the perfect Gabriel who never seemed to come within a light year of sin. I was the worst of the four of us, though. I was an archangel. I was so much more worthy of her affections than a lowly gate guardian. That was a horrible thing to think. I might be the least powerful of the archangels, but I still had more than the average angel, and far more than a gate guardian.

But I was tired of angels only wanting me because of my status. I was tired of the passive-aggressive slights, the subtle and not-so-subtle lack of respect. I was tired of mine being the least valued of the choirs. And I was tired of angels trying to woo me who had no interest in who I really was. It would be nice for once to have an angel want me for the crazy, just-barely-an-Angel-of-Order that I was. For the first time I felt I'd met an angel who might appreciate the real me. And I wasn't about to back off because some gate guardian had discovered her fifty years before I had.

Nisroc raised his chin, eyes flashing. "I've vowed to protect her, and protect her I will, even if that means I go against my vow to the heavenly host, or you as a member of the Ruling Council, even if I go against the vow of service I made to the Grigori, even if it means my vibration pattern degrades with sin. I cannot allow you to take her against her will, to hurt her."

Hurt her? I shook my head wondering what the hell Nisroc was thinking. "I would never take her against her will or hurt her. She's an *angel,* for creation's sake! I vowed I wouldn't kill her, and beyond that I would never harm her."

A muscle tightened in Nisroc's jaw. "You're part of the Ruling Council. You fought with the Angels of Order in the war. You, of all angels, made the choice to fight instead of use your position to promote peace and reconciliation. You fought them, killed them, and signed the treaty that banished them. You agreed to the treaty. And according to the treaty, she should be either killed or thrown into Hel. That was your vow before all the angels of Aaru. Why would she want you? Why would she want an angel that slaughtered others just because they were of Chaos?"

That hit hard, but it wasn't anything that I hadn't already punished myself over. I'd been designated an Angel of Order, but one with enough Chaos that I'd always felt I'd betrayed my own in the war. Plus, Samael...our brother. I was three billion years old, yet had aged more in the last three million years than in my whole lifetime. Things were changing, though. It was time to do the things I'd been too cowardly to do before, time to stand up for who I really was inside.

"There *will* be peace. There will be reconciliation. That's why there is a rebellion in Aaru. The Ruling Council recognizes we made a mistake and wants to rectify it, but others resist. There are changes taking place both here and in Aaru. You've met the new Iblis, you've seen how Michael's heart has warmed. I admit my shameful part in what fractured us so long ago, and I will not betray my brethren again. And I hope that she'll see that."

Nisroc's eyebrows shot upward. "You're frivolous. You're irreverent. You're swayed whichever way the wind blows. I doubt you will stand strong for anything of value, that you'll resist sin and improve both yourself and those of your choir. And I don't think you'll be good for Ahia. You'll seduce her, have your fling, then leave her to go frolic in another pasture. Don't ruin her potential purity with your smut."

I hadn't been an exemplarity angel in the past, and I wasn't sure I could ever live up to the standards of vibration that pure Angels of Order demanded. But my intentions toward Ahia were sincere. Which is why I'd somehow managed to keep myself from falling into her bed tonight. "I have no desire to make Ahia a casual fling. I tell you now that if she chooses me, I'll not abandon her to frolic in any other pasture."

Nisroc eyed me doubtfully. "Don't ruin her. She's special. She's got more Order than any other Angel of Chaos I've ever known. I think with proper guidance, she can strengthen that pure part of herself and achieve an admirable vibration level."

Ugh. He was the one who would ruin her. Let her be as she was created — perfect and pure in her own way. Ahia was on the edge of Order just as I was on the edge of Chaos. She was one of the rare angels that straddled both designations, and her vibration level was just fine as it was.

Already my thoughts raced into a fanciful future. Ahia. It was a beautiful name, although it didn't really work for an angel. If she attained status, she'd be Ahiael. That was a whole lot of vowels. Although I was definitely putting the cart before the horse on that one. She wasn't mine…yet. And angels didn't reach the title of 'el' for several million years.

And there was that sticking point of her being an Angel of Chaos and forbidden entry into Aaru. From what I could see, that was just a matter of time, though. Possibly a ten-thousand-year matter of time, but it would happen. I'd told Nisroc things were changing in Aaru and I meant it. Plus, if Micha could get his imp there as the Iblis, I could certainly get Ahia there too. Maybe make her a part of the Iblis's household.

Yes. Cart and horse. Definitely.

The priority was supposed to be to secure and stabilize this area, to ensure the rifts didn't derail the positive evolution of the humans, or destroy the ecosystem of the planet or threaten the gateway to Hel. I had responsibilities. And those responsibilities weren't supposed to include seducing the lovely Ahia.

Screw it. There was no reason I couldn't do both. Nobody set a time limit on my project up here. I'd already agreed to team up with this intriguing angel, find and close rifts, determine the pattern of occurrence, and before I completed this project, and within the next three days, I had every hope that she'd be mine.

I turned to Nisroc and gave him my honest vow. "I won't ruin her. I'll do my best to win her heart within three days, but I can promise you I will do nothing to change who, and what, she is."

The angel eyed me suspiciously. "Three days. Then you're gone?"

I nodded. "Three days."

CHAPTER 13

AHIA

We were up with the sun, Pop-Tarts consumed, and ready to fly. Our breath clouded in the cool spring air, birdsong filled the sky, and pale golden sunlight filtered through the trees, casting long dark shadows like stripes across the three-acre field that served as my front lawn.

Humans in Alaska had known about us for hundreds of years, but I still tried to be stealthy when flying. My front lawn gave me a nice runway, and my nearest neighbors off the narrow gravel road were over a mile away and were-wolves. Once in the air my main concerns were that tourists not see a woman with wings soaring overhead, and that some idiot wouldn't shoot me out of the sky.

I wouldn't die, but it would piss me off and I didn't want to be responsible for a hunter returning home with his rifle melted into a lump.

"Ready?" Raphael revealed his wings and I eyed them admiringly. I did the same and he made an "ooo" noise. "You've got some dramatic wings there, Hot-stuff."

They were. I spread them out, brushing the tip against Raphael's. Mine were nearly the opposite of his — iridescent black on the tops, like an oil slick in a midnight ocean, then fading to light gray at the bottom. The flight feathers were a shocking pure white, a dramatic contrast against the dark background. His wings reversed the shading, although instead of black and gray, his were a muted purple. And next to mine, the color appeared richer and deeper than when I'd first seen them.

"Back at cha', Pretty-boy." I ogled his wings, rubbing mine against his.

"Keep that up and we'll never get out of here."

He was right. I sighed, pulling my wing from his and stepping forward. "Ready?"

I didn't wait for his reply before I started to run, angling my wings so that I could get enough lift to be above the tree line before my front-yard runway ended. Eight steps in I felt hands on my hips grab me from the ground and launch me straight upward into the air. I tumbled ass over wings, my ascent slowing. Righting myself, I held my wings tight to my back, dropping down nose-first, then spreading my wings and swooping upward on a thermal. I squealed. He laughed and pulled in just off to my left, following my lead.

We took the scenic route northwest, swooping low to feel the splash of water off whale tails as they dived, and hovering at treetops to peek into eagles' nests. Seeing some dark shapes on a buoy, I took us on a slight detour to harass a huge bull seal and his harem. Swinging toward the shore, we wove in and out of trees, banking close to see where the old mines and trails had been.

All too soon I landed, my feet becoming soaked from the dew still on the grasses and scrub. I'd sensed the rift just as we'd rounded the last copse of trees, and now could clearly see it close to where Brent had indicated, just a few hundred feet from the icy waters of Goat Lake. The energy coming off the rift was sharp and cold. It reminded me of the way frozen iron pipes taste. And yes, I knew what frozen iron pipes tasted like. Rafi landed beside me, his grin huge. Shaking his wings, he folded them close to his sides and walked over to admire the sunrise barely visible through the trees.

"Pretty, isn't it?" I loved my home, and showing all this to Raphael was *my* version of peacocking.

"Well, it's not quite a nude beach at Cannes, but Alaska clearly has one of the greatest beauties of the world."

He flashed that adorable dimple at me, and I felt the brush of his spirit-self against mine. Flirt. But I was more intrigued by the other part of his statement.

"Is there really a nude beach at Cannes? Have you been there? Is everyone nude, or just you? And do you sunbathe with your wings out? Do they bring you drinks with little umbrellas in them? Do you party on movie-stars' luxury yachts?"

His eyes grew warm. "I'll take you, then you can see for yourself."

Was this one of those things people said on impulse or out of politeness that they had no intention of ever following through on? I hoped not. "I've never been out of Alaska. Would I be safe?"

It was as if a shadow fell across his face. "Probably not. There are extremists in Aaru, and while I'd protect you with my life, I wouldn't want to take the risk that something would happen to you. Soon. Soon all this will be done and you'll be free to do as you please. When that happens, I'll take you to Cannes, and anywhere else your heart desires."

Soon might never happen, but at least I had now. I could show him my world, enjoy his company and hopefully more. I could create memories that would carry me until 'soon'."

So I smiled and extended my arms. "The rift is here. Go on. See if you can figure out where."

"Here?" Rafi turned and put his hands on his hips. He was facing a completely different direction from the rift.

"Yep. Right there." I couldn't help it. I was a troublemaker, and seeing him stare intently at a pine tree was just too funny.

He patted the air in front of him and shot me a perceptive look. "Do I look like a fool yet?"

I snickered. "Yep. It's actually over here. Warm. Warm. Warmer. Hot. Smoking hot."

"I know." He wiggled his eyebrows at me and I smacked his shoulder.

"Here, silly." I stuck my hand into the rift and shrieked as something bit me. When I yanked it out two fingers were bleeding and it was Raphael's turn to snicker. Before I could chastise him for his unfeeling mirth, a giant chicken head shot through the rift, grabbed me by the arm, and yanked me to the other side.

Instinctively I shot a bolt of lightning into the bird-thing. It squealed and dropped me about five feet onto a bed of white, fluffy, snow-like stuff, flying off as I tried to catch my breath. This side of the rift wasn't as cold as I'd imagined, given the landscape, although my breath did send little clouds of gray into the air. The snow was dry, like the fake stuff they use to decorate store windows during the holidays. The air was dry too. I felt like every bit of moisture was being sucked from my skin. Looking down I saw my hands whiten, bones becoming prominent as my flesh shrank against them.

I panicked, frantically trying to fly up and out of here through the rift before I dehydrated into nothing. Then something changed. It was as if my body were an article of clothing to be shed at will. When I shifted form into a wolf, or hawk, or even a bear it always seemed as if my body vanished and reformed. This was a twisting sort of feeling. Right before my eyes, my hands returned to normal, and the dry feeling vanished.

I glanced backward, relieved to see the rift still above me. Then I turned around and gasped at what I saw. There were five shapes on the ground — mummies in coveralls and camouflage. Their skin was flaked and pale as it stretched tight over bone. Three had blond hair that stirred lightly in the breeze. Two had short dark hair pressed tight to their skulls. Vacant eye sockets stared at me, teeth shining in a horrific grin between lips stretched tight. Brent had said the bird-things had dragged two hunters through the rift. I'd assumed those two were dead, most likely eaten. This could be them. And the other three must have been others who perhaps fell through on their own.

It brought home Raphael's words as well as Brent's. Was this what I'd see if I went through the other rifts? Were they all dead, as these ones were? I was too late to save these humans and I got the feeling that even if I'd gotten here five minutes after they fell through it would have been too late. This area was clearly not able to support human life, but it did support life of another sort. The bird thing that grabbed me seemed to have gotten reinforcements. As I looked up I saw winged beings with long, thick tails circle closer.

I should have flown back through the rift and had Rafi close it before these things got out, but curiosity killed the cat, and it probably would end up killing me too. I'd been shot, frozen, burned. I'd fallen off a mountain onto rocks, fallen into a narrow crevasse in the ice, fallen off a sea kayak into the freezing water where a polar bear had tried to eat me. Five thousand years was a long time to live and I never had much in the way of self-preservation instincts. I'd always survived, healing critical wounds quickly. I seemed destined

to live forever, unlike that polar bear whose fur still decorated my living room floor.

So I stayed, shooting a quick glance up at the pulsing
gateway to make sure it was still there. The winged-things
lost their caution and dove toward me at top speed, their
bodies aligning in a V formation as they flew.

Their upper bodies and wings looked like a half-plucked
chicken. They had sparse iridescent feathers, and pebbled
pinkish-gray skin. Long hair streamed from their heads in
clumpy strands. Sharp claws curled from their hands and
equally sharp-looking teeth snapped in their beaks. Their
lower halves were like serpents, scaled with a twisting tail
and no legs. Every instinct screamed at me to run, but
instead I was rooted in place staring at the horrible things
because they were naked. And they had boobs.

Duh. Of course they were naked. I think humans were the
only crazy beings in all of creation that needed to cover up
their bodies with the skins of others, even in warm climates
where body heat preservation wasn't an issue. Heaven forbid
another human saw their reproductive parts. I didn't understand it. The werewolves didn't understand it either. If they
didn't run the risk of getting arrested, I'm sure most of them
would run around with their dicks flapping in the wind.

But these five creatures had no dicks flapping in the
wind. They did have breasts so large that back home they'd
need to special order bras, although it was pretty obvious
these women-bird-things had never seen a foundational
garment in their lives. It was interesting to see how gravity
took a toll on body parts even in other worlds.

They swooped down, claws outstretched. That's when I
stopped gawking at their boobies and flew.

I could hear the sound of their wings behind me. Soft dry
snow swirled up in clouds with each step. The gate pulsed
above me but just as I was about to dive through it, I smashed

head-first into Raphael. We tumbled to the ground in a heap, me on top.

"By all that's holy, are you okay?" Lavender eyes stared up into mine. "I half expected to find you pecked to death, or standing over a flock of dead bird-things. Either scenario was just as likely."

I wasn't paying attention, since I was trying to get off of him, accidently elbowing him in the face in my haste. "Incoming!"

That was the only warning he got. The five winged, boobed creatures landed on us like a swarm of insects. Claws dug into my shoulder, tearing through muscle right down to bone. I did the only thing I could think of doing at the moment and grabbed the creature's bumpy arm, sending a surge of electricity through it.

Cooked chicken smells wonderful. Electrocuted boob-birds do not. The claws dug in deeper and the creature screamed. It was the most horrible high-pitched sound I'd ever heard. I wouldn't have been surprised if my ears were bleeding along with my shoulder.

"Get through the rift. Get through the rift," Raphael shouted, punching and kicking at two of the bird-things.

Hey, how come he only had two to fight off where I had three? I continued to electrocute the one and try to shake the other two off my back. Raphael managed to free himself of his two and grabbed onto one of mine, yanking it off me. Unfortunately, a chunk of my shoulder went with it. Before I had a chance to heal, the other one was digging into my thigh while the electrocuted one sank talons into my waist, biting down on the very shoulder the first one had ripped open.

These things were like a plague — a very determined piranha kinda plague. I could see Raphael was continuing to have problems of his own. I tried the electricity again, this time raising it up a few notches, but the only effect was the horrible odor.

If lightning didn't kill these things, what would? Pain was derailing my ability to think, and panic was taking hold. Sadly, beating the boobie-birds with my hands didn't seem to deter them either. Neither did the stop, drop and roll technique. I caught sight of Raphael out of the corner of my eye. He was barely visible from the blur of bumpy skin and ratty feathers covering him, but it looked like the angel was trying to pry the things off of him and stomp them into the ground.

"Fucking birds!" the angel shouted. Before I had a chance to laugh at his unangelic language, a blinding light filled the air, followed by a sonic boom. The birds let go, squawking, and something else grabbed me, rising through the air. I squirmed for a moment before realizing it was Raphael, trying to fly us through the rift.

The rift he couldn't see.

"Left, left, left!" I shouted. "No, your other left."

I have no idea how, but he managed to clip the edge of the rift, finally sensing it and spinning around with enough force to push us through. Unfortunately, the boobie-birds had recovered from whatever he'd done and followed us.

They were pissed. Seriously pissed. So pissed that I considered running for it and attempting this again some other time. The only reason I wasn't flying top-speed out of here was because Raphael had decided to make a stand, yanking a small tree out of the ground and trying to bat the boobie-birds back through the rift.

The rift he couldn't see. Which meant all he was doing was whacking the things across the snow and grass. One hit the water's edge and screeched, its tail smoking and dissolving into a pile of scaly goo.

Ew. But at least I now knew how to kill them.

Raphael finally managed to launch one through the rift. One down, four more to go.

Nope. Five more to go. Damn thing came right on back through the rift, heading straight for my bleeding leg.

"They won't stay. Get them to the water. Drown them in the lake." I was close to entering full blown, pissed-off-Ahia mode. Bullets and fire hadn't killed me. It would really suck if these things did, and right in front of a sexy angel too. Determined not to let such an embarrassing death happen, I redoubled my efforts, throwing myself onto the ground, rolling toward the lake's edge and kicking like a crazy woman. The boobie-birds squawked, only digging in harder.

This was not looking good. I wasn't sure how much blood I'd lost, but my left leg, the one with a boobie-bird attached to it, was soaked and cold from the knee down. Out of desperation, I tried the electricity thing again, yelping as the charge cycled through the screaming bird-woman and zapped back at me.

Wet. My leg was in water. I was right here, I just had to get these things into the water with me. Punching one of them in the face, I started rolling again, feeling the icy wetness move up my leg.

It worked. The boobie-bird screamed, this time in a very different pitch. Steam rose from her skin, which was expanding at an alarming rate. I ignored the one attacking my shoulder and watched fascinated as she swelled up like a giant, partially-feathered, boobed tick.

Holy shit these things were ugly. The bloated one let go of my leg and thrashed around in the water, giving me the opportunity to concentrate on the one still gnawing at my shoulder. Stupid thing hadn't even noticed her friend was like an overinflated balloon. These boobie-birds might be nasty, vicious things, but they lacked any sense of empathy or community spirit toward each other. What creature keeps trying to kill and eat dinner while her bestie is two seconds from exploding into a pile of wet feathers? Bitch.

Her self-centered attitude worked to my advantage. I rolled again, gasping as I slid off a narrow ledge into deep water. Down I went, my diaphragm freezing in place with the shock of the icy lake. A thousand years in Alaska, and I never quite got over how cold water could feel before freezing.

One of the advantages of being underwater was that the boobie-bird's screams were muffled. She'd expanded like a puffer fish the moment we went under and released my shoulder, flailing as she tried to get back to the surface.

Oh no you don't. It was my turn to grab the boobie-bird, wrapping my one functional arm around it as well as the leg that wasn't hanging numb from my hip. I held my breath and watched as she kept swelling. Her skin lost its just-plucked texture and became a shiny, stretched pink-gray. Her eyes disappeared under bulging half-circle eyebrows. The serpent half swelled into a ball of scales. Feathers began to pop from her skin, filling the icy water around us with iridescent color. I held tight as her struggles slowed, determined to see this thing die once and for all.

Yep, I held a grudge that way. I really didn't have any problem killing these things. Maybe it was five thousand years of seeing birth and death repeat like an overused laundromat washer. Maybe it was my temper which lately didn't seem to tolerate human, or other creature, stupidity easily. Maybe I was just a blood-thirsty angel with no morals whatsoever. Either way, this thing was going down. The boobie-bird kept swelling until I felt like I was holding onto a giant, slimy, pillowy balloon. And then it exploded.

Exploded. As in little bits of skin, bone and internal organs decorating the waters along with the feathers.

Suddenly I wasn't so thrilled. It was probably going to take me forever to get the smell out of my hair.

I let go of the pieces I was still holding and surfaced, gasping and frantically trying to spit the nasty taste of bloated boobie-bird from my mouth.

"Ahia!"

Hands grabbed me, and hauled me out of the icy water. Strong arms came around me and pulled me tight against a warm, muscular chest. I slumped against the angel, hoping that if I played the hurt and injured routine I could stay here in his arms for the whole day. Or at least an hour or two.

"You okay?" Hands smoothed my wet hair. I felt his lips on the side of my head. This was the life. But as much as I wanted to stay here, we needed to close the gateway before more boobie-birds came through.

"Yeah. You?" I took advantage of the occasion to do some exploring of my own, running my hands all over him. He had no shirt on. And his wings were still out. If only his pants weren't on.

"Physically yes, although I think I'm mentally scarred for life. Did those things have boobs? Giant, saggy boobs?"

I laughed. "And did you see their hair? What the heck were those things?"

His arms tightened around me. "No idea. I thought at first they were cockatrice, but I've never seen them with boobs before. Maybe I've only seen the male ones."

He's seen cockatrice? As in real live cockatrice? Actually there was a more pressing question on my mind. "Did they have dicks? I mean, if they're called cockatrice, they have to have dicks."

"They've got the lower half of a serpent. Serpents don't have dicks."

"Serpents don't have boobs either," I retorted. "Neither do

birds. If the females have boobs, then I demand the males have dicks. And saggy, floppy balls."

He chuckled. "If my beautiful angel commands it, then it must be so."

I loved this, nestled up against him, laughing about these boobie-birds. He was gorgeous. He had a sense of humor. He'd just called me *his* beautiful angel. And he was damned handy in a fight.

And there was something else he was good at. I sighed, pulling my head away from his wonderful, tanned chest. "Guess we better close this rift before more of them come through. I'm sure the next round will be the penis-birds looking for their women."

Raphael shuddered, standing up and letting me slide to the ground along the front of his body. "Now *that's* a terrifying thought." The angel walked over to the rift, patting in the air as I watched him.

"How do you do this? Closing the rift, I mean."

"It involves a direct application of a specific type of energy, aligning the patterns from each side then melding them together seamlessly." His hand vanished as he found the edge. I noticed that *his* fingers didn't get bitten on the other side.

With a wave of power that nearly flattened me, the rift lit up white. Light and colors flashed like strobes in a club, red then purple, orange then green. The rift turned gold, narrowing. And then there was sound — like a combination of church bells and broken glass. White light exploded everywhere, blinding me. I ducked, covering my head as I tensed for the inevitable explosion, but there was nothing. After a few seconds, just to be sure there was no delayed reaction, I poked my head up to look at a very smug angel.

"So, what do you think?"

That I so want to fuck you right here, right now. "Not bad for a minor angel," I teased.

He grinned, but there was something in the way he stood that made me think the whole process had taken a lot out of him.

"Want to take a break? We can go grab brunch and take care of the other ones afterward."

The angel looked as if he were about to protest the need for a break, then he paused, a sly expression on his face. "Brunch sounds wonderful. I'll cook while you change out of those wet clothes."

CHAPTER 14

RAPHAEL

Thankfully she'd decided to shower and wash the boobie-bird gunk out of her hair because I had an epic brunch to make and not a lot of time to pull it together. I was an angel. And I put that to good use, teleporting all over the place to grab the ingredients I needed. By the time she walked into the kitchen, I had everything set up and was busy frying pancakes.

I might not be able to make a huge variety of food, but I'd gotten this pancake-making thing down to an art.

Ahia stopped and stared at the table open-mouthed. She'd put her tank-top on before she was fully dry, and had fore-gone a bra. I heartily approved. And if I didn't stop gaping, I was going to burn my pancakes.

"I'd expected cereal in a bowl, or maybe scrambled eggs if I was lucky. I never imagined this." She walked over and stuck a finger in the clotted cream, tasting it. "Oh my God, this stuff is amazing. And fresh raspberries? Where did you get those?"

Score. I don't care how much they denied it, angels loved food just as much as any human. And since Ahia was an

Angel of Chaos, she was more open to indulging in sensory pleasures. I felt myself stir at the thought of all the other sensory pleasures I wanted the pair of us to indulge in. "I know a guy in the lower forty-eight who has an early berry harvest, and there's an amazing dairy in France. And then I swung by that farm in Virginia to get some of that bacon I was talking about last night." I flipped two pancakes onto a plate and set it on the table next to the plate of thick, crispy bacon.

"You are amazing. I never expected an angel would know how to cook." She sat down, grabbed a piece of bacon and waited for me to join her. "Or eat. I had this vision of angels wearing hair shirts and existing off air and water."

"That's Gabe, my brother. He's the austere one of the family. I'm different." Very different.

She dug in, heaping raspberries and cream on the pancakes and eating as enthusiastically as she had last night. Watching her enjoy something I'd made with my own hands, that I'd provided, was one of the best feelings I'd had in a million years.

"You have a brother? I mean, I guess angels have to come from somewhere, but I never really thought about angel families, or babies or anything like that."

I sat down and started in on a stack of pancakes. "I have four siblings. As I said last night, we're genderless, but we have preferences. Right now two are in male form, and one is a female."

"What about the other one?" she asked, mid bite.

My chest felt like someone had piled boulders on it. "He's probably dead."

I hadn't meant it to come out like that — so harsh and abrupt. I could still barely stand to think about Samael, the one most like me, the one I'd not stood beside when every-thing in Aaru fell apart.

The fork froze halfway to her mouth. The sympathy in her eyes was almost more than I could bear. "I'm so sorry."

I usually never wanted to talk about the brother I'd lost, but for some reason the timing seemed right, the wound finally ready to begin a slow process of healing. She hadn't been there. She was probably the only angel that wouldn't judge me for what happened. And I needed someone to know.

"Remember when I said there are Angels of Order and Angels of Chaos? Well, Samael was the only one of the five of us who was an Angel of Chaos. He was the Adversary, the Iblis. He was the one who questions, who made us see another point of view. Angels of Chaos keep us from being too intractable, they break us out of our tunnel vision. They keep us from stagnating. They bring us alive."

"You sound more like one of these Chaos angels then an Order one," she commented.

"I am. Occasionally there is an angel born that straddles both sides. They are designated whichever type they hold the most in common with, but they never truly fit in with either group."

"And that's you." Her voice was soft, full of sympathy. I had to take a breath to pull myself together. In billions of years, there hadn't been anyone who truly understood. No one except for Samael.

I nodded. "There was a war. The Angels of Chaos lost and were banished to Hel. They've interbred and produced demons. We…we can't interbreed. Aaru has become grid-locked in our own piety. We're stuck. And we're too proud to admit it and reach across the distance to reconcile with the demons."

She shot me a sad smile. "Isn't pride a sin?"

"There is a whole lot of sin in Aaru. Probably as much sin as in Hel."

"And your brother died in the war? This Samael?"

I swallowed hard. "We don't know. We're pretty sure he didn't die in the war itself, but he may have died soon after the Angels of Chaos were banished. It's been nearly three million years and none of us have seen or heard from him. His seat on the Ruling Council sat empty until a few years ago when an imp showed up with Samael's sword and took his place."

She reached across the table and took my hand. The sparkle of tears in her eyes made me want to cry too. "And you blame yourself for not taking his side, for opposing him with your other brothers."

Like a scalpel, her words cut right to the heart of the matter. "I was designated as an Angel of Order, but I could have gone either way. Samael begged me to stand with him. And in my heart I knew he was in the right on these matters. If I had stood with him, maybe he wouldn't have died. Maybe there would have been some reconciliation."

"Or maybe you would have been banished like the rest of them. And Aaru would have been a far worse place without you there to shake things up a bit." She smiled. "Why did you choose to fight on the other side? The side of Order? I know you had your reasons."

She was the only one ever to ask. In three million years, no one had bothered to ask me why in that pivotal moment I had chosen Order over Chaos.

"Samael was in the right, but he was brash. He wanted change to happen at a pace that would have caused unacceptable disruption. If he just would have exercised some patience, gone through the prescribed channels, then he would have gotten his way in the end. I loved my brother but he was all about smashing the status-quo and less about enacting a gentle, sustainable change."

She squeezed my hand, and I felt her spirit-self reach out

to mine. "Spoken like an Angel of Order. You might think you don't fit in, but from my viewpoint, you sound like the only voice of reason in this whole madness. Maybe if both sides had listened to you, there wouldn't have been a war."

I felt the weight on my chest lift. There was nothing I could have done to prevent the war, but it was so freeing to actually share this with someone.

"What about you? What has your life been like so far?" I asked.

She laughed and tried to retrieve her hand. I held tight, not wanting to let her go, and she relented.

"Let's see...it was hard to find my place with the humans. They called me Little Crow because every time someone followed my advice they got into trouble. I'm contrary, always questioning authority, stirring things up. I guess like your brother, in that way. About two hundred years ago, a werewolf caught sight of me and recognized me as a Nephilim. The humans were reluctant to let me leave, but once there was an established pack, they finally agreed."

"You didn't have any say in all of this?"

She squirmed, looking down at the few scraps of pancake still left on her plate. "Yes, I guess so. But what was I to do? The humans took me in as an infant. I'd been living off their charity ever since, and now I live off the werewolves' charity. I have a job, but it's not enough to support me. Everything I have I owe to them — the humans and the werewolves. Without their care, I would have been alone in the wilderness."

"You're nobody's charity case," I argued. "Those years with the humans, and now with the werewolves...you contribute. You're out there killing chimera, trying to kill a hydra. How many times did you defend your humans from attack? How many times did you provide food for them when they had none? You've protected them. You've kept them safe. They live off *your* charity."

They were lucky to have her. An angel walked among them, watched over them, and she thought she was like some homeless beggar on the corner?

She stared at me a moment, then looked down at our joined hands. "I love them, really I do, but they die, and I don't always understand their priorities, or how they live their lives. No matter how much they welcome me, and consider me part of their pack and family, I've always been the outsider. I've always been the crazy half-angel. I'm the only one like me here, the only one here for five thousand years."

She was lonely. And that was something I completely understood. "You're an angel, like me, like Nisroc, like all the angels in Aaru. You might be an Angel of Chaos, but you're definitely not an outsider. Someday I'll introduce you to the Iblis. She's an Angel of Chaos too. And she's so crazy that you'll look completely sane in comparison."

I felt the muscles in her hand tense as she pulled it from my grasp. "There's another? And she's not in Hel? Or dead? I just assumed when you said 'imp' that she was a demon."

"She used to be a demon, but she re-evolved or something. I'm not sure the exact details. She's the Iblis though, so she gets to be here and even in Aaru as part of her duties on the Ruling Council." I smirked, deciding to answer her unspoken question. "She joins with my brother, Micha. They're quite a devoted pair. And no, we've never been an item. She's like a sister to me."

Ahia squirmed. "I didn't......I mean... So, when an angel *joins* is it like getting married? This Iblis and your brother?"

I grinned, happy to discuss one of my favorite activities — one that I hoped I'd be participating in with this angel. "Joining is to angels what sex is to humans. Our spirit-selves align and merge outside of a body. Two become one. It's an incredible rush. When we are perfectly unified, a pair of angels becomes one and is in a state of grace, approaching divinity."

She snorted. "Grace and divinity? Leaving my body? Ugh. Give me naked, sweaty, heart-pounding human sex instead."

I leaned forward. "Both. At the same time. You have to leave a portion of your spirit-self inside the body to feel the physical sensation of orgasm. That means you won't get the full rush of joining, but the two together, both sensations simultaneously, would be explosive."

Her eyes were wide. "Holy cow. You've done that?"

"Never at the same time. I'm waiting for the right angel, one who appreciates my kind of crazy, a like-minded someone who is a little bit of Order and a whole lot of Chaos. Once I find this special angel, I'll need to woo her, convince her of my worthiness, persuade her to take a walk on the wild side."

"Woo her, huh?" She raised an eyebrow then looked down at the pancakes. "Like with flowers, chocolates...or pancakes."

Flowers and chocolate coming right up. I motioned to the remains of our breakfast. "I'll admit to having ulterior motives."

Her lips curled up in a smile that went right to my heart — as well as other parts of my anatomy. "Good. I'd be terribly disappointed if you didn't have ulterior motives."

There was one of those moments, and I wished there wasn't a table between us. I could make the table vanish, but then there'd be plates and pancake scraps and clotted cream all over her floor.

Her spirit-self touched mine, merging along the edge. "Like this? Only more?"

"Most definitely like that," I whispered. The table needed

to go. Right as I was wondering whether it would be wise to make the dishes vanish as well, she pulled away and stood.

"These dishes can wait until tonight. Let's go close some rifts and bowl with drop bear heads."

I watched her ass as she strode from the room then stood. Patience. It was a virtue that seemed to be quickly vanishing as I reveled in the sin of lust.

CHAPTER 15

She took me on another scenic tour as we flew to the next few rifts, then played the same guessing game, laughing while I tried to find the correct spot all on my own. What she didn't know was that her eyes gave it away every time. I just went along with it all because I loved to hear her laugh.

We checked in each rift for survivors. On the other side of every last one we found dead. Each time it was like Ahia had been stabbed in the chest. It made me try even harder to make her laugh with my mime routine at each rift. It made me wish that just once we could find someone alive, that I could give her the satisfaction of actually saving someone, reuniting them with their friends and family. But each time, we only found corpses near the opening on the other side of the rift.

Today I'd closed three rifts, fought off a host of boobie-birds, raced all over the world gathering foods to impress her. I'd brought all my power to the surface, showing her every bit of the archangel I was. I was tired. The battles in

Aaru, all the fighting… I hadn't expended this much energy since the war nearly three million years ago. I desperately needed to rest and recharge, but there was no way I'd let her see any weakness. Raphael, the least powerful of the archangels, the frivolous, silly, not-completely-an-Angel-of-Order. So many in Aaru thought me unworthy. I didn't want her to think that, so I kept onward. There would be time to recharge in a few days. I had plenty of strength to keep running flat-out until then.

So I glowed, shifting my wings in the sunlight, pushing the weight of my power into the air around us as I looked up into the trees. They were up there, little furry bundles with shiny black noses and adorable round ears. I was beginning to rethink the appeal of bowling with drop bear heads.

"They're kind of cute. Maybe we should just round them up and send them back through the rift."

Ahia looked at me open mouthed. "Cute? Did I tell you they shredded me like a plate of pulled pork? That Brent had to flee before they took him completely apart? Brent, an Alpha werewolf, had to run away."

I snorted. "So Brent's a pansy. Look at them. They're like big squirrels. No, they're like animated teddy bears. I'm sure you just got on their bad side."

She folded her arms across her chest and shrugged. "Fine. You go round them up, Pretty-boy. Have at em'."

I rolled up my sleeves. "Okay. Go stand by the rift so I can tell where it is." They were cute, but I'd been scratched by adorable kittens before. If these things were going to get feisty, I wanted to be able to run over and push them through to the other side as quickly as possible.

Ahia walked over near a tree and framed it with her hands, posing as if she were on a game show. She had a little smirk on her face, so I shot her a narrow-eyed glance and tiptoed my way over to the trees.

Yeah. I was an idiot. I knew what was going to happen, but I just wanted to hear her laugh again — that deep belly laugh that made her double over and tears run down her cheeks. I loved that laugh the best.

The furry beasts stirred in the trees, one sending up a loud, chilling cry. "Here, bear, bear, bear. Time to go home, bear, bear, bear."

The trees erupted with noise as the animals jumped from limb to limb approaching me as a group. One jumped down and I opened my arms to catch him. Then they all jumped, a hoard of twenty furry teddies landing on me all at once, claws and teeth flashing. I felt my skin shredded as if the bears were armed with box cutters. Dancing around, I tripped on a root and felt to the ground, teeth sinking into my torso and every limb.

That's when I heard it — that laugh. "Help," I shouted, gratified to hear the laugh reach breathless proportions. About then I decided to get serious about these things. One by one I ripped them from my flesh and hurtled them like fuzzy footballs into the rift. Ahia held her arms in a circle as a target. Three made it through, but I got a little careless on the fourth and it whacked her in the face where it clung like a demented furry leech.

Okay, I wasn't careless. I'd done it on purpose.

She did a funny scream-laugh then spun around, pulling the drop bear from her face and kicking it through the rift. Then she turned to face me, grinning with red, bleeding stripes down her face. "Did you see that? I drop-kicked the drop bear!"

I wanted to clap my approval, but I had sixteen drop bears trying to devour me alive.

"Here. I'm open. I'm wide open." I tore another bear from my leg and threw it to Ahia, who caught it like a pro wide-receiver and tossed it through the rift. "Another! Another!"

I obliged then launched another and another and another at her. She squealed as she caught one, and two more latched to her, biting and scratching as she threw the first one through the rift. "You bastard!"

"You have no proof of that," I shouted back. "But I don't either. I'm pretty sure we all were formed by the Creator itself."

"Pfft. I know a bastard when I see one." Two more bears went through and I launched two more, aiming for the same spot. One went through, the other hit the edge and spun, squealing as it rolled across the ground. Ahia dove for it, tossing it from the dirt into the rift.

We continued, goofing off and throwing bears until all twenty were gone and we were both torn up and bloody, laughing as we rolled on the ground.

"Hurry up and close this before they come back," she told me, wiping her eyes with the back of her arm and smearing red across her face.

I looked up in the trees, just to make sure there weren't any more of them up there. I was assuming that they'd all jumped down on me at once. If there'd been any holding back, then they would have already made their presence known. I got the feeling they weren't the run-and-hide type.

Unlike Brent. Haha.

"Hustle your cute ass, Pretty-boy."

I stood and healed all my wounds, leaving my clothing torn and blood stained just for the effect. Then I paused, tearing the ruined T-shirt from my chest, and throwing it on the ground.

"Woohoo!" Ahia clapped, then again outlined the rift, doing her game-show routine.

I sealed the rift between the worlds, forcing myself to remain upright once it was done. As I turned around, I felt her slam into me, her arms wrapping around my neck.

"God, that was fun." Her breath was warm against my cheek. I grabbed her ass and pulled her up against me and she wrapped her legs around my waist.

"First I'm a bastard, now I'm a god. Pick one, woman."

She leaned her head back to look me in the eyes, her face so near mine. "How about a little of both?"

Then she kissed me, her lips soft and open, her tongue tangling with mine. I dug my fingers into her rear, crushing her against me. I'd had plenty of fun in three billion years, but never had I been so on the edge of completely losing control, never had I wanted to share so much of myself with another angel.

My knees buckled and we rolled on the ground, coming to a stop with her straddling me. Her mouth never left mine, and now her hands were all over me, feeling the muscles of my chest as her fingers worked their way downward. I let her play, just holding her hips tight against me and thoroughly enjoying for once having another angel take charge and both initiate and drive our encounter.

Her hand drifted lower, popping the button on my jeans. At the same time her spirit-self reached for mine in a soft, shy caress, merging tentatively at the edges. Again my control began to unravel and I bucked my hips against hers, struggling to keep from snatching her spirit-self from her body and joining with her completely. Patience. Patience.

She pulled her lips from mine, her eyes glowing silver as she looked down at me. "I want you. Right here, right now."

I pulled her down to me kissing her, loving the soft feel of her lips, the sweetness of her tongue against mine. "Nope. Not yet."

She sat up, a pout pulling those beautiful lips together. "Not yet? What do you mean 'not yet'?"

Clearly few people had ever told this angel no. Rocking

my hips against her, I watched her eyes lose their focus, a soft sound escaping her mouth.

Mine. Mine, mine, mine. But I didn't want to rush this, not when it, us, was so very important. "I'm not done wooing you yet."

Definitely a pout. "Dude, you had me at pancakes. Actually, you had me long before pancakes. I'm wooed. Trust me, I'm wooed."

I slid her off my lap and stood, unable to resist giving her another quick kiss on the forehead. "You're not wooed until I say you're wooed, angel."

Her eyebrows shot up. "Bossy. Are you going to demand I get in the kitchen and make you a sandwich?"

"Hardly." I held my hand out and helped her to her feet. "Given that you tossed me a package of Pop-Tarts for breakfast, I assume your culinary skills end at boxed mac and cheese. A sandwich might be beyond your abilities."

"I'll have you know I make a mean bologna, cheese, ketchup and potato chip sandwich."

"By the Creator, are you trying to kill me?" I held my stomach, grimacing. "You don't seriously put potato chips *on* your sandwich, do you?"

"Absolutely. Otherwise it's kind of mushy. The other ingredients don't have much texture. The chips give it a refreshing crunch."

I sighed, putting my arm around her. "Is that going to be your cooking show entry? Bologna and potato chip sandwiches?"

"No, it's our dinner tonight. You'll love it."

"What if I don't love it?"

She batted her eyelashes. "Wooing me, remember?"

I grinned. "Ah, yes. Then I'm sure I'll love it so much that I'll ask for seconds."

"And after the sandwiches, the oral sex?"

There was a tease in her eyes. Did I get the order wrong? Maybe it was flowers, pancakes, oral sex, *then* chocolate and a shoulder massage? "Maybe. They better be darn good sandwiches, though."

CHAPTER 16

On the way home, Ahia took a detour. I didn't argue, since I wasn't all that eager to choke down a bologna, ketchup and potato chip sandwich and pretend to like it. Still, I was surprised when she lit on a narrow, rocky ledge looking down into a broad meadow.

"Want to have some fun?"

"Always." I grinned, wondering what she was up to. Boobie-birds, drop bears. What now?

"See that dark shape down there? The one by the tree?"

I squinted. It was pretty far off, but I could make out that it was a bear. "Grizzly?"

She gave me a thumbs-up. "Bingo. Except it's a grizzly shifter — a weregrizzly."

Okay? "Is he or she a friend of yours?"

The angel laughed. "It's a love-hate thing. He messes with me; I mess with him."

I was catching on. "So we're going to mess with this weregrizzly?"

"Absolutely. Here's the rules. You have to be totally silent on our approach. We'll land about fifty feet away in that copse over there, but not touch the ground. Then we need to float over to him. Once we land, no flying. That's cheating, and I don't like cheating. Got it?"

No. We were going to all this trouble just to sneak up on a weregrizzly and say boo?

"Trust me," she said, patting my shoulder. She had that naughty smile going on that let me know this was probably going to end badly — and be a whole lot of fun.

"Okay. Let's do this."

We flew in a wide circle down to our landing spot, hovering just a few inches off the ground. Then we slid forward as if we were on an invisible moving walkway, approaching the grizzly from the back. He was seated, one shoulder against a tree. And he was snoring.

Ahia waved me around the other side of the bear. I raised an eyebrow but complied, eyeing the line of drool extending from the guy's half-open maw to his massive paw. The angel made a downward motion with her palm and we both lowered ourselves to the ground, careful to remain silent. The bear snorted, his nose twitching in his sleep.

In two steps Ahia was on him, shoving him over onto the ground. "Bear tipping!" she screamed at the top of her lungs. Then she ran. I hesitated, which in hindsight was very poor judgement on my part.

The grizzly's eyes flew open as he hit the ground. A roar shook the air, spittle flying as he scrabbled to get onto his feet. Then he saw me standing right in his line of sight and snarled. Oh, that angel was so naughty. And she also had a head start of nearly five seconds on me.

I ran, feeling the thump of four huge paws hitting the ground behind me, hearing the harsh breath of a pissed-off werebear. Claws swiped at my leg and I put on a burst of speed, catching up to Ahia, and giving her a dirty look as I ran by for making sure I was right in front of the grizzly and ditching me without warning.

She stumbled. The bear launched himself at her and I acted from instinct, knocking her aside and rolling out of the way of the huge claws. This bear was fast, and I wasn't sure how serious this fight would be if he caught us. Killing boobie-birds was one thing. I had no desire to be known as the angel who had to use lethal force against a were. Seeing him recover and jump toward us, I made a quick decision: I grabbed Ahia tight and teleported.

Not far, because I was downright exhausted after everything I'd done in the last twenty-four hours. We found ourselves a few miles away, Ahia sprawled on her back under a tree, me on top of her.

"You're crazy," I muttered into her hair. "I thought I was crazy, but you're Sam-level crazy. Good grief, Ahia, what did you intend to do? Were you going to fight to the death with him over a prank? Lay down and let him rip you to shreds? Were you going to seriously hurt a guy who was just taking a nap when you rudely woke him up?"

The sparkle in her eyes dimmed and she squirmed trying to get out from underneath me. "It's just Karl. He welded all my fry-pans together last month. And this past summer at the cookout he gave me a sandwich with a plastic hamburger in it. It squeaked when I bit into it. Neither of us would have killed the other. If he'd have caught me, he would have shoved my head in his mouth and slobbered all over it. Then he probably would have thrown me up into a tree."

Oh. I know she'd said there was mutual pranking going on, but with a roaring grizzly nearly on top of us, I'd gotten…serious? Protective? More Order and less Chaos? I was Raphael. I was the angel who should be all on board with were-tipping and silly pranks, but out of the blue I turned into someone else and lectured her.

"Yes, I'm crazy." Her eyes sparkled, and she blinked hard. "I'm sorry, I just am. And I thought for once in my life that I'd…oh, never mind."

She pushed and this time I rolled off of her, watching as she stood and turned her back to me. I gave her a moment to compose herself then went over and wrapped my arms around her. "I'm sorry. I don't know why I was channeling my brother Gabe there for a moment."

I did know why. A weregrizzly was about to slice our heads off, and I felt the need to protect her. And then snapped at her because she'd put herself in danger. She was an angel. She was tough. But she was also only five thousand years old. And the thought of anything happening to her twisted my stomach into a knot.

"We'll do the hydra and chimera rifts tomorrow along with the others, then I'll just have Nisroc contact you if any new rifts pop up." Her voice was wooden and bruised. I'd hurt her.

"No." I breathed the word into her hair then turned her around, taking her face in my hands. "Ahia, I'm sorry. I didn't know you guys did these pranks back and forth. I thought he was trying to seriously hurt you. I thought I'd have to kill him and fill out a two-hundred-page report, then face the angelic equivalent of the Spanish Inquisition. I freaked out. I'm sorry."

There was this uncertain look in her eyes — the look of someone who'd always been an outsider, been different, and been lonely. I rubbed my thumbs along her cheekbones. "I adore crazy. I'm not exactly sane myself, throwing drop bears like footballs and drowning boobie-birds — and enjoying every minute of it. Actually those activities wouldn't be at all fun without you. I'm coming to the conclusion that nothing is going to be fun without you."

"Does nobody expect it?" She asked, her face serious.

I had no idea what she was talking about. "Expect what?"

Her lips twitched. "The Angelic Spanish Inquisition."

I laughed, relief flooding through me. Then I kissed her, gently, my lips moving slowly against hers. With an impatient noise she deepened our kiss, brushing her tongue against mine. She tasted of warm honey, her tongue tangling with mine as her hands came up to bury themselves in my hair. Fire ran down my spine and I pulled her closer, crushing her chest against mine and trailing kisses from her mouth down her jaw to her neck.

Her hands left my hair to grab my hips and pull me tight against her. "We're done wooing, aren't we? Please tell me we're done with the wooing crap."

"What, you don't want me to make you pancakes anymore?" I teased, slowly nibbling my way down her neck.

She arched her back. "Sex first. Pancakes later. Then more sex."

I hesitated. Then she took my earlobe in her mouth and nipped, grinding herself against me. "Come on, sin with me, Rafi. Show me how wicked you can really be."

My willpower crumbled. Sneaking my hands under her shirt I ran my fingers up her ribcage to cup the fullness of her breast. "Like this? Or, like this?" Licking the sensitive skin along her collar bone, I rolled her nipple between my fingers and felt her shiver.

Her hands yanked at my waistband. "Now. Get these damned clothes off now."

"Your wish is my command." I made her shirt disappear then dipped my head down to draw her nipple into my mouth.

She gasped and swatted me on the shoulder. "No. Well, yes, but I meant your clothes not mine. Well, mine too."

I chuckled. "Patience, patience." But still I removed both of our clothes. The cool spring air hit my skin, heightening every nerve ending. She was warm and wet against me, her fingers gripping my rear as she slid herself along my length.

"Fuck patience," she gasped.

Indeed. I rocked my hips against her, losing myself in the feeling. She whimpered, her breathing ragged as she worked herself against me. I brought my mouth back up to hers, pressing her body against mine and lifting her to her toes. My hands grabbed her hips, to help her keep her balance and her rhythm.

"How do we…?" She kissed me again, tugging me downward. I had a better idea and scooped her up, taking three steps to press her back against the rough bark of a tree. I'd barely maneuvered her into position before she jerked her hips, pushing forward. I felt her stretch around me as I sank into her heat.

"I think we should stop and have more pancakes," I teased.

"You do and I'll rip your wings off. Now shut up and do me."

I laughed, rocking myself in and out of her, touching her spirit-self with mine. She grazed her teeth along my shoulder, nipping at the skin.

"Harder. More," she urged.

I complied, grasping her waist and rolling my hips. My spirit-self merged with hers in a swirl of translucent white. I felt her shudder, felt her muscles tense as she tilted her face to the sky. Harder and faster I drove into her until she clenched tight around me, her orgasm pulsing through her like a wave. I held back, enveloping and merging my spirit-self with hers to prolong her release, then when I could take it no more, I let myself go, filling her, joining with her spirit as much as I could while still retaining corporeal form. Sparks danced at the edge of my vision and I fell against her, my muscles quivering, the tree the only thing holding both of us upright.

Then I kissed her lips, and her face, whispering all the things I'd wanted to say, all the emotions I felt, and when I looked into her dark eyes, I knew I'd found my other half, I'd found the angel that made me, complimented and completed me. I'd found the angel that made me whole.

CHAPTER 17

AHIA

*B*ack home we curled up on the couch, argued over movies, got into an incredible wrestling match for the remote. And we had sex — lots and lots of sex. This playful seduction of ours was intoxicating. When we had joined — both physically and with our spirit-selves —the planets halted in their orbit, the moon fell from the sky, the stars sang. Rafi made good on his promise, doing things with his mouth that surely no angel should ever imagine doing. We made love in the kitchen, on the sofa, on my polar bear skin rug. And when we weren't exploring each other's bodies and spirit-selves, we were talking and laughing. Each interaction entwined us together with another silken strand, on their own fine and fragile, but combined they were becoming an unbreakable bond. My life was forever changed. Not even twenty-four hours and I couldn't imagine being without him. I'd never believed I could fall this fast. Lust at first sight, yes. Love at first sight? That was a myth. Until it wasn't.

He ate my sandwiches, admitting that the potato chips were a brilliant addition. Then I fell asleep with my head on his lap. And the next morning when we awoke, curled

123

together on the couch, I felt a sense of joy I'd never thought possible. We did rock-paper-scissors for breakfast. I won, and grinned as I tossed him the packet of Pop-Tarts.

We were on my front porch, hand-in-hand, munching our breakfast and drinking coffee when my phone beeped.

"Crap," I said as I read the text. "Morgan is out sick today and they want me to cover her shift." This was seriously cutting into my Raphael time. We'd closed quite a few of the rifts yesterday, but there were still more, and we still had to deal with that hydra. And then there was sex. I wanted to block out lots of today's schedule for carnal pleasure.

"Do we have time to take care of this hydra before you go in? I hate to leave it till tomorrow." His voice was casual, but his spirit-self-touched mine. We were having such fun together. I didn't want my job to interrupt what was shaping up to be an amazing day, but I had responsibilities. They needed me at work, and I couldn't let them down. Besides, if Jess had to do a double shift and cover for Morgan, the shoplifters would rob us blind.

But I didn't need to go in until two. We had time for a little hydra action. "Yep, as long as I can be back in time to shower and change beforehand. I can't show up to work covered in hydra guts." Or puffy from hydra venom, but hopefully the swelling would have receded by the time my shift started.

"Do I get to see where you work?" He asked, our fingers still entwined, his spirit-self still against mine.

I blinked in surprise. "Sure. I guess. If you want to."

His hand gripped mine tight. "I want to. I want to know everything about you. Besides, I need to buy tacky Alaska-themed gifts for my family."

I grinned. "A shot glass for your sister-in-law the Iblis?"

"And a pair of bear-butt boxers for Micha. A mother-of-pearl whale-tail necklace for Uri. And for Gabe…" He gave me a wicked smile. "For Gabe a giant stuffed beaver."

I laughed. "Stuffed. Because beavers were meant to be stuffed, you know."

He wiggled his eyebrows. "Some beavers more than others."

Love didn't begin to describe what I felt for this angel. "Beavers and boxers later. Right now, let's go kill a hydra."

* * *

FIRST STEP WAS to close the rift. This was one of the few that hadn't taken any humans, and, so far, only the one hydra had come through. It would really suck to go to all the trouble to kill one hydra only to discover a family of five had arrived while we were fighting it.

"Here?"

This had become a game between us — guess the location. "Warm. Getting warmer," I added as he shuffled forward and to the left. "Warmer. Hot. You are so hot."

He smirked. "Thank you. And back at cha'."

I rolled my eyes, tempted to shove him off the edge of the cliff. Although that particular action wouldn't have much of an effect on an angel who could just sprout wings and fly right back up.

"Smoking hot, Pretty-boy." His hand vanished and I laughed at the absurdity of it all. If someone had told me a few days ago that I'd be working side-by-side with an angel, flirting with him, having lurid thoughts about him, screwing him every chance I got, I would have proclaimed them insane. Yet here I was.

"Do we need to look in?" Raphael asked.

"No humans fell through this one. The hydra has killed a bunch, including two werewolves, but this isn't a well-traveled spot, if you could call anything in Alaska well-traveled, that is." The rift was on the edge of a cliff. There were better places for mountain climbing, and most of those who came here to fish weren't interested in scaling the rock face.

"So you're not the slightest bit curious about where hydra come from?"

It was my turn to smirk. "Well, the male hydra inserts his hydra-cock into the female's hydra-pussy. There is a bunch of friction and an eventual ejaculation, and if the timing is right the female will give birth to a minimum of one hydrette."

"You make it sound so clinical. Where's the romance? Where's the earth-moving, stars-standing-still passion? Where's the making-pancake seduction?"

Oh, Lord. I was so going to do this angel, preferably before lunch. "Well they're hydra. What do you expect, foreplay?"

"I do hear they give good head."

Haha. I really loved this guy. It wasn't just the pretty face and incredible body, it was his silly, light-hearted approach to life. He was fun. He was kind of goofy, like the class clown. And from what he'd said, the other angels didn't appreciate this sort of behavior.

I appreciated it. And those other angels were idiots to let this one get away.

"You sure? Not the slightest bit curious? Going once. Going twice–"

"Oh, all right," I said, walking over to him. "Let's see where hydra come from. With any luck, maybe we'll catch two of them in the very act of procreation."

"Eww, I hope not." He grabbed my arm just as I was about to go through. "Me first."

Chivalry was not dead. And I wasn't an idiot. This angel

had billions of years of experience on me. If he wanted to stick his head through first, I wasn't going to argue.

Raphael's upper half vanished, his hand still firmly gripping my arm. After a few seconds he popped back out, his hair wet, drops of liquid on his face.

"Please tell me that's water and not something horrible like hydra spit," I said. "Or hydra cum."

"Water." He pulled me forward. "Come look. It's beautiful."

I shoved my upper body through the rift and gaped at the sight before me. I'm pretty sure some people would not have found the scene before me beautiful, but I agreed with Raphael. The cave extended back past where I could see, an inky blackness that echoed the sound of water dropping from the low ceiling. Hundreds of thousands of bat-like creatures crawled along the walls with six legs, their membrane wings glowing a pale yellow that gave the cavern a golden glow. I heard a splash and looked down to see we were inches above the water that covered the entire cave floor.

A drop hit me on the head, icy cold as it ran down my face. I caught my breath and the soft sound was amplified around the cavern. The bats took flight, golden wings making them seem like iridescent butterflies. A few dove into the water, becoming more like stingrays than bats. It was magical. I hated having to seal this world away, but it was for the best — both for the residents of this world as well as the ones here.

I pulled myself back to the cold spring Alaska air, the sunshine, the rocky mountain ledge, and the angel who'd never let go of my arm the whole time I'd been halfway through the rift.

He was grinning. "Cool, huh?"

More than cool. "I wish I could go to places like that, see

other worlds. Heck, see other states. I barely remember the life I had across the ice. This world is my home and I love it, but these glimpses of something else…"

He tugged and pulled me forward into his arms. "You can love home and still enjoy experiencing new places. Aaru has a special place in my heart. It will always be my home, but my life would be less rich, less fulfilling, if I didn't explore, if I didn't give myself the chance to fall in love with new places, and new experiences."

I wanted that too, and before I could stop myself I was envisioning new places and new experiences with this angel by my side. Would he share that with me? Because doing that on my own didn't seem nearly as much fun as doing it with someone else — someone to share the excitement, the novelty, the sensation. I was all about sensation, and in spite of all I'd ever been told about angels, I got the feeling that Raphael was too.

Maybe, just maybe a minor angel from Aaru would be interested in a future with a young, inexperienced angel who lived with a werewolf pack and worked in a tourist shop.

Raphael's arms tightened around me and I felt him kiss the top of my head. "Do you want to help me close it? The rift?"

I looked up at him, bringing my lips tantalizingly close to his. "Can I do that? I thought I couldn't. I see them. You zip them shut."

He closed the distance, giving me a feather-light kiss. "Together we can do both. Together I can see the gateway, and you can close it. When an Angel of Chaos and an Angel of Order join, they both experience a bit of the other."

Now that had to be the smoothest line I'd ever heard. "Are you trying to get into my pants?" I teased.

"Yes, I am." Again that soft kiss that promised so much more.

"I do want to close the rift with you."

I wasn't sure what I expected. I'd seen him close the rifts yesterday, and it had been all power, light and sound. This time was magic. His arms remained around me. I could feel the hard planes of his chest against mine, his breath against my face. But even as he held me, I felt him envelop me, felt something white-hot where our incorporeal selves touched. Then we eased together in a swirl of color and sound. Aside from some tiny part that anchored us to our individuality, our physical selves, we were one.

He caught his breath and I knew he could see the rift with its splash of blue in a field of gray, that he could hear the discordant sound it made, jarring against the harmonious world around us, that he could feel the sharp jagged energy which radiated from this oblong shape that had rent a hole between two worlds.

Then he reached with his spirit-self, and the power that poured from him, through me and into the rift nearly brought me to my knees. He steadied me, and I saw what he was doing, the millions of mathematical formulas that he processed faster than any computer. He, we, tailored the energy flow to match the fluctuating resonance of the rift, and it seamed together, sealed with sound and light. His energy changed to a perfect match of the Alaskan landscape, and with a burst of white, he filled the gap.

It was incredible. It was awe-inspiring, the mental process, the sheer power that it took to do such a thing. I felt like a nobody next to him. I'd always been the big fish in the pond but in this ocean I was a minnow. Once more I wondered how someone like Raphael could ever find anything of value in me.

Without you, I could never have seen the terrible beauty of that rift.

Oh crap. He could hear me think. Had I thought something incriminating while we were joined together like this? This had to be one of the most embarrassing moments of my life. Far more embarrassing than that time I set my own boat on fire and had to swim three miles back to shore.

Without you I would never have seen that cave, or battled a bunch of boobie -birds. And how in all of creation did you manage to set your own boat on fire?

I pulled back enough that I could keep my thoughts to myself, enough that once again I realized how good his body felt against mine. "We were night fishing and I thought it would be helpful to have a globe of light. Seems I'm not very good at globes of light. Thankfully I was the only one in my boat at the time."

He chuckled. "I flew into a billboard a few years back. I was messing around and not paying attention and *whack.* Gabe swore he'd never tell anyone. He'll probably blackmail me for it a thousand years from now."

I giggled at the image of Raphael with his beautiful wings, smashing into a huge sign advertising a golf course or something. "Thank you for letting me help you with the rift, for sharing that experience with me. It was amazing."

He leaned close, resting his forehead against mine. "I hope to share other things with you. Lots of other things."

"What, like things involving beavers and streams, and friction?"

"And lots of bodily fluid exchanges."

I snorted. "Who's the romantic now? Bodily fluid. That's some silver tongue you've got there, Pretty-boy."

"Hey, you started it with your hydra sex-ed. Which reminds me, we still have one to kill before you go to work."

I really didn't want to go to work later. What I wanted to do was roll naked in the sheets with this angel. Maybe before work. What was I saying, totally before work.

"Okay, Pretty-boy. Hydra. Then perhaps there will be friction and bodily fluids in our very near future."

He wiggled his eyebrows at me. "Sounds like a plan, although don't blame me if I try to rearrange the order of things."

Now, *that* was a plan.

"See? Hydra."

We were perched on the ledge where I'd made my swoop attack yesterday, wings at the ready. I stretched one of mine out to touch Raphael's, marveling at the contrast. His were light descending to dark, mine the opposite. Mine black where his were the palest lavender. Yin and yang.

His wing brushed along mine, and more. Once again his spirit-self connected with mine. I hadn't quite gotten used to the sensation. It was a strange mix of comforting and sexually stimulating. All I knew was that I liked it. I liked it a lot. And I liked this angel a lot. He was funny, gorgeous, and had a depth to him. And he made pancakes. How awesome was that?

"I thought it had three heads?"

"Yeah, well it *did* have three heads. I kinda screwed up with my little salt experiment and now it has five."

He laughed. "Pfft. What's another two heads in the grand scheme of things? Five isn't a big deal. If that Hercules dude can take down one with nine heads, two angels should be able to wrap this up, have a lengthy shower together, grab lunch, and have you to work in plenty of time."

Mmmm, shower. "A very lengthy shower. And I know a spot in Juneau with incredible fried halibut that's on the way to work." What can I say? I liked food, too.

"It's a date." His wings spread out, the dark sections reflecting the light. "Let's go."

"Wait!" It was too late. He'd already begun his free fall, and the hydra was looking right our way. So much for the element of surprise. I was tempted to sit up here on the ledge and watch him try to do this one solo, just to teach him a bit of patience, but I really wanted in on this action. I had a score to settle with this hydra. And it wasn't like patience was my virtue either.

He might be reckless and impatient, but the angel was damned impressive. He slammed into the hydra at full speed, taking half a dozen bites before managing to rip one of the heads off with his bare hands.

"Hey! What the hell?" I hovered just out of biting range. "I'm supposed to cut heads and you're supposed to cauterize."

"Oops." He tossed the head onto the shore, then quickly beginning ripping the tiny ones that began to sprout in its place. "Change of plans. Now get in here before it winds up with fifty heads coming out of this stump."

That got me moving. I flew in, slashing at the other heads and hiding my wings the moment I got to Raphael. He had his arms wrapped around the thrashing hydra-neck, so I had nowhere to cling to but on his back like a monkey.

And it was awesome. He'd hidden his wings too, keeping the sensitive appendages from the hydra bites. That meant I felt every flex of his muscles against me. I wrapped my legs around his chest, making sure the back of his head fit nicely in my cleavage.

"Any day now."

He wasn't pissed off; he was amused — even though we were both being mercilessly bitten by four hydra heads. Well, I was being bitten the most since I was draped across his back. It was so worth it.

"Ahia. I promise you can rub yourself over my naked back all you want later. Just cauterize this hydra's neck before the damned thing bites us to death."

We wouldn't die, but the bites were starting to send numbing poison through me. Guess I better get to work before I was a drooling, limp mess on the shore and Raphael had to finish the job himself.

I grabbed the thing's neck, scooting up Raphael's back and leaning over his head. He laughed again, unable to see as my boobs were now draped in front of his face. I smirked and sent a bolt of lightning into the hydra's wound. It did cauterize the neck, but the electricity also reverberated through the monster and back into the pair of us.

Raphael yelped. "Cauterize. Not electrocute."

"I can't do fire. Or anything hot enough to sear it besides lightning," I shouted back. My lack of skill in that area had been a terrible disappointment to my early human families, who were hoping for fire with a snap of my fingers.

"Oh for Aaru's sake." He was still laughing as he reached up and grabbed the back of my shirt, yanking me free from him and throwing me to the side. I squealed and flung out my arms, grabbing hold of another hydra head. "You cut. I'll cauterize."

This was a total farce. I was bitten all over my back and limbs. I was swelling up like a very pink, very bloated tick. I'd just shocked myself with what for a human would have been a lethal dose of electricity. I was having the time of my life. Where had this angel been the last five thousand years?

I held on tight to the hydra's neck with my legs and yanked out my knife to start sawing away. Raphael jumped from the neck we'd just finished to the one I was working on, landing opposite me and wrapping his arms around both the hydra and my body.

"Hey, babe. Come here often."

Worst pick up line ever. "I almost cut *your* head off. Idiot. Now get ready."

With a jerk of the knife the hydra's head came off. Raphael slammed his hands onto the bloody stump and it sizzled with the aroma of cooked eel. Two down, three to go. I tossed the head to the shore and made a dramatic leap to the next neck. Unfortunately, I was beginning to resemble a balloon at the Macy's Thanksgiving Parade, and my joints weren't working in an optimal fashion. I bounced off the hydra neck, my puffy hands scrabbling to gain purchase as I sank down the long column and onto the creature's' base — which lay a foot under the icy water.

Holy mother of a biscuit, that was cold. I felt it even through my numbed legs.

"The head's up here," Raphael shouted. He was above me, his hair whipping wildly about as the creature tried to toss him off.

Jerk. I pulled out my knife and turned so he couldn't see what I was doing. Then I cut off the hydra's neck at the base. It toppled like a tree and I heard Raphael yelp as he hit the icy water. Just for good measure, as I cauterized the wound with lightning, I made sure to send some through the water, to zap the angel a bit extra.

Two left. And I was beginning to think we might need to come back and finish this thing off later. I could barely feel my legs. I was one more bite from losing my knife into the lake. And my face felt like it was about to explode. If I'd been alone I would have called it a day, but there was no way I was giving up in front of this angel. So I stuck the disgusting, hydra-bloodied knife between my teeth and grabbed another neck by the base, shimmying up it as best I could.

And now my mouth was going numb. Stupid venom. Raphael had learned his lesson and was sawing away at the head on the neck I wasn't trying to scale. I abandoned my efforts halfway up and just began hacking at the thing's neck — a difficult task given my hand was three times the size of my knife by this point.

"Done! Beat you."

Fucker. "It's not a race," I shouted back. Actually it sounded more like "Mfmph mmf ugh pstlf," because my mouth was numb. It would have been a good time to get a root canal.

"Here."

Raphael was beside me, wings unfurled to support him midair as he twisted the head off and tossed it to the side. I was almost done. He didn't have to help me. To illustrate my capabilities even puffed up to twice my size, I electrocuted the hydra once more. Raphael pulled his hands away just in time, his wings fluttering like a hummingbird's as the electricity sparked through the hydra.

No more heads. The thing began to slide into the lake and I jumped, summoning my wings. The wings didn't come and I found myself falling deep into the water. Hands grabbed me and hauled me upward, dropping me unceremoniously on the shore next to the pile of hydra heads.

Raphael sat down a few feet away, hiding his wings and throwing his hands in the air. "Yeah! That was awesome! Wasn't that the most fun you've had in centuries? More entertainment than even the boobie-birds. I can't wait for dragons and phoenix to start appearing. Bring em' on!"

Did I say I liked this angel? I think I changed my mind. I was exhausted. I felt like an over-ripe peach. I was covered in hydra guts. And I had to work in four hours. I healed fast, but last time it had taken me a good eight hours to recover. How the heck was I supposed to show up at the tourist shop looking like this? I couldn't even talk.

But it had been fun. And if I was being completely honest, I did want to ditch work and go take a cruise around Alaska, looking for other creatures to take out with this angel. Well, as soon as the venom was out of my system.

Crap. I couldn't even get my wings to show. Four hours until work. Damn it, in four hours I'd probably still be here flopping on the rocks.

"Pftfm mfft pwllt," I told Raphael, throwing a hydra head at him. It landed with a squelch against his chest before bouncing to the ground. How was he not all puffy? He'd been bitten just as much as I'd been.

The angel picked the head up and tossed it back at me. Then he grinned one of those dimpled-cheek, totally hot grins. "Come here."

There was an edge of command in the words that totally turned me on. I was puffy, therefore crawling to him with my best sexy-stalking-panther impression was out of the question, so I just flopped onto my back and gave him the finger.

"I said, come here."

I opened my eyes to find Raphael on all fours above me. Then he leaned down and kissed me.

My first thought was that he was a seriously kinky motherfucker to want to kiss me all puffed up to twice my size and covered in hydra guts. Actually my first thought was that he was a darned good kisser and I wished my mouth wasn't so numb. My second thought was that he was a kinky motherfucker.

Wait. I could feel my mouth. And I could feel a whole lot more too. He was healing me, and darn if this wasn't sexier than a Band-Aid and two aspirin. My arms went around his shoulders and I returned the kiss, arching my back to try to press myself against him.

Too soon his lips left mine and he stared down at me, those violet eyes lit with flecks of sky-blue. My arms slid upward so my hands twisted in his hair and caressed the column of his neck. My gaze drifted to his gorgeous full lips, then back to those mesmerizing eyes.

"Want to fly?" he murmured, swooping down to give me a quick hard kiss.

"Yes — fly home and take that lengthy shower together that you promised."

"Later. First I want to fly, if you're feeling adventurous, that is."

We had been flying, and although it was one of my favorite things, I'd never considered it particularly 'adventurous' in and of itself. But maybe he meant something else? "Is that angel slang for sex? Angel mile-high club?"

He sat back on his heels, pulling me up against his chest. Wings unfurled from his back and without conscious thought mine did the same.

"Six thousand feet isn't enough for what I have in mind. More like the six-mile-high club."

I blinked. "I don't think I can breathe at that altitude."

He grinned. "You're an angel. You don't need to breathe."

Maybe not, but breathing was a nice perk — one I was rather fond of. "And why forty thousand feet? I mean, if we're going to try to somehow manage sex while hovering in the air why not do it at a distance we actually can breathe at? And not freeze?"

The grin got bigger. Damn, those dimples were amazing. "Who said we're hovering? I was thinking more like a freefall."

He was crazy. I mean, I was crazy, but this angel made me look like the staid, sane one.

"Freefall? Sex during a freefall?" I did the math and didn't like the answer. "Dude, that gives us less than a minute. That might be fine for you, but that's a bit fast for my enjoyment."

"You're not taking terminal velocity into consideration. We'll top out at around two hundred miles per hour, not four hundred and eighty."

Sheesh. Mister Physics here. "Okay, roughly four minutes."

"Give or take." He narrowed his eyes as he thought. "That's if we do a nose dive. If we spread our wings out, we might get six minutes."

I laughed. This had to be the most insane idea ever. I liked it. "All right, Pretty -boy. Count me in."

CHAPTER 19

RAPHAEL

’d discovered my soul mate. Ahia fought those boobie-birds like a rabid Chihuahua. She liked my pancakes. Her sense of humor was just as twisted as mine. She wasn't wearing a bra. She'd thrown a bloody hydra head at me.

Did I mention she wasn't wearing a bra? I wanted her, and I wanted this to be an experience she could only have with an angel, that she could only have with me. And I'd need to act fast because acceleration and terminal velocity weren't our only issues. She had to be at work, and I wasn't about to be the one to make her late. For an Angel of Chaos, I got the impression responsibility was high on her list of important traits. Her co-worker was sick. She'd promised them she'd take the shift. She'd be there on time. And she'd be there breathless and sore in all the right places.

I looked into those eyes, so dark brown that they were almost black. "Ready?"

The edge of her mouth quirked up. "Catch me."

And off she flew, like a missile straight up in the air. I watched, partly to give her enough of a head start to make this fun, and partly so I could admire her ascent. Most angels flew in this form like they were drunken penguins. We didn't approve of physical manifestations, which meant we didn't get to use our wings in this plane, or for this type of activity. There were few angels who'd be able to fly like her, with the muscle control, the knowledge of thermals and cross winds, the mastery of aerodynamics as it applied to a human body with wings. I waited until she was barely a speck in the sky, then rocketed up after her, gaining altitude with powerful thrusts of my wings, then letting the thermals ease me up in an ascending circle.

Watching her vanish into the white mists, I sped up and burst through the clouds. They were a thick floor beneath us, reminding me of Aaru except for the sharp blue of the sky and the golden heat of the springtime sun.

I caught up with her at about twenty thousand feet. I was faster, and stronger, and I'd made it a habit of flying here every chance I could slip away from Aaru. As the distance narrowed between us, she pushed harder to keep her lead. And failed. I saw why once I got within ten yards of her. She was breathing hard, struggling to produce effective muscular action with the thin oxygen at this altitude.

I scooped her up in my arms, plastering her against me chest to chest. Her wings still pushed, but I was the one driving us upward.

"Can't breathe up here." She tried to put her arms around me and came upon my wings. Instead she gripped me at the waist.

"Then don't breathe. Stop thinking about it. You're fine. Breathe or don't breathe. It doesn't matter."

"What are you, Yoda?" she muttered.

She was scared. And she wasn't about to let me know it either.

"Mine, you are. Know it, you will," I teased. Then I hiked

her up further along my body so I could hold onto her ass. And I kissed her.

She tasted of honey, cinnamon, and cayenne all rolled together. Her legs came around my hips and my hands dug into her rear. For good measure, I oxygenated her blood, and felt her melt into me. There were times for lessons, and there were times for fun. This was the latter and I wasn't about to put all this effort into wooing an angel who was worried the whole time she was going to suffocate. Casanova now. Yoda later.

With a thought, her shirt was gone. She squealed in surprise, pulling her lips from mine. I scooted her up higher, putting her breasts right where I wanted them. Then dipping into a barrel roll, I took one of her nipples in my mouth, flicking it with an undulation of my tongue as I sucked. She gasped, arching her back. The g-force, the feel of my mouth on her, the adrenaline of all we'd done today had her right on the edge. It had me right on the edge too. So I did what any good angel would do, I reached out with my spirit-self and enveloped her, merging and joining, taking enough of her that she felt a bit of what it was like to be an angel, but leaving her enough in her body that she still felt everything our flight and my mouth were doing to her.

She tensed, then fell apart in my arms. Her surrender shocked me so much that I almost did the same, holding myself back at the last moment. I leveled out and eased her down my body slowly, pulling back my spirit-self, and kissing my way up to her neck.

"Less than four minutes, and we didn't even need the full distance," I teased. "Quite the record."

"That was completely unfair," she complained breathlessly.

"It was totally fair. And so is this." I made her jeans vanish and felt her warm and wet against my lower stomach. Everything south of my belt tightened painfully, straining against the unforgiving fabric of my pants.

"I need to go to work." She laughed, rubbing herself against me. "And I want to have time for our shower."

I groaned, nipping at her shoulder in retaliation. "We've got time for one more, this one at forty thousand like we planned."

She glanced upward, and I felt a spark of fear run through her.

"I've got you. Do you trust me?"

She looked down into my eyes, and I swear I could see right into her heart. "Yes. I trust you."

Her words took the breath right from my lungs. I was Raphael, the crazy one, the barely-an-Angel-of-Order. Besides my long-lost brother Samael, I was the archangel least loved in Aaru. No one trusted me — sometimes not even my own siblings. But she did.

"Good." I held her tight and shot upward, growing harder at her squeal of delight.

The greatest pleasure always has an element of fear along the edge, so I took her all the way to forty thousand feet, feeling her shiver and gasp in my arms. Then I spun around lazily, making my pants disappear and feeling the bite of cold air against my balls. Thank the Creator I was an angel, because a human would have been the size of a bean sprout in this cold. Actually a human would have probably been dead long before he hit the ground at this height. It was good to be an angel. And it was beyond good to have another angel in my arms, warm and soft, her face pink with excitement.

"Ready?" I dropped her hips down lower, feeling her warm folds brush against me. She better be ready, because I was not going to be able to hold on for long.

Her pupils dilated, her lips parting as she breathed out an 'oh' noise. She arched her back, pulling her hips away from mine and sliding deliciously along my shaft, angling herself to hold me in position.

"Ready."

She shifted her hips and drove them forward, shoving me balls deep inside her. Everything went white and for a moment I lost complete control. We plummeted from the sky in a freefall, twisting and turning. I began to rock my pelvis against hers, again enveloping her spirit-self with mine. My wings were useless, I could do nothing to stop our descent. All I could do was fill her, complete myself in her softness.

I heard her make a soft cry and her lips claimed mine, confident and demanding as she matched my rhythm. Faster we fell, everything becoming a blur of sensation. I had no idea how far off the ground we were, how fast we were going. This was supposed to be me in control, carefully managing the experience for her. Instead I was frantic, desperate, her body and her spirit fulfilling a need that had gone unmet for all of my three billion years. She tensed, tightening around me and I felt myself swell and tighten in response. Somehow I managed to hold back as she came, the rhythmic clenching of her on my cock my undoing. I crushed her against me, my mouth plundering hers as I followed, spilling every bit of myself into her sweet warmth.

And then I surfaced from this heaven, snapping my wings outward and twisting us into lateral movement just feet from the ground. The heels of her feet skimmed the icy water of the lake and she laughed, the sound like the voice of God in my soul.

CHAPTER 20

AHIA

I was pretty sure everyone at work knew I'd been screwing Raphael like a monkey. The way we walked into together, our hands brushing, the lust rolling off of us, the way our eyes met — it was like a giant neon sign over our heads that said "Fucking. Whole lot of fucking going on."

We'd played in the air as we flew back to my house after the frankly earth-shattering flight sex, having a round two on a mountaintop. Rafi ended up teleporting us back supposedly to save time — time we used to climb into the hot steam of the shower and do it all over again. I didn't want to be at work right now. I wanted to be riding him in my kitchen, or bathroom, or on the living room couch, or out on the front lawn for all the neighboring werewolves to see. Heck, with the hearing they had I'm sure any driving by heard us in my shower. It wasn't like either of us was particularly quiet or discrete.

"I want you," he muttered, wrapping an arm around my waist and pulling me against him. Oh lord, this angel would be the death of me.

And there was a little voice deep inside my head that told me he probably *would* be the death of me. He was gorgeous. He was fun. He made love like he'd been perfecting the art for billions of years. I was falling for a guy who was known for flitting from one entertaining experience to another, and when our project was finished and he left Alaska, he'd take my heart with him. But I was in too deep to back away now. Crazy, careless, reckless woman that I was, I'd move full steam ahead, giving every bit of myself — body, heart, and soul to this angel. And as painful as his leaving would be, our time together would be worth every tear shed. These were the kind of memories that made life worthwhile, no matter how bittersweet they might be.

"I want you too, but I have to work." I couldn't resist giving him a quick kiss, running my hand down his back to squeeze his ass. Wasn't like anyone was watching us. Okay, maybe they were, but I didn't care.

"Nine o'clock?"

My quitting time. "Maybe ten after. I have to lock up and pull the bank deposits."

His fingers stroked my cheek. "I'll be back."

He better. "Not soon enough."

"Oh, I will definitely be back to get you, Hot-stuff." He kissed me again, and this time it was more like we were making out smack in the middle of the store where I worked. The door chimed. We broke our kiss, and with a wink he left.

I immediately felt cold and lonely without his presence. Yeah, I had it bad. How could I fall so hard in two days? It was crazy, but I was crazy. He was crazy too. And the feelings I had for him went so far beyond simple physical attraction. I'd never met anyone so fun, so powerful, but so light-hearted. He was an Alpha without all the seriousness. He was someone I'd love for the rest of my seemingly immortal life.

Because I did love him. In this short time, I'd gone from

not even knowing him to feeling like he was a part of me, like I'd only be half a person, or angel, without him by my side. Grinning like a fool, I turned around and saw who'd just come through the door — Brent and Zeph.

Zeph's eyebrows were practically on the ceiling. "Okaaaay. I'm going to just go to the Fjord for a few beers right now. Leaving right now."

He backed his way out the door and practically ran once his feet hit the sidewalk. That left me, and a scowling Brent.

"I need to clock in." I turned around and marched to the back. He was still there when I came back, leaning on the counter next to the register. I had customers, but they were all browsing. Ignoring the elephant in the room, or werewolf in this case.

Jess shot me a perceptive glance. "I'm leaving. Try not to get blood on the jewelry display, okay? I just cleaned it."

"See you Monday," I told her, watching as she grabbed her purse and headed out.

Brent still stood at the edge of the counter, looming. Scowling. Waiting. I decided to put the whole thing off and made the rounds asking the various customers if they needed assistance. Two teen girls off the cruise ship looking at wolf figurines. A woman and her two sons checking out the T-shirts. An older guy perusing the salt-and-pepper shakers. And a woman who looked to be in her early forties, who smiled sheepishly when I asked if I could help her and admitted that she was just waiting for the bus to pick her up for a hiking and rock-climbing tour.

There was no avoiding him. Brent wasn't going to leave and I couldn't circle around the shop for seven hours. Readying myself for battle, I walked back to the register, putting the counter between us and folding my arms across my chest.

"Yeah?"

He glared. "I thought you told me there would be no romantic encounters in hunting down monsters."

I shrugged. "I didn't realize that things like lopping the heads off a hydra would be such a turn-on. There's an attraction there, Brent. I'm not going to deny it."

"You have no restraint, do you?" he snapped. "You want it, you take it, regardless of who gets hurt. Regardless if it's *you* who gets hurt."

"Well, why not?" I snapped back. "Try living for five thousand years, watching those you love age and die right in front of you like time lapse photography on super speed. I've got to take what I want right away, because tomorrow it's gone and I'll never get the chance again."

The anger drained out of him. His eyes full of sympathy as he reached out and touched my cheek. "He'll hurt you, Ahia. He'll waltz out of your life, break your heart and toss it aside without a care. He's an angel. Even if he doesn't tell the others about you. Even if he keeps your secret, he'll ruin your life."

"You don't know that. I think...I think he really cares about me."

Brent's mouth twisted. "He might care about you, but that doesn't mean he won't happily walk away in a few weeks once he's done here. He'll go back to Aaru, back to all the other angels, and remember you fondly. He'd probably be surprised at how you wanted and expected more. I know you, Ahia. You love deeply. You'll want what this angel will never be ready to give."

Brent was right. Even if Rafi did care, even if he loved me, I had no idea what that meant for angels. The only reference for any sort of relationship I had was humans and werewolves. I doubted I'd get the white picket fence, his and her four-wheelers, and a three-tier wedding cake with Rafi. My parents obviously hadn't stayed together or reunited. And they'd dumped me. Even if they meant to return, it had been five thousand frickin' years.

Maybe that was normal for angels. We'd love, then he'd leave and maybe in a hundred thousand years or so swing by to catch up and reminisce. And he'd be confused and surprised that I'd ever wanted something different, something like what the humans had.

Whatever Rafi's intentions were, it was too late for me to back away now. And I was determined to enjoy what we had. "I can't help myself. Let me have this one moment, Brent. Let me have a day in the sunshine, then I'll go back to the same thing I've been doing for the last five millennia."

His smile was sad. "I guess I can't forbid this as your Alpha?"

I snorted. "I'm not a werewolf."

"You are to us. For hundreds of years you've been our First, a Nephilim. And I'm still your Alpha."

They were my family. I might have more in common with Raphael than this werewolf before me, but he was right. He was my Alpha. They'd sheltered me, given me a home, loved and cherished me for their oh-so-short lives, which was more than any angel had ever done.

But I still wasn't giving in. "You can forbid all you want, Brent. I'm your First. I'm not bound by your orders, I'm your counsel. I'm the devil in your ear making sure you think through your decisions. I'd be a crappy First if I let you order me around. I'm going to have my wild fling with this angel, and I hope you'll be there to pick up the pieces when he's gone."

He cupped my chin in his hand, leaning across the counter to place a quick kiss on my forehead. "Always. I'll bring the ice cream, a stack of movies, and a strong shoulder to cry on."

And he would too, because that's what best friends did.

With a quick pinch of my chin he turned to the door. And everything exploded.

Literally exploded. One moment there were tourists shopping, a woman waiting for her tour bus, my best friend headed toward the door. The next there were chunks of concrete and glass flying. Something hard hit my midsection and flung me across the room, smashing my back into the wall. I felt bits of glass cut my skin, a metal pole stab through my shoulder, the cash register whack me in the head. Light so bright it was like knives stabbing into my eyes filled the room. Bits of metal and cabinet embedded themselves into my legs. I felt the warm trickle of blood drip down my face.

When the dust cleared the store looked like a demolition zone. Cars screeched and crashed in the street outside. I heard people screaming. Racks and display cases were destroyed in a circle radiating out from the rift that had opened to encompass nearly ten square feet of what had been the store. Two dudes in beige raggedy clothing, hoods over their heads, stood, staring at torn T-shirts and shattered coffee mugs.

Wait. Who were these guys? They looked like a cross between scuba divers and Bedouins. Like something from a science fiction movie, only without the lasers.

One spread out two sets of arms, the first set from where I'd expect his shoulders to be and the second from some-where around his waist. From under the hood came a clicking noise. The other extended a stick-like item, and shot a pulse of light that hit what was left of the jewelry case.

Great. They did have lasers.

Time seemed to hold still while my mind worked in over-drive. I was cut and bleeding, a pole sticking through my shoulder. The jewelry case, at least what was left of it, was now on fire. One of the raggedy guys had turned toward me, treating me to a view of goggle-covered eyes and a scaled, elongated jaw that extended a good seven inches from his face, ending in what looked like a metal grill of a mouth.

Where the heck did this rift lead to? The danger of monsters in downtown Juneau didn't escape me, but I held back judgement on these guys. For all I knew they were just as confused as I was, and might not be violent. Well, at least not violent to anything but jewelry cabinets.

"Hey, it's all good." I put my hands up in what I hoped was the universal sign of peaceable intent. "I know this is as weird for you as it us for us."

The stick swept my way, and pain seared through my chest. The next shot skimmed the broken counter top, carving a black groove in the surface before boring a hole in the wall behind me.

I couldn't breathe. My lungs were full of blood, my heart stuttering. It hurt, but luckily the brief pain was the only thing I'd suffer. Placing my hands on my chest, I focused. A white light burst from my fingertips and my lungs filled with air, my heart rhythm stabilizing. Now if I could just get this pole out of my shoulder, I'd heal that too.

Another shot ricocheted off the cash register inches from my hip. I decided the pole in my shoulder was the least of my worries right now and scooted behind what had once been the door to the back room. The guys-in-rags continued to shoot at me, but I managed to make it behind the broken metal door without further injury.

Once there I realized my dilemma. Keeping their focus on me meant that hopefully they wouldn't be shooting at the humans in the street, but I couldn't keep taking and healing damage. I needed a distraction so I could get the weapons from these guys and take them down.

What I really needed was an angel. Where was Raphael? Why couldn't there be a romantic psychic link between us that would let him know I was in danger of having my head blown off? For all I knew the guy was on my couch watching CSI reruns, or perusing my collection of VHS tapes.

"Brent? Ahia?" The shouts were from a voice I recognized. I heard the sound of shots fired directly after, the ping noise of them bouncing off something metal, and a hurried curse.

I didn't have an angel, but I had the next best thing. A werewolf.

CHAPTER 21

"Zeph!" I shouted, yanking the pole from my shoulder and popping my head above my shelter to see the werewolf by the ruins of the front wall. He had a car hood in one hand and was using it as shield to deflect the shots. He was still in human form since most werewolves took ten to twenty minutes to change form. It was definitely a genetic drawback.

The raggedy guys turned their sticks back to me. Just before I ducked back down for cover I saw Zeph launch the car hood like a giant Frisbee at them. There was an ear-piercing shriek, then the rapid-fire sound of shots. I crawled to the other edge of the door and peeked out to see one down, the edge of the car hood impaling him against a shelving unit and nearly severing him in half. The other guy was clearly panicking, alternating his aim between me and Zeph.

One shot took the top off a clothing rack and clipped Zeph's shoulder, spinning him around. I couldn't wait any longer to act, so I jumped on top of the counter and launched myself at the monster, plowing into his back and knocking him to the ground. The guy emitted series of growls and those weird clicking noises. Now that I had my hand on this guy, he was done for. I'd killed boobie-birds and a hydra today. This guy wasn't going to get the best of me. He was going down, but first, I needed to take care of his weapon.

I might be reckless, but even I knew better than to break a stick that somehow shot lasers out of the end. So I broke the raggedy guy's arm instead. That's when I got my next shock of the day. What I'd thought were worn and dirty bits of clothing were actually part of his body. Instead of soft flesh and a bone core, the arm had floppy rag-scales that were like boiled leather covering a brittle skin. Under that was gooey flesh and light gray liquid that I was going to call blood.

I had no idea how to use the laser-stick, so I tossed it and the amputated arm across the store, giving a quick prayer that the weapon wouldn't go off when it hit the floor. That's when something needle-sharp stabbed into my neck. I couldn't move. Icy cold poured through my veins, locking muscles and misfiring neurons. I gasped, but as quickly as I could repair my body, the toxic liquid attacked again.

This sucked. This really sucked. If raggedy-guy got the best of me and Zeph had to swoop in for the save, I'd never hear the end of it. Zeph rescues Ahia from a monster. There was no way that I was letting that happen, so I gave up my fight against the toxin and did the other thing I was good at, I shot a bolt of lightning into the raggedy-guy.

Dude might be a monster with four arms, a laser stick, and poison teeth or claws or something, but electricity was not his friend. The hardened skin bubbled up under my hands. Dark gray spurted from joints, steaming in the air. The monster shrieked like nails on a chalkboard and bucked underneath me. It gave me the chance to jerk free from the needle-like talon in my neck and repair pretty much every muscle and nerve in my body.

They might be innocent monsters, attacking us out of fear, but all bets were off. My fragile leash on my anger-fueled blood lust had slipped and I was on the fast lane to berserker rage.

Everything became a blur. I grabbed the half-cooked raggedy guy and began slamming him into the floor. Another needle jabbed into my neck, but evidently my souped-up angel adrenaline overcame the toxin this time. I grabbed the creature's shoulder, and repeated my electricity trick.

"Ahia?"

The blur, the hot white light slid away and I found myself covered in gray ooze and bits of cloth-like flesh, smashing little pulpy chunks of monster into the ground.

"Ahia, I'm pretty sure he's dead. They're both dead."

Yep. And once again I'd shown one of my packmates just how crazy I was. "You wouldn't happen to have a towel handy, would you?" I asked Zeph.

He handed me a torn sweatshirt from the floor and I stood, trying to wipe the goo off myself as best as I could. Sirens sounded in the distance. Humans stood in the street next to a traffic jam of parked cars, staring at Zeph and me. He had a blackened mark on his shoulder and through it I could see angry red flesh and white of bone. "You okay?" I asked, worried. Werewolves could heal just about anything, but I wasn't sure how their recovery skills coped with alien-monster lasers.

He grimaced. "No, but I'll live. Thing almost took my arm off."

Which would have taken him months, if not the entire year, to regrow. I looked around the demolished store. We had two dead raggedy-guys, a whole lot of debris, and…wait, where was Brent? Where were the shoppers? Were they buried somewhere in the rubble of the store? I looked around, but couldn't see legs sticking out from under anything. There was no sign of either Brent or the seven humans. I could imagine a werewolf moving fast enough to possibly get clear of the blast, but the humans couldn't. Where were they? Or at least where was the spray of blood and guts and random body parts?

"Did Brent go outside?" I envisioned him grabbing the humans and rushing them all to safety before the blast went off, but I'd seen him when the blast went off. None of us had any warning. There simply hadn't been time for even a fast werewolf to clear the area. Besides Brent would never have run from danger. Even if he'd taken the tourists to safety, he would have come back to fight with Zeph and me.

"No." The look of horror on Zeph's face was probably mirrored by mine. "Where is Brent?"

I looked to where the glowing rift had been dancing in midair as it expanded and contracted. It was gone. Walking over I reached out a hand to pat the place where it had been and felt nothing. I couldn't even sense any residual energy to pinpoint its location. It was gone. And so were Brent and the shoppers.

Humans had disappeared through the rifts before. But before it had been clear that the humans had fallen through, like stepping into a crevasse in the ice. Rifts had never exploded like this before. I closed my eyes, remembering the mummified bodies I'd seen when I'd been pulled through one of the rifts by the boobie-birds. Oh, no. Were they dead? They couldn't be dead. Brent dead. It would destroy the pack. It would destroy me.

I'd seen so many humans and werewolves die during the

course of my life. Some of old age, but many from illness, injury, violence, and accident. It always hurt, but losing someone had never hurt like this. Brent. He was my friend. He was my Alpha. I wasn't ready for him to go. I wasn't ready for him to die.

"Ahia? *Where's* Brent?" Zeph's voice this time had an edge of panic to it.

I looked around the store once more. He'd been too far from the rift to fall in. Maybe it sucked him and the humans in, exchanging them for the two raggedy guys. It was the only explanation that made sense.

"He's gone." I tried to hold down my fear, my grief.

"Gone where?"

"I think…" I bit my lip, that grief breaking free and roaring through my mind to grip my heart in a vise. "I think he's on the other side of the rift, where these monsters came from."

Zeph sucked in a breath. "Can you get him back? You can see the rifts. You're more powerful than any of us wolves. You're more powerful than any Nephilim is supposed to be. Please tell me you can get him back."

"The rift is gone. Trust me, if it were still there, I'd already be on the other side trying to get to him."

The werewolf's eyes filled with tears. "Then what? Can you open a gateway? Or maybe if we sit here and wait, the rift will reopen? I can't…I can't just accept that he's gone. Not Brent."

I was a crazy angel living with werewolves. I'd always been a freak. And what good was it to be a freak if I couldn't do freakish things, like find or somehow create a gateway and go through to find my friend, my pack's Alpha? Five thousand years of hanging out and watching the humans, and werewolves, live and die around me. I'd had enough of death. I'd had enough of loss. I was a fucking angel. It was time for me to do angelic things. It was time for me to pull a miracle out of my ass. Alive or dead, I was going to bring Brent home. And if I had to spend the rest of my insanely long life doing it, I'd find him.

CHAPTER 22

BRENT

I hit the ground with a force that knocked the wind out of me, gritty sand doing little to cushion my fall. Screams and cries told me I wasn't alone in this bizarre situation. I'd been in the tourist store, arguing with Ahia about what at best would be a heartbreaking affair with an angel, then everything blew apart and I'd found myself falling — falling through a red-orange tunnel then falling from the sky. Spitting the sand from my mouth, I caught my breath and opened my eyes.

And saw a landscape that had nothing to do with a tourist store, or even Alaska. Gone were the jagged mountains, deep blue rivers, thick forests. Heat washed over me in waves, shimmering up from the coarse sand. Scattered away from me were others. Humans. Even with the odd smell of iron and copper in the air, I smelled humans. There were humans in the tourist shop, seven or maybe eight? They must have fallen through with me.

Last year I would have had no idea what had happened. I'd never seen a rift come into being before, but us being on the other side of one was the only reasonable explanation.

Either we'd fallen through a rift or I was dead and this was a very unexpected sort of afterlife. If I was dead, I'd just have to go with it. If we were alive, there was a chance for rescue, as long as Ahia was somewhere around here. If that Raphael angel felt anything at all for Ahia, he'd come after her, and he if didn't, Nisroc would certainly enlist help. Plus with Ahia here, we had a good chance of surviving until help came. An Alpha took all the help he could get. It was the spirit of teamwork that made a pack strong, and there was no one in my pack I'd rather have by my side in a crisis than Ahia.

But was she even here? I didn't smell her nearby. Had she been thrown outside the range of my heightened senses? Had she somehow been left behind when we had been taken? I refused to think about the chance that she might have been trapped in that rift, or died in the explosion. I refused to think that, especially when the cries I'd heard meant humans were hurt and needed my help.

A woman about twenty feet away stirred, moaning. I tried to stand to go to her and immediately fell back to the ground. Heat burned through my leg, a thousand needles of pain as a torn ligament began to heal. Super-healing was one of the advantages of being a werewolf. It would hurt, but I'd be completely fine within the hour. In the meantime, people needed me so I crawled over to the woman, careful not to twist my healing knee. She looked to be in her late thirties with shoulder-length highlighted hair. Her khaki pants and white T-shirt were torn and she was missing a shoe. As I reached out to touch her shoulder, she turned to face me, her cheeks streaked with blood and tight with pain.

"My boys."

Her first. "Where are you hurt?"

"My ankle. My head and it hurts to breathe."

I checked her head. The cut had already clotted and didn't look too serious, but I was no expert. Werewolves all knew basic medical training. Given our rough and ready lifestyle, even those who healed quickly needed to have wounds bound and sprains wrapped. Concussion. Cracked or bruised ribs. Hopefully the ankle wasn't broken.

"Which ankle?"

She grimaced, trying to sit up. I helped her, realizing that her ribs must not be bad if she had this much mobility.

"The one with the shoe." She shook her head. "Figures. I somehow manage to lose one shoe and it's from the uninjured foot."

"Can you move it at all? Do you think it's broken?" I was afraid to take the woman's hiking boot off, worried that a break would be better supported by the structure of the shoe than leaving the woman barefoot in what seemed to be the desert.

"A little bit. It's not like I can move it much in hiking boots anyway."

I reached out to touch the foot, gently squeezing and turning it. "What's your name?"

The woman panted as I tried to turn her foot. "Renee. Where are my boys? Are they here too? Am I dead?"

Renee hadn't screamed when I'd moved her ankle, so I was going to hope it was just a sprain and move on. "I don't think we're dead. I'm going to check for others including your boys. Stay here, okay?"

She nodded, tears filling her eyes.

My leg twinged as I crawled, reminding me that I should be holding it still as it healed. Gritting my teeth, I moved on, encouraged by the sight of movement ahead. As I drew near I saw two boys that looked to be about twelve or thirteen wearing jeans and the requisite Alaska themed T-shirts that all the cruise-ship tourists seemed to sport. The closest one was covered in dust and dirt, curled into a ball. And right next to him was a torn hiking boot. At least the mystery of

Renee's missing shoe was solved, although I wasn't sure how it had managed to come off her foot.

"You okay? I just came from your mom and she's all right." I should have asked the woman to give me their names. I was assuming these were her two boys. I thought back on the tourist shop right before everything blew. Ahia. Renee with these two. Two girls — late teens, maybe. An older guy. And some woman waiting by the door with a backpack.

"I think I'm okay. Sore. Had the wind knocked out of me. Is David okay?"

"Aside from eating some sand, I'm fine." The boy a few feet away stirred, pulling himself onto hands and knees to shake the grit from his hair. "What happened?"

I examined the first boy, then shifted over to check the other boy — David. Bruises. Possibly concussions. Hopefully the others weren't any worse than these three were. It would be a huge stroke of luck if I, the one with the ability to heal rapidly, had suffered the worst injury. "I don't know yet. Your mom is worried about you and your brother here. She's over there? Can you see her? Do you think you can go over to her then stay there until I check for others? Oh, and take her shoe over to her, please."

The two boys nodded, getting to their feet and grabbing the hiking boot. I did the same, wincing as I put weight on my knee. David. Renee. And… "What's your name?"

The first boy coughed, brushing his arms and shirt. "Jason. I'm eleven. That's David. He's thirteen."

"All right, Jason and David. You two go over to your mom and wait. Don't let her get up until we get back. She's hurt her ankle and I don't want her to stand."

Both boys staggered through the reddish-brown sand over to their mom. I limped to the next closest person, fighting back a wave of nausea as the pain in my leg increased. Lights danced in front of my eyes, sweat beading on my skin. Clearly this was more than just a torn ligament. And a fever? Since when did a soft tissue injury and a possible fracture cause a fever?

About twenty yards off an elderly man gasped quietly, his nose a flattened mess of blood. That was the least of his worries. One arm was at an angle that made me wince.

"Hey there, sir. Anything besides your arm and nose hurt?"

The man's dark eyes met mine "My face hurts so bad. And my arm. I think it's broken."

"Legs okay? Any pain in your chest or back?"

How the heck was I going to set this man's arm, let alone find something to splint it? I could tear up a shirt into strips to bind Renee's ribs, and support this man's arm. Were there sticks anywhere? This place didn't seem to have any trees. What could I use as a splint? And how would I manage to keep their wounds clean unless I found some water? Water. They'd need it for more than cleaning wounds. Where *were* we?

"No. I don't think so. No. Just my face. What happened?"

I sat up and yanked my shirt over my head. "I agree that your arm is probably broken. I'm gonna make a sling. I can make it immobile, but I'm not a doctor. Hopefully it doesn't require anything besides this. Bad news is it's gonna hurt worse, once the adrenaline fades. Your nose too."

The old guy shot me a twisted smile. As horrific as the grin looked with all the blood and his mangled nose, the effort made me like this guy all the more.

"What's your name?" I tore strips from the shirt, making sure I tucked a few into my waistband for Renee. Hopefully I wouldn't need any for the others.

"Ray. Hurry and get this over with before I have a panic attack and pee myself."

Yeah. I was really liking this guy. I gently took hold of the man's arm and supported it as I wrapped my shirt around where the break seemed to be and tied the ends behind the man's neck. Ray's eyes widened as I moved the arm, then unfocused.

"It really hurts. Wish I had some drugs."

"Me too." I stood and looked around. "Stay here while I go check on the others. I'll be right back."

The man put out his other hand to halt me. "Where are we? What happened?"

Those were the questions of the day. "I don't know. We'll figure it out. Right now I need to see who all is here and make sure everyone is okay."

The man nodded, and I moved on. In the distance were two figures, another approaching them on foot. As I drew near I heard the sounds of crying. The girl's blonde hair was stained pink with blood, and she was crying over a motionless figure on the sand.

"Sarah? Sarah, please. Oh God, please, please, please." The blonde woman began to rock. Hobbling closer, I squatted down to face the crying girl. "Is this your friend Sarah? Can I look at her? I know some first aid. Maybe I can help."

There was no helping Sarah, but I had to do something before the other girl completely lost it. Gently I turned the motionless figure over, smoothing reddish hair away from her face. The girl wasn't breathing. Her eyes stared blankly at the horizon.

"I landed on her. I killed her. I landed on her."

There was no time for this. It was hot and dry. People were injured. We needed to clean and take care of the wounded. There wasn't time for grief and guilt.

"I'm so sorry this happened to your friend, but we need to find shelter." We needed to find water and food, too, but first we needed to get out of this sun and somewhere defensible. I had no idea where we were or what sort of dangers this place might have, but heatstroke was the most pressing problem we were going to face, followed by dehydration.

"I can't leave her. I can't leave her." The girl wailed. They were all going to fall apart on me. An injured elderly man, an injured woman with two children, this emotional wreck, and a dead teenager. I was an Alpha, a leader of werewolves, not a leader of hurt, frightened humans.

"Let me help. Can I get through here? Coming through. Excuse me."

I turned around, then looked down. Standing in front of me was a woman who had to have been over a foot shorter than me. Her dark brown hair was escaping in wisps from a stubby ponytail at the nape of her neck. She was slight, with delicate features and the most amazing eyes. They were so dark brown that they were almost black, heavy lidded with long lashes. Bedroom eyes. The sort of sultry, sleepy eyes you wanted looking up at you the morning after an amazing night of sex. Her skin was creamy pale, but her features had a Mediterranean look, as if she were a Spanish film star or an Italian model.

And those sexy bedroom eyes were looking at me with a commanding confidence that many werewolves couldn't even muster. Her gaze drifted past me to the body on the sand and she caught her breath, for a brief instant allowing the mask of authority to slip. She'd seen dead before. She'd seen lots of dead before.

Then abruptly the cool confidence was back as she turned her attention to the crying woman. "Let me see where you're bleeding from, hon." She blew a strand of dark hair away from her face and plopped her backpack on the ground, pulling out a flag-patterned bandana, a first-aid kit, and a bottle of water.

"Out of my way, Muscles." It was said with a good-natured twinkle in her dark brown eyes and an elbow to my ribs that effectively moved me to the side. She reminded me of the pack females, used to holding their own surrounded by males. She moved in front of me, blocking the crying woman's view and giving me a chance to quickly close the dead girl's eyes. Sarah. Sarah's eyes. Hopefully it would make her seem peaceful, as if she were sleeping, and give her friend a bit of comfort.

The woman knelt down and examined the blonde's head with gentle but thorough hands. The whole time she made soothing noises, telling her it would all be okay, and that she'd help. Help with what? She could slap some antibiotic cream on the woman's head, but nothing was going to help with her grief. It wouldn't be okay. And I was pretty sure if they didn't get out of this heat to some shelter, it would be far from okay.

"We need to go," I said. It was like I was talking to the air. No one moved or responded to my firmly worded edict. That was a first. Humans and werewolves alike jumped when I gave orders. Ahia was the only one who argued back or ignored me. This…this just didn't happen.

"Ooo, that's a nasty cut. I'll clean it best as I can now and put a butterfly bandage on it. Hand me that bottle of water, will you, Muscles?"

I stared at the woman's outstretched hand for a moment, then picked the bottle up off the sand and placed it in her palm. "We should conserve water. I don't know when we'll find more."

"I don't intend on washing her hair with it, just cleaning the worst stuff out of the cut." She moistened a corner of the bandana and dabbed it against the cut in the woman's temple, examining the wound before capping the bottle and handing it back to me. "Can you hand me the antibiotic cream and a butterfly bandage from the kit? I don't have anything with me to stitch it, so I'll have to hope this holds."

I stared at her a moment, wondering how I'd completely lost my authority to a human with do-me eyes and a backpack. Before my ego could get too out of whack, I gave myself a mental slap. Yes, she was a human, but she clearly had more first-aid experience then I did, and she had supplies. Time to stop thumping my chest and be grateful that there was someone else with leadership skills.

"Here." I handed her the bandage and the cream, putting the water bottle back in her pack.

She squeezed the cream out and applied it to the cut, smoothing the woman's hair aside then squeezing the edges of the wound together as she put the bandage on.

"I killed her. I fell on her and killed her," the blonde woman told her.

She stood and put the antibiotic cream back into the first-aid kit, stashing both it and the bandana back into her pack. "Let me take a look."

"We need to get going." I repeated. Again, no one paid any attention to me.

Bedroom-eyes knelt down beside the dead girl, examining her. "I don't think you killed her, hon. We didn't fall that far, and landing on her wouldn't have caused instant death. I think she may have died in transit to wherever we are."

The girl looked up, her eyes and nose red and swollen. "Really?"

"Really. We need to bury your friend. We can't just leave her here exposed, but we need to find shelter. Can we bury her? Is there something you'd like to leave with her? Something you'd like to say?"

The blonde girl gulped and pulled a gold chain from around her neck, and the other woman pulled a small package out of her pocket. She placed them all on Sarah's chest, folding the girl's arms, then scooping sand over the body. The blonde watched her for a few moments, tears still spilling from her eyes, then she knelt down and helped bury her dead friend.

Pushing enough sand over the body to barely cover it, the woman stood and picked up her pack. "You're right. We need to get shelter," she said to me under her breath, glancing over at the crying girl. "Do you have any orienteering experience? I've got a compass in my backpack, but the iron in this sand will probably screw it up. Besides that, I don't know the landscape around here. I'm assuming you're a resident?"

I helped the blonde girl get to her feet. We'd eventually have to deal with her emotional state, but for now there were other priorities. "I'm a resident of Alaska, but we're not in Alaska anymore." I couldn't help an ironic smile at my words, envisioning a yellow brick road opening up before us.

"I didn't think there were any deserts in Alaska, but where else could we be? Did a tornado suck us off to Oz? Did we fall through an interdimensional rift to a land of lizard people and sand monsters?"

"I suspect the latter." I headed off with a supportive arm around the blonde, and the woman on the other side of me.

"Nice dry humor. Very good delivery," she teased. "So you've got no idea where we are either? And you're hurt." The last was said with a sharp, accusatory tone, as if I'd done it on purpose.

"It's no big deal. I'll be fine."

"You're limping. I saw you in the tourist shop. You're the strongest, most fit among everyone here. We need you, which means we need you not to be hurt."

Brutally practical. And she, as well as the others here, had no idea I was a werewolf. Local humans did, but those facts were always kept from the tourists.

"I'm fine. I promise you I'll be one-hundred percent in a few hours. Pinky promise."

She snorted. "Okay, tough guy. I better not see any limping by tomorrow, or you're under my care."

Bossy. "What, you're a doctor?"

"Yes, I am. A trauma surgeon. I work in the ER."

"And you were on the cruise ship?"

"No, I flew up for a few weeks to do some hiking and rock climbing. Doctors get to take a vacation every decade or so if we're lucky," she teased. "I thought this would be a fun trip."

"Is it living up to your expectations?" What was I doing? We were trapped, surrounded by hot sand in another country, or planet, or dimension, and I was carrying on a flirty, bantering conversation with a bossy, incredibly sexy doctor.

"Expectations exceeded. I can't wait to write my online review. 'It was like an episode of Land of the Lost, only with more people.'"

I chuckled. "I'm hoping without the dinosaurs."

"Me too."

My brief levity vanished when I saw the older man and once again realized the gravity of our situation. Ray was pale and looked as though he might be going into shock.

"Crap." The woman muttered, hurrying forward. She knelt down in front of the man, and I noticed her left leg seemed off, as if she was favoring it when she bent the knee.

I doubted she'd been packing for an emergency medical situation, but for someone I assumed had been about to go on a hike, she had a good amount of survival items in her pack. The first thing she did was unfold a lightweight, metallic emergency blanket and wrap it around Ray.

"What do you need?" I asked, taking the backpack from her outstretched hand.

"Water. Gauze. One of those ice packs."

I pulled them out, and assisted as she examined his arm first. She was fast, efficient, and had a calm air about her that elicited confidence in her skill. She was also kind, speaking to Ray and smiling warmly at him as she worked. When she was done, Ray had an icepack supporting his arm that was now back in the T-shirt sling and some gauze packing in his nose.

"Can you walk?" She asked, getting to her feet and holding out a hand for Ray.

The older man took her arm and got up nodding. "I think so. I want to warn you that I've got my blood pressure meds back at the cruise ship. We were only supposed to be off the boat for a few hours, so I didn't bring anything but my wallet and my pocket knife."

The woman patted his arm, but shot me a grimace. "I'll keep an eye on you, Ray. We've got a bit of walking ahead of us, but we'll go slow. Think you can make it a few miles?"

The man paled. "I don't have much choice, do I?"

I saw a muscle twitch in her jaw. "We'll go slow. And if we need to rest, I'll stay with you. The others can go ahead."

I'd be darned if I left any of these people behind, but the sun was hot and we probably didn't have any water beyond that one bottle that the doctor had in her backpack. I looked around to some mountains in the distance. It was hazy out and it was hard to tell if they were huge mountains that were fifty miles away, or smaller ones five or ten miles off. I wasn't sure Ray would be able to make it even if they were only five miles away.

When we joined up with Renee and the two boys, I felt a slight sense of relief. At least we were all together, and beyond Ray and Renee, none of the others were injured.

"Doc? Can you check on Renee's ankle?" I asked.

The doctor muttered a curse and went over to the

woman, easing herself down, then pulling supplies out of her backpack.

I sat in the sand, willing my leg to heal faster. Ahia wasn't here. We'd all fallen fairly close together, and she'd not been anywhere. Part of me wanted to go search for her, just to be sure I wasn't leaving a pack member—my First, my best friend—behind, but I couldn't abandon these people. They all looked to me with hope and expectation in their eyes. I'd need to find shelter first, then water, then food. Doc could take the medical treatment off my hands, but the rest would be up to me.

I couldn't smell water nearby. I couldn't smell anything beyond heat and the metallic odor of the sand. The haze was clearing a bit, and I guessed that the small mountains in the distance — —more like big rocks — —were about three miles away. But I didn't want to head there if water was closer elsewhere. Closing my eyes, I inhaled, willing that faint extrasensory directional ability I had to find something, anything that would point me in the right direction.

Iron. Copper. And the cold clear smell of granite, but no water. My eyes popped open. It would have to be the mountains. There we'd at least have shelter. And there was a chance of a stream or pond, and possibly edible plants and animals that I'd be able to smell once closer.

I stood. "Renee, can you walk?" I'd carry her if I had to, but hopefully she could walk at least some of the distance.

"I don't know. Can I, Doc?"

The other woman nodded. "You'll never get this boot on again if I take it off. I'm thinking this is just a sprain. If not, the boot will help stabilize any break until we get somewhere for the night. I might have to cut the shoe off, but..." Doc looked over at me, then back at Renee. "We'll figure something out for footwear if I do."

She helped Renee to her feet, and the woman hobbled a

few steps with the help of her sons. "I'll be okay if we go slow."

I looked out at the endless expanse of sand toward the mountains. I had no idea how long it would take us given our injuries. Hopefully we'd make it before nightfall. Hopefully we'd make it at all.

CHAPTER 23

AHIA

I needed to talk to Nisroc and Raphael, to figure out how I could find or replicate the rift that took Brent. But first I needed to talk to the pack. They'd just lost their Alpha — quite possibly forever. Sabrina had been the next in line, but she wasn't ready to take over the pack. No one was. As the last person who'd seen Brent, it was my responsibility to tell them. And as the pack's First, it was my responsibility to support them, to help Sabrina pull together the leadership, authority, and alliances she'd need going forward.

So I'd sent Zeph to my house to fetch Raphael and tell him to bring Nisroc, then I'd driven to Brent's place to hold what was fast turning into a press conference.

It wasn't just the pack that was affected. A human establishment had been destroyed. Humans had vanished — tourists. Those who lived here were well aware of the supernatural and had been working with the pack and me to take care of the monsters who came through the rifts as well as cordon the areas off to prevent further human disappearances. They all knew but what were they going to tell the cruise ship? One or two tourists running late and missing the boat wasn't a big problem. It happened a few times per season and we just sent those people via boat or plane up to the next port-of-call to meet the ship. But seven humans? Seven humans who weren't all on the same sightseeing bus, and were all seen shopping in the demolished store just a few blocks from the port.

Word had spread fast, and by the time I'd pulled down Brent's long driveway to the huge hacienda-style house designated for the pack Alpha, it was lined with cars. Everyone had access to the Alpha's house. It was more a pack meeting place than a real home, so I wasn't surprised to see all the lights on and people milling about the porch as well as inside.

I'd barely put the car in park before the sheriff was knocking on my car window, Sabrina by his side. I rolled it down and he leaned in.

"The cruise ship officers are being very cooperative. I told them of the explosion, and that we were still sorting out who was hurt and in the hospital, who might be buried in the rubble, and who was unaccounted for. Understandably, they don't want to alarm families without cause, so they've agreed to wait, but they won't be able to give us more than a day, max. They gave me a list of those who didn't report back to the ship, and will stall as best as they can, but they need answers and they need them now."

Sabrina made a choking noise, her eyes red and puffy. This wouldn't do. Our next in line for Alpha couldn't be falling apart like this, not when I was leaving the pack in her hands to go find Brent.

"They're dead, aren't they Ahia?" she asked. "We've assumed all the others are dead, either killed on the other side by the monsters or unable to survive in whatever conditions are through those rifts. They're dead. We should announce it, and start trying to pull ourselves together."

An image of the mummified bodies flashed through my mind and I almost started to cry myself. "We don't' know that. I'm able to go through the rifts. If I can somehow get this one to open again, I'm going to go through and bring them home."

Most likely I'd be bringing their bodies home, but I didn't want to face that myself let alone smash whatever hopes the others might have.

"How? How are you going to open the rifts?" Sheriff Marsh seemed to have no more hope than Sabrina.

"Angels." Their faces both fell. I didn't blame them. It wasn't like the humans had experienced much in the way of angelic intervention — positive or negative, and the werewolves only knew angels as heavy-handed enforcers. Nisroc had been the exception. Raphael had shown to me that he was an exception too. I was banking on there being other exceptions — ones who might have enough mojo to open a gateway where a rift had once been, and make it stable enough for me to travel through then return a few hours, or days, later.

"The Ruling Council sent an angel here to close the rifts. We've closed several of them and killed both the hydra, and the creatures who attacked the hunters near Goat Lake. Angels made the gateways to Hel. If they can do that, if they can close the rifts, then they can open one."

It was a stirring speech, but neither the werewolf nor the human appeared moved. "I appreciate your dedication, Ahia." Sabrina smiled like she was humoring a small child. "You've always been there for us when something extraordinary needs taken care of. Yes, the angels might be able to open a gateway, but first they'd need to send an angel who could do it — probably an archangel and they don't come down from heaven often. Then they'd need to determine *where* Brent and the others went to. All that takes time, and angels aren't known for expediting things on a human timeline. Let's say they hurry and it takes them three days. Even if they're in a place where there is enough oxygen, and it's not too cold or too hot, the chances of them surviving for three days is slim to none. As much as I don't want to do it, I think we need to announce that they all died in the explosion, their bodies unable to be recovered."

No. I wasn't going to give up. I might not get there in time, but I'd get there.

I got out of my car, forcing both the sheriff and Sabrina to jump out of the way. "Announce whatever you want. I'm going to go find them."

"Pigheaded First," Sabrina muttered. She was right.

Every member of the pack and a good number of our local human contacts were inside. Someone had brought half a dozen deli trays, a cooler full of cold beer, and enough chips to last us until the apocalypse. Typical werewolves, a crisis always made them hungry.

Everyone fell silent as I walked through the room and hopped up on a chair to be better seen and heard.

"As you've no doubt already heard a rift opened today inside Tracks and Trinkets. Unlike the other rifts, this one exploded, significantly damaging the store. There were no remains found, and my belief is that in the explosion, the rift took everyone from inside the store except me. In their place were two…creatures. Zeph returned upon hearing the explosion and the pair of us killed the intruders, thankfully before they could injure or kill any of the nearby humans."

Everyone spoke at once and I held up a hand to get their silence. "Among those taken were seven humans and our Alpha."

I let that sink in, let everyone work through the ramifications before I continued. "Sabrina is in charge of the pack until further notice. I'm going to find a way to open another rift, a gateway, to wherever Brent and the humans are and bring them back."

Dead or alive. I didn't have to say the last bit. Everyone was well aware that I'd most likely be hauling corpses through the rift. Their Alpha gone. He was only forty-five. He'd only been Alpha for the last five years. His loss would be devastating to the pack. And his loss was devastating to me.

CHAPTER 24

I came in right as Ahia was giving her speech, just in time to hear the grief in her voice as she announced that werewolf of hers was gone.

What in all of creation had happened? A rift swallowing up every living being in the store except the angel, then closing immediately after. I'd never heard of one that did that. Yes, they occasionally closed on their own, but not for days at the least. And I'd never heard of one exploding.

Unless two rifts had opened in the same space. And if that were the case, the werewolf and the humans would be no more than scattered atoms somewhere in the universe.

"She loves him, you know," Nisroc whispered to me. "There may be others, but that werewolf has a special place in her heart. She'll never love anyone else like she loves him."

I couldn't breathe. I was torn between an urge to throttle the gate guardian or fly off to a cave somewhere and wall myself in. The one angel I'd met who seemed to really connect with me, the only one I'd felt a bond to in my whole life, and she'd given her heart to a mortal? Was Nisroc lying? Detecting falsehood had never been a strength of mine, but his words rang true. I might have had a chance to eventually win her away from the werewolf, but there was no competing with a dead lover. His faults would be forgotten, his attributes exaggerated until there was no way even an archangel could live up to his memory.

Was I willing to be second choice to a werewolf? A dead werewolf? How pitifully desperate of me that my answer was yes.

When Ahia was done speaking I went up to her, Nisroc trailing behind me and, no doubt, chafing at the order of precedence he had to comply with.

"You okay?" I asked, pulling her close and wrapping her in a big hug.

"No." She held me tight for a moment then pulled away. "I was the only one left behind, Raphael. Why wasn't I taken? If I was with them, I might be able to help them get back."

Or watch them die. I felt a stab of fear at the thought that she might have right now been on the other side of a closed rift — in any one of billions of places. I'd never find her. And if what happened in the shop was what I thought, she would have instantly died. I would have lost her forever. Gone, after only knowing her for a few days.

"I'm glad you weren't taken. I don't know what I would have done if you were gone."

I would have flown straight to Michael and Gabe, begged them to help me find her is what I would have done. Begged like I'd never done before. And if they didn't help, I would have torn the world apart attempting to get to her. I wouldn't give up even though she most likely would have been dead. The rest of my immortal life would have been spent searching for her.

Was that how she felt about Brent? Would her entire life from this point forward revolve around searching for a lost love?

"How can we find him?" she asked, confirming my thoughts. "The rift closed, but you can open one, right? You can create a gateway there and we can go find them."

At least there was a "we" in her request. I'd been relegated to assisting her. I guess it was better than being cut out of her life entirely. It was better than nothing.

"You need an archangel to create a gateway," Nisroc spoke up. His voice was smug. I knew just what he was doing. Jerk.

Ahia turned her face to me. "You know archangels. The Ruling Council sent you, and you must at least know the head of your choir. If you ask, will one come to help us? Please?"

She was begging for help, just like I would have done if it were her on the other side. "Even an archangel would have no way of knowing where to open the gateway. It's like a passage, a hallway. We…they need to know where we're going before it's created."

"The dead monsters. Will they help? They must have some residual energy that might be familiar enough to identify where they came from. The rift opened twice in same spot in the store. Maybe there's some marker left there. And I know. I saw it. If the archangel joined with me, I might be able to help him, or her, find the right spot."

There was no way in Hel I was letting her join with any other angel. Over my dead body.

"Ahia, you said there was an explosion. That usually happens only when two rifts open in the same spot. That's what got me sent here in the first place. Nisroc told the Ruling Council that a rift had opened close to the gateway to Hel. If they touched, half the state would have been blown to bits. If that's what happened in the store, then we'll have no way of knowing which location to build the bridge to. And there's a good chance any gateway we open will connect with another rift and explode again. This time it could take out the city. This time, we could be right in the middle of it when it blows."

"I wish I could help, Ahia." Nisroc sighed dramatically. "If I had that kind of power, I wouldn't hesitate to help you regardless of the risks."

"I know, Nisroc." She moved away from me and put her arm around the gate guardian. I glared at him over her head.

"I'll sit with you where the rift opened. We'll wait together until it opens again, then I'll go through and help you," the guardian continued.

"You would?" Ahia, looked up at him, her face shining with hope. "You think it will open again? You think that there's a chance they're alive."

No he didn't, that snake in the grass. He was just saying anything to gain her favor. It was bad enough I had to try to win her affections from a dead werewolf lover but now I was in competition with a gate guardian.

"Ahia, it's too dangerous. Even if the rift opens again, it might not be stable…" Damn it all. I couldn't believe I was thinking of going along with this. And I called Michael whipped.

"I'm going." Her jaw was set in that determined line. "Nisroc will ask the Ruling Council if you won't. And if they refuse to send an archangel to help me, I'll wait. And I'll go through every rift that opens until I find them. They might be dead, but I'll still know I didn't give up, that I tried."

This was such a bad idea. We were both going to die, but better us together than her alone thinking I didn't care enough to help with something, someone, so important to her. "I'll do it. I'll open a passageway. I can't guarantee I'll be able to find the right place, but I'll try. But if I can't create something stable, a gateway I'm sure won't get us killed, then we're not going. I need you to trust my judgement on this."

She blinked, a suspicious glint in her eyes. "You've done

this before? You know enough to decide if a gateway is stable or not? I thought only archangels could create gateways."

Nisroc had a little smirk on his face, the little sneak. He knew I'd kept this from her, and figured the deception would work in his favor.

"I'm an archangel. My siblings and I head the Ruling Council. We run Aaru. And we are the only ones who can create the gateways. I'm not the strongest or the best, that's Michael, but I can do it."

Nisroc sniffed. "Then perhaps we should request the Ancient Revered Archangel Michael to assist. We wouldn't want to entrust such a difficult and important task to the least powerful of the archangels."

Ahia ignored the gate guardian, her eyes still fixed on my face, so I let the dig slide. For now.

"Why did you not tell me you were an archangel before? Why did you let me think you were some minor angel?"

I needed to be honest with her, although I hated exposing myself like this in front of Nisroc. Stories traveled like wildfire through Aaru, although it wouldn't be the first time I'd looked like a fool in front of the heavenly host.

"Because I *am* the least powerful of the archangels. Even my youngest brother was more powerful than me. The only reason angels petition to join my choir, the only reason any of them ever expressed interest in me as a potential partner is because of my status. I'm barely an Angel of Order. Most consider me to be immature, unpredictable, and unstable with a vibration pattern scarcely within acceptable limits. My only redeeming quality in their eyes is that I'm an archangel and can get them access to my more powerful siblings." I took a deep breath and watched her carefully, hoping she'd understand. "I wanted you to like me for me, not because of my position on the Ruling Council, or because I head a choir in Aaru."

She tilted her head, her lips twitching upward in a sideways smile. "I do like you. And honestly I don't know if I would have been as comfortable with you had I known you were an archangel. I probably would have been intimidated into silence. I might have peed my pants every time you spoke to me."

I felt weak with relief. She wasn't mad. She didn't hate me. "Any angel that single-handedly takes on three boobiebirds would never be cowed into silence by an archangel." I felt like a small asteroid had just been lifted from my back. It didn't matter to her. My title didn't matter to her. I might be second to a werewolf, but at least I was in the running.

"I really think we should ask for another archangel," Nisroc interjected.

"No." She didn't take her eyes from mine. "I trust Raphael. I've seen what he can do, and I think in this particular situation, in *any* situation, he's the archangel I want by my side."

My heart took wings and nearly launched itself out of my chest. "Then we'll start first thing in the morning. You need sleep. I need to recharge a bit from the day. I know you're in a hurry, but we won't do your friend any good if we mess up because we're exhausted."

A little frown creased her forehead, but she nodded. "Okay. Let's go home and go to bed and we'll start at dawn."

Home. Not "my house", but home. And hopefully the reference to bed meant I wouldn't be sleeping on the couch. Not that I'd sleep, but I'd rather have her in my arms, guarding her slumber, then tossing on a lumpy couch in another room.

I can't recall the last time I rode in a human conveyance. I'm sure it wasn't nearly as hair-raising as the trip to Ahia's house in her Jeep. Clearly her skills at flying didn't translate to driving. I'd need to teach her to teleport before she managed to kill herself with this thing — or kill her passenger.

We got through the front door, and she stood there, lost, like she didn't know what to do. I could feel her exhaustion. I'd exerted far more energy than she had today closing two rifts not to mention teleporting everywhere to get the best pancake ingredients, but she was young. And I could tell most of her exhaustion was emotional.

"Sit." I led her over to the couch — the couch I hoped I wouldn't be sleeping on — and gently pushed her to sit. Then I took her phone and called the number in her directory for pizza.

"Thin crust meat-meat-meat with black olives and hots." I raised my eyebrows at her and she nodded, giving me the thumbs-up.

The pizza-man said dinner would arrive in thirty minutes or less, so I headed to the kitchen and got a bottle of wine from the fridge and two glasses, flicking the music on and the lights to dim with a wave of my hand.

"You're useful to have around," she told me as I handed her a glass of what had to be the cheapest Pinot Grigio in the state.

Then I sat down, pulled her to me and began to massage her shoulders. She relaxed into me, the back of her head resting on my shoulder.

"You're trying to get laid, aren't you?" she teased.

"Guilty. You know it would be easier for me to rub your shoulders if you took your shirt off."

"And it would be a lot easier for you to rub other things too." She laughed. "The pizza guy will be here soon. I'm not answering the door in my bra."

"Then take the bra off too." I tugged at her shirt and she squealed, fighting me to pull it back down. "You know I can just make this flimsy piece of fabric disappear?"

"You wouldn't dare!"

I would. And I did, making her pants vanish for good measure. She shrieked, splashing wine out of her glass. It ran over the top of her breasts, down into her cleavage. I chased the drops with my tongue and she sighed, leaning back into me. "Can you do it? Can you really open a gateway?"

I was so not going to get laid. "Maybe. I assisted in building the gateways to Hel. I can teleport, and creating this sort of passage is a similar skill."

"But you haven't done it before," she pressed. "You had help with the Hel gateways. You've never created a gateway on your own, have you?"

I suddenly felt every bit like the weakest branch of our family tree. "No. I haven't done it before."

There was that look on her face, like she was beginning to think Nisroc right and that we should call for a better, more skilled archangel. Once again I wasn't good enough. When things really mattered, I wasn't good enough. I couldn't fail at this. Ahia was depending on me. I needed to validate the faith she'd shown in me, prove to her that I was the right archangel for this, and any other, need she had.

"I hate to not-eat and run, but I need to pop out for the night. Save me some pizza?"

She turned her head and gave me an odd look. "Yeah, I guess. You're leaving? For the whole night?"

I didn't want to tell her why or where I was going. "Yes. Something…suddenly came up. I'll be back tomorrow."

She stood, recreating her clothing and hugging herself with her arms. "I guess I'll see you tomorrow then."

The tone of her voice made me wince — wounded and uncertain. I didn't want her to know. I didn't want to let her see my insecurities and feelings of inadequacy. I was an archangel. I was supposed to be strong and powerful. And when I fell short, I just did something crazy and irresponsible and laughed it off as being part of my Chaos. I didn't want to play the fool anymore, but I also didn't want her to think less of me.

Rising from the couch I gave her a quick kiss and then I was gone.

CHAPTER 25

BRENT

J'd found the cave just as the sun set, and not a moment too soon. We were all shivering in the sudden chill. Ray wasn't looking good. Renee was practically being carried by her two sons. Crystal, previously known as Blondie, was like a walking zombie. Doc looked like she could barely take another step.

Inside the small shelter, I turned to the humans. "We need to unpack everything we have — purses, backpacks, pockets, everything. It's going to get dark soon and I've got no idea if we'll have a moon or any stars to see by. We need to figure out what we have and what we need to survive here."

We'd already gone through two of Doc's water bottles, leaving one. Thank the stars she'd packed for a hiking trip and had them as well as the first-aid kit or we would all have been screwed. Even so we were all thirsty, and only had the one bottle to share between the eight of us.

What was I going to do? It was less than a twelve hours since we'd fallen into this world and it seemed the humans had already given up. Not that I had much cause for optimism. Solo I might survive, but every Alpha instinct

187

screamed for me to protect these humans. Actually, my chances for survival weren't especially good even solo.

Renee had a big purse, and so did Crystal, although the girl's was tiny compared to the giant bag the other carried. The teen upended it, dumping cash, and ID and a pass key.

"I dropped Sarah's purse on the way here," she said, her voice wavering. "I think she just had the same as me, though. I can't believe I dropped it."

"It's okay sweetie. It's okay," Renee comforted her.

"We've got some change and a stick of gum," the two boys announced.

"I've got a pocket knife," Ray chimed in, his voice strained. "Someone's going to have to get it *out* of my pocket, though."

Doc reached into the man's pants pocket, looking somewhat embarrassed as she pulled out what actually was a small multi-tool, and added it to the pile.

Renee winced and slid the bag off her shoulder, opened it and placed the contents on the ground next to the rest. Hand sanitizer. Aspirin, and a wallet with cash and cards. Chapstick, a notepad and three pens, and six granola bars. Best of all, she had a small bottle of water. Including Doc's remaining one, that left us with two — enough to get through tomorrow if we conserved them and stayed out of the sun.

"We need to conserve the water," Doc commented. "Ray and Renee, can you take aspirin dry?"

They nodded, and Doc handed them each two pills from the little bottle. "That only leaves six plus what's in my first aid kit." She walked over to her huge backpack and brought it back, carefully lining the contents up next to Renee's stash.

In addition to the first-aid kit and bandana, she had sunscreen, a head lamp, a multi-tool, five protein bars, matches in a waterproof box, climbing equipment, and a leg.

At least I thought it was a leg. The foot part was about half the size of a normal foot with a toe that came to a sharp point and an articulated ankle connected to a spring and something that looked like a bungie cord up to a knee with a similar system. Everyone stared at the device.

"What's that?" Jason asked, picking up the leg.

"That's a climbing leg. It's a prototype. The one for below-the-knee amputees is in production, but one for above-the-knee amputees is a bit trickier to design. I'm beta-testing it for the designer."

"You're an amputee?" I felt like an idiot asking the question. Of course she was, otherwise why would she be testing a prosthetic leg? But she hadn't said one word about her disability the whole hike to the cave. She'd walked miles through the sand with an artificial leg. The thought made me feel a whole lot less like the bad-ass of the group.

"Yes. The one I'm wearing now has a computer-controlled knee, and I've probably only got five days or so before the battery runs down." Her brow furrowed. "The climbing leg isn't meant for walking, especially long distances, but I don't know how stable this one is going to be once the battery dies on the knee. If we're here for a long time, you might need to carry me, Muscles."

Was she joking? I wasn't sure until I saw the corner of her mouth twitch. "Just call me Atlas. Pile everyone on my shoulders; I can take it."

Actually I probably could carry three of them if I could figure out how to efficiently balance their weight and keep them from falling.

She gave me a sideways smile and gestured to the pile. "Let's each take half a granola bar and a sip of water. It's getting cold and we only have the one emergency blanket, so we'll need to huddle together and share, being careful of Ray's arm and Renee's ankle."

I put Renee in charge of dividing the food, then picked up a protein bar and nodded for Doc to follow me to the entrance of the cave. It was cold outside, the temperature having dropped at least fifty degrees since we first fell into this world. Stars blinked above, and two moons lit the desert before us with an eerie blue-gray glow. I sat, then scooted close to Doc once she lowered herself to the ground, offering her the protein bar.

She broke it in half and handed me a section.

"Ray's not going to make it, is he?" I asked.

"Depends on how long we're here and how serious his heart condition is. The long walk, the heat, the lack of food and water — it could be a problem. I just don't know *when* it will be a problem."

I grimaced. "Water and food are going to be a problem for all of us sooner rather than later. Can you find out more about his heart? Is there anything you can do for him?"

"Probably not." Her voice was emotionless. I got the feeling that she'd developed a kind of numbness to steel herself against the inevitability of death. She'd probably seen more than her share in the hospital. "I'm not an ER doc, I'm a trauma surgeon. I get the accident victims, the falls, the burns. The other doctors get the heart attacks, pneumonia, and strokes. I can find out what he was taking, get his medical history, but there's not much I can do. Heck, even if I was a cardiac specialist, there wouldn't be much I could do. I don't have anything besides aspirin, and we're having to force the guy to walk around in the heat."

"Should we press on or wait here?" I asked, thinking out loud and grateful for someone to bounce ideas off. "I hate to torture Ray by hauling him through these mountains, but we don't have enough food or water to last more than another day here. If we wait we might not be strong enough to make it to somewhere with more resources. Maybe you can stay with the others while I go off and try to bring water, and possibly food, back here."

"With what, four plastic bottles? If we climb up and get a good look around in the morning and see there's water nearby, that will work. Given that there's a desert out our front door, I think we'll need to be on the move."

I bit into the protein bar and thought. "Let's see what's on the other side of this mountain range tomorrow, then think through our options.

Doc nodded then sighed. "Do you have *any* idea where we are? Do you know if there's even potable water or anything edible a few days' hike from here, if at all?"

I hated to admit this. "No. I have no idea what this place is or what to expect. Plus, I haven't been able to smell water, although I'm hoping in the morning I'll be able to catch a scent. If not, then we'd be heading out on instinct."

She smoothed back an errant lock of hair and tucked it behind one ear. "Every bit of my training says to stay put, to remain as close to our entry point as possible in order to facilitate rescue. Given the uncertainty of our finding food and water, plus Ray's condition, I'm voting to stay put. We could build a fire to signal our extraction team and indicate our location."

I eyed her curiously. "Are you ex-military?"

"Army, but that was a long time ago right after I graduated high school." She smiled. "I was a medic. When I got out I went straight into college and med school. Eight years of school in total, a five-year residency, and a two-year critical care fellowship."

"That's a whole lot of schooling."

"Yeah." She sounded sad, and I knew she was probably thinking what a waste it all had been if she was going to die out here.

"The problem is that I don't have faith that there *will* be an extraction team. We only have enough food and water to hold us another day. Even if someone is coming, I doubt a rescue team can get to us by then." I swallowed hard, not wanting to say the fear that had been lurking in the back of my mind ever since I'd hit the sand. "Remember when you asked if we'd fallen through an interdimensional rift? Well, we have. If it's still open, I know someone who will definitely come after us, but if it's closed, we might be screwed."

Silence greeted my words.

"There might be someone who can open the rift and come for us," I added, "but it's a long shot. They might not be able to do it. They might not be able to find the right location. And they might not want to do it." Stupid angels. Half the time it seemed they didn't care one bit about humans, let alone werewolves.

"You're serious? About this rift thing?" She let out her breath in a whoosh. "Normally I'd think you were crazy, but I went from a shop just off the port in Juneau, Alaska to a desert unlike any I've ever seen. And two moons? I'm either having some sort of coma dream, or I'm dead in hell, or you're right. I'm not sure which of the three is worse."

"I'm right. Rifts have been opening up for a few weeks now, but never in a populated area like this one did. They're being closed as quickly as possible, but I don't think anyone knows how to prevent them happening."

She sniffed. "Nice of you guys to alert the tourists. I mean, I might have gone to Colorado instead had I know there was a risk I'd be sucked through an interdimensional rift while waiting for the tour bus. Or at the very least demanded a hazardous-location discount on my trip."

I grinned. I couldn't help it. She was so matter-of-fact, so dry in her humor. There was an instant sort of camaraderie between us, a respect, an odd kind of partnership built on the stress of our situation. And if I were completely honest with myself, an attraction. Doc was striking rather than conventionally beautiful. She was lean and strong, fresh-faced with a slim nose, a wide mouth, and those beautiful eyes. She was smart, capable, calm in an emergency. And all of that together attracted me far more than a dolled-up bleach blonde. I reached out a hand and tucked that darned stubborn lock behind her ear, noting how soft the fine hair was, like strands of silk against the rough callouses on my fingers. "You doing okay?"

She laughed but this time it was short and bitter. "Interdimensional rift. Falling roughly six feet into gritty metallic sand. Trying to help traumatized and injured people while tromping across a hot desert with limited water. Facing the prospect of shivering all night in a cave, lying on a stone floor. Slowly starving to death, or dying of thirst or exposure, or being eaten by a dinosaur. Yeah, just peachy. Every muscle in my body aches, and I think I've got sand in places there shouldn't be sand."

She reached down and zipped open her left pants leg, then pushed something. There was a whoosh sound and before I knew it, I found myself holding a leg while she peeled off a silicone sleeve and massaged a stump that ended just above where her knee would have been. "Man, this hurts. If we're up in the mountains tomorrow, I might switch to the other and save the battery on this one."

I admired the complex piece of equipment. "This is pretty sweet."

"It better be. It costs one hundred grand for that thing."

I nearly dropped it. "You're joking."

She grimaced, still rubbing her leg. "I wish I wasn't. I love it though. I can walk on rough terrain, down stairs foot over foot, and with a quick adjustment, I can stand for hours in surgery without fatigue. It's waterproof, sand proof, shock proof. It was worth every penny, although when I'm chilling at home I tend to leave it off and just use crutches."

It really was a marvel of technology, with complex joints and electronics in both the knee and ankle. A far cry over what I'd ever expected a prosthetic leg to be. "And you have the beta-test one. Any others?"

"The climbing one is a design test, so it's with me on loan. I've got a jogging leg that's got a carbon fiber blade, too. I drive a ten-year-old piece of junk, live in a crappy, basement-level efficiency. Every dime I make goes to student loans from med school and this expensive leg."

I chuckled. "And trips to Alaska. Didn't the government pay for your college?"

"G.I. Bill only goes so far. And I do splurge on the rare vacation. Priorities, my friend. Priorities."

Didn't I know it.

"So what do you do?" She turned her face up, looking at me with those sleepy, bedroom eyes. "Professional body builder? Calendar pin-up model? Grizzly wrestler? Have you got military experience yourself?"

I'm the Alpha of a werewolf pack didn't seem like a wise announcement, although I was pretty sure I'd need to reveal that to these people soon enough. "No military. I'm a manager of sorts. I organize and lead hunting trips. That sort of thing."

She nodded, then we both sat there in awkward silence, looking up at the moons.

"What's your name?" I realized I'd never asked her, instead assigning her nicknames of Doc and Bedroom-eyes.

"Kennedy. Kennedy Duke."

I grinned. "Doctor Duke? Seriously? That sounds like a character on a kid's show."

"Don't I know it. My mom's last name is Cruz. I've been

tempted to go with Spanish tradition and be Kennedy Duke Cruz, but my dad would be crushed."

"I thought so. I was guessing Spanish or Italian."

"Italian? Them's fighting words. Andalusian. My dad was in a college exchange program and met my Mom in Barcelona. How about you?"

I grimaced. "My mom died when I was twenty in a hunting accident. I lost my father five years ago." It was the same fishing accident which had taken our pack leader. Which meant I'd taken on the Alpha role at the same time I was mourning the death of my father.

She narrowed her eyes, as if she were trying to do the math.

"I'm forty-five," I confessed. "Been in Alaska since birth, five generations of us. I've got no idea what our ethnic ancestry is." I did, but this wasn't the time to tell her we were descended from Nephilim, our angelic blood diluted to the point where healing, strength, speed, and the ability to shift into a wolf form was all that was left of our heavenly powers.

Her eyebrows shot up. "Forty-five? No way. You don't look a day over thirty. I thought I was older than you. Doesn't Alaska weather a person, or is that just a stereotype?"

"Moisturizer, sunscreen, exercise, and good genetics." Mostly genetics, but I occasionally remembered to slap on some moisturizer.

"Ah, healthy living. No doubt you eat your vegetables and do yoga every morning."

I snorted. "I hate vegetables. Meat. Fruit. Nuts. And more meat. And I wouldn't know a yogi if he knocked on my door."

She chuckled and we fell silent again.

"So what's your name? I can't keep calling you Muscles. Well, I can and probably will, but it might be nice to know the given name of someone I've fallen through an interdimensional rift with."

"Brent Phillips."

She nodded. "Well, Brent Phillips, aka Muscles, I'm dead on my one foot. Can you give me a shoulder so I can hop off to sleep on the cold stone floor?"

I looked down at the top of her head, at the silky, shiny dark hair that had nearly all escaped from the elastic. I was still holding her leg, feeling the warmth of her next to me. Suddenly I was reluctant to join the others, to take her back. What would happen if we stayed out here? If I kept her warm?

This wasn't the time. As much as I wanted to lose myself in passion, to see the look in her sexy eyes as I made love to her, there were injured and scared people in that cave. So I got to my feet and held out my hand, pulling her up and helping her balance on the one leg. Then, unable to resist, I tucked her prosthetic under my shoulder and scooped her up in my other arm. She gasped, throwing her arms around my neck and pressing herself against me. Her rear was resting on my forearm, completely supported by the muscles in my arm and shoulder. Not that this was any amazing feat of strength. The woman had to have weighed no more than a hundred ten pounds soaking wet.

I felt her breath, her breasts against my shoulder, her mouth brushing right above my ear. "I think I *will* call you Muscles."

Breathless, husky. I grew hard just hearing that seductive note in her voice. Maybe later. If we all survived the next few days, then maybe I'd do more than just imagine taking this bossy doctor to bed. Maybe.

CHAPTER 26

"Glad to see that Alaska survived your visit," Micha drawled. "And your timing couldn't be better. Things are unstable in Aaru and I foresee some battles in the next few days. We'll need you."

"The situation in Alaska isn't stable. There are more rifts to close, plus one opened in Juneau, exploding a store and taking seven humans plus the local Alpha. If others similar to that one occur, the whole area is at risk."

Micha waved his hand. "Perhaps I'll send Zatiael. He can handle things for the next few years, and let us know if the gateway is in danger."

I'd promised Ahia, and I intended to keep that promise. "It's not just the rifts and the hydra and the drop bears, and the boobie-birds, it's that exploding one. It's a serious danger, Micha."

"Boobie-birds?" The angel shook his head. "Like the seabird? Genus Sula? Blue-Footed Boobies?"

"No. Half-plucked birds with serpent tails and pendulous breasts."

Micha's mouth dropped open. "Birds with breasts? Well,

no matter. You can investigate all this later, after we stabilize Aaru."

"No, now. I need to go back and see if I can reopen the rift, create a stable gateway and try to rescue the humans and the Alpha that are on the other side."

"Let me get this straight, you want to go back to Alaska and expend an enormous amount of energy constructing a gateway so you can rescue seven humans and one werewolf." Micha shook his head. "It took four of us to build the gateways to Hel. It's not worth the effort, my brother. It nearly drains me empty to haul that dragon back and forth."

The Iblis had roped him into that one, making a deal with the dragon who had taken up residence in the British Museum. But beyond that I got the meaning behind his words. This task would be a challenge for Micha, the most powerful of us by a mile. It would be impossible for me.

I'd been underestimated for three billion years. I wasn't as powerful as my siblings. I was barely an Angel of Order, and I had a habit of wandering off when things got boring. But I could do this. I *would* do this. If only I knew how.

"It needs to be stable for a day or two at most, not two million years. And I'm only bringing seven humans and a werewolf through, not a dragon." And an angel, but he didn't need to know that.

Micha sighed. "Where does this rift lead to?"

I tried my hardest not to squirm. "I don't know. We've got a dead…thing that came through it, so I'm hoping to get enough read on it to make a connection. There should be some residual energy around the area of the rift too."

"Your odds of succeeding are less than winning that Powerful Sphere lottery my Cockroach likes to play. These humans and the werewolf are dead. Even if you could manage to produce a stable gateway on your own, you'll never be able to connect to the right location. We need you in Aaru. Stop goofing off in Alaska and for once in your life be a responsible archangel."

"By responsible you mean do as you say? Because clearly it would be impossible for me to have priorities that differ from yours."

Micha gritted his teeth. "Rafi, are you telling me that seven humans and a werewolf that are all mostly likely dead are more important than fighting for your homeland? That these futile efforts to establish a gateway, efforts that will most likely mean you won't be strong enough to assist us, are your top priority?"

"I need to try. If I can't manage to establish the gateway in the next twenty-four hours, I'll be back."

My brother shook his head. "Rafi, we could lose Aaru. If I call, I need you to come whether that's in an hour or in a week."

He just didn't understand. "I will make every effort to come, Micha. This is important, though. And yes, this does take priority. We can always fight another day. We can win Aaru back if we lose it."

"We can't lose Aaru," Micha thundered. "We can't."

"I heard the same plea when we fought the Angels of Chaos. Look how that turned out. Winning that war meant losing in the long run. I don't want these idiots to take our home, but we have billions of years to win it back. There are things in this world that are more important than Aaru. This is one of those things."

For a moment I thought Micha was going to continue to argue, but then he hesitated, and gave me an odd look. "Very few things are more important than Aaru."

"Family is."

Micha winced. "Yes. I learned that lesson too late."

"We all did," I said softly. "I won't make that mistake

again. Family. Love. Friends. My homeland will always be there. These other things might not."

My brother nodded. "You're right. Make sure you support the thresholds and that they transition the energy appropriately. Try to see if the corpse has any residual memories. You might recognize the location."

I nodded. "Thanks. I'll return as soon as possible."

My brother's voice halted me as I turned to leave. "Rafi? I'm sorry. You were right two-and-a-half million years ago, and you're most likely right now. Just because you're different from the rest of us doesn't mean you're less of anything. I won't doubt your judgement or dismiss your counsel again."

I felt as if everything inside me were about to burst. My eldest brother had just apologized and realized that I might have something of value to contribute. Hel was most definitely freezing over right now.

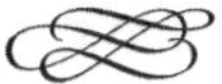

isroc paced across my living room, hands behind his back. "We'll set up a watch near where the rift appeared in the shop. It's bound to show again, and this time we'll be ready. I can teleport short distances. I'll get you there, we can go through and find Brent and the others."

I was the crazy one, but even I saw how incredibly dangerous that plan was. "The two times this rift appeared it was only open for less than a minute. That's not enough time for someone to alert us and you to transport me. Even if we get lucky and it's still open, how are we supposed to get back?"

"We wait for it to appear again. Ahia, it's the only way."

"And risk being stuck on the other side, possibly with injured humans? Rafi is trying to figure it out. I appreciate your offer, Nisroc, but I think it's better to wait for an angel that can open gateways, so we can be sure of at least having a chance at returning."

The angel's mouth twisted. "Ahia, he's not coming back. He can't do this. He can't figure out where the original rift went to recreate it. He can't put together a stable gateway on his own, and he sure as heck wouldn't be able to get you back. He's left, giving you some lame excuse, and he won't be back. That's how he is. This is what he does."

What was he trying to say? "He can do it. He probably needs to get some information from one of his brothers, or meditate or something. He'll be back. I trust him. He said he'd open a gateway, and get us there and back. I trust him."

Nisroc reached out a hand to caress my hair. "Oh my dear, you do not know Raphael as I do. In all of Aaru, he is the considered the flighty one, the undependable, the angel whose vibration pattern isn't to the level expected of an Angel of Order, let alone an archangel."

"I don't care about that," I interrupted. "Vibration pattern or designation doesn't matter to me. I've seen him close the rifts. I've felt his power. I know he can do this."

The angel shook his head. "Maybe. But even if he could, he won't. Raphael is all about fun. He's irresponsible. Any time matters become serious, whenever it's no longer a rollicking good time, he vanishes."

"He promised me."

"And I'm sure he meant it. But when something else catches his eye, he'll forget about his promise. Or he'll remember ten years from now when it's too late."

"He's not like that."

"He is." Nisroc grabbed me into a hug. "He'll realize that he can't do this thing you're asking of him, and be too embarrassed to come back, or he'll get distracted, or he'll decide this is no longer fun and go off to do something else. I've been alive ten million years, and during that time Raphael has always been the same. You're such the optimist. You always see the good in everyone, even if it's not there. It's one of the things I adore about you. But the Raphael you are imagining isn't the real archangel. Trust me."

No. I refused to believe it. Raphael might be lighthearted

and fun, he might be more chaotic, more seize-the-day than other Angels of Order, but that didn't mean he lacked a sense of responsibility. Deep down, I knew he was a rock of strength, that he was an angel of his word, one that I could depend on. Rafi wouldn't let me down, no matter what Nisroc said.

I promised the gate guardian that I'd think about what he said and contact him in the morning, then after he left I sat down to plan for tomorrow.

What would I need if I were to go through a rift into an unknown world? I thought about the ones I'd poked my head, and more, through in the last few days. It could be a short trip. As much as I didn't want to admit it, there was a miniscule chance I'd find Brent and the others alive. It was far more likely we'd get to the other side to find frozen bodies, or mummies, or mangled corpses.

But I didn't want to think about that, so instead I tried to figure out what I might need to take with me, given that I couldn't exactly drag a set of luggage through a gateway. Whatever could fit into a good-sized backpack would have to do.

Seven humans and a werewolf. Eight emergency blankets. Rain ponchos. A first-aid kit. A rope. An entire box of survival foodstuff. My multitool and hunting knife. A water filtration system with spare filters. My 9mm and spare bullets. Or maybe I should take the rifle instead? Oh, what the heck, I'd take both. Never know when you'll need to shoot something. My lightning might not be enough if we needed to face off against two dozen of those raggedy-guys. They seemed susceptible to physical attack, given how the one had been taken down with a car hood, so I was hoping bullets would do the trick.

I crammed it all, except for the rifle, in my backpack and stared down at it. What if he didn't come back? What if he came back and told me that he couldn't do it? What would I do?

The reality of the odds I was facing crashed down on me. I mourned the loss of humans, but Brent... My best friend. The Alpha. My heart ached to think I'd never see him again, never run through the forest on four legs beside him, never share pizza, enjoy a pitcher at the Fjord, argue with him, tease him ever, ever again.

Slumping beside the backpack, I cried. I sobbed until I felt there was no more in me to give, then stood, uncertain whether to lay sleepless in my bed all night or try to gain a moment of escape through a movie. Before I'd decided, there was a knock at my door and it opened.

Only the werewolves came right on through my door without waiting for an invitation. It wasn't rude, it was just a pack, a family thing. At least they knocked. They used to just burst in until that time they found Brent and me rolling around naked on my living room floor. After that, Brent was the only one who walked on in without a knock.

"You okay?"

It was Zeph, and he looked like he'd been crying just as hard as I had. Brent was like an older brother to him. After Sabrina, Zeph was the third likely candidate for Alpha. If Brent didn't come back, he'd become a second at the ridiculously young age of thirty. And I knew this wasn't at all how he'd wanted to advance in the pack.

"No. You?"

"No." He grabbed me in a hug. Unlike with Nisroc, this one was bone-crushing. His warmth surrounded me, powerful arms tight around my shoulders, rock-hard chest smashing my face. I let him squeeze the breath out of me as long as he needed, then patted him on the back as he choked out a sob.

Finally, he pulled away, wiping his eyes on his sleeve.

"Sabrina has us watching for any recurrence of the rift and making sure everyone stays away."

It was a good idea. "If we can record the frequency of the rift appearances, maybe we can figure out a pattern and be there to go through."

Zeph's eyebrows shot up. "I thought that angel of yours was going to open up a gateway?"

"He's not sure if he can do it or not." I paused, Nisroc's words returning to me. "If he can't we'll need some way of getting through to the other side."

And possibly not getting back. It scared me, but it scared me more that there were people on the other side, desperately hoping for rescue. What if I got trapped over there? Would Raphael come for me? Would Nisroc go to the Ruling Council and ask them to send a rescue party? If Rafi were with me on the other side, would his brothers come for us?

"Zeph, what do you think of Raphael? Nisroc thinks he's not coming back."

"Are you kidding?" Zeph patted my shoulder. "Nisroc wishes he wasn't coming back. I saw the way that Raphael looked at you at the shop and again at the Alpha house. Trust me, he's coming back."

Good. It wasn't just me being a foolish angel in love, then.

"I don't know anything about angels," Zeph continued, "but if he were a werewolf I'd say his intentions were honorable. Well, maybe not honorable, but at least sincere." His eyes twinkled and he elbowed me.

Brent was worried for my heart. Nisroc was speaking out of jealousy. But Zeph wasn't my Alpha, my ex, nor had he ever had a thing for me. I trusted his judgement.

"Stay with me?" I asked, putting a hand on his arm.

He wiggled his eyebrows. "In your bed?"

I snorted. As if Zeph ever wanted in my bed. "No, on the couch. Just until Raphael gets back."

He grinned. "Yeah. That angel would tear my limbs off if he found me in bed with you. Couch it is."

We kept each other company until Zeph was snoring in front of the TV. Then I went to bed and was surprised by how quickly I drifted off and how soundly I slept.

CHAPTER 28

KENNEDY

Gold light was beginning to filter through the cave entrance when I finally gave up on sleep. The others were asleep, huddled together to keep warm, Ray sharing his emergency blanket with the two boys. I'd tossed and turned on the hard ground, dozing in short chunks. It wasn't the first time I'd gone without decent sleep or bedded down on hard ground without so much as a blanket. It wasn't the first time I'd marched through the sand and heat, although doing so with a prosthetic leg had posed additional challenges. It wasn't the first time I'd weathered an explosion only to get up and race to the aid of the injured.

Although I'd never expected an explosion in a tourist shop in Alaska, or one that sucked me and the others through into some other dimension. But years of facing my fears made it easier to ride the panic out, and the knowledge that others needed me threw me into an automatic response.

The night hadn't been completely sleepless. A few hours in I'd felt a warm body curl up to me, pulling me over to rest against him. Brent wasn't particularly cushy, but he was better than the granite floor. A little better. When I'd first seen him shirtless next to Crystal, I'd thought I was halluci-nating, or maybe dead and gone to heaven. I'd spied him at the tourist shop, watched him argue with the native girl at the counter and thought *figures. All the hot ones are taken.*

And he was totally hot. Dark hair, neatly trimmed beard, warm brown eyes. He towered over me, probably had a hundred pounds or more on me, had taken charge of the situation like a born leader. He had an air about him — confidence, good judgement — the sort of person you could count on to think of the team first and himself second. But leaders needed strong team members, and this team needed a doctor.

According to him there was a faint hope of rescue. But if that miracle didn't happen, we might be here forever, in a place that could possibly have no water or food. This was when being a doctor sucked. I knew full well how horrible death by dehydration was. Land of the Lost indeed. We hadn't seen another living thing since we'd arrived. At least if there had been dinosaurs I would have known water and food were a possibility. But now...

I sat up and stretched, reaching over for my climbing leg. Brent had left just before dawn, no doubt to scout around. I'd known that even curled up next to me, he'd stayed awake. Vigilant. Watchful. Protecting us like a giant guard dog.

Leg attached, I made my way to the cave entrance, grab-bing a sip of water on my way. Outside, the view was breath-taking. The sun was huge in a pale blue sky, the reddish sands stretching out to the horizon. We were at the edge of a range of tiny mountains, red and brown rocks pitted from what were probably sandstorms. There were other outcrop-pings farther up, separated by vertical rock. The big question was what was on the other side. A small set of mountains might not mean an environmental difference on the other side, but it was worth checking out.

Eying the rock for the best route upward, I jumped and grabbed a narrow ledge as a handhold. Wedging the pointed toe of the prosthetic into a crevice, I began to climb. It wasn't steep enough to warrant tying off or using my harness, and within an hour, I found myself at the top. The view there was equally breathtaking — a valley down the other side far lower than the desert side. I nearly wept to see that there were some sort of odd tree down there. Trees meant water, and hopefully they meant something edible. The difficulty would be getting everyone up here, then down the other side. I had climbing equipment, but not enough for everyone. One at a time, it would take all day, and the effort would probably be beyond Ray and possibly Renee.

Brent was right. It might be best to send him off to get water, even if we only had the four bottles. I ran through the inventory of items, trying to decide if there was anything else that might hold liquid. Perhaps one of the purses?

Movement off to the side caught my attention and I spun around, mouth dropping open.

"Uh. Hi."

Good grief, it was Brent. Naked. Looking just as embarrassed as I felt. "You don't have any clothes on," I announced. As if he were unaware of that fact.

"Yeah." He'd frozen the moment he saw me, but now took a few steps forward, bending down to pick up a pair of pants from behind a rock.

"Is this some religious thing? Climb to the top of a mountain, get naked, and go for a walk?" I'd thought he was scouting out the area, checking for food and water. What about that would require he be naked?

And I wasn't about to look away. Nope. Gorgeous, ripped hunk of man naked in front of me and I was going to stare all I wanted. Wow. Too bad we needed to get back to the others.

Too bad we were in a crisis situation. Although crisis situations did tend to spark passion.

"Putting my pants on now," Brent announced. There was a bit of a laugh in his voice as he held the pants in front of him, blocking my view of one of the best parts of his anatomy.

"Don't hurry on my behalf. Take your time."

He grinned, sliding the pants on and easing them up slowly. When he was done buttoning them, I looked back up to his face. Still grinning. Still gorgeous as ever.

"So, what do you think?" He gestured down at the valley.

"Hang on. I'm still processing the whole naked thing." After a few seconds, I sighed heavily. "Okay. Plant life. Most likely water. Hopefully food. No way we're going to get Ray up and over this mountain."

He nodded. "Short and to the point. I like it. You've got that climbing harness and gear. We should be able to use that to help everyone up one side and down the other."

I winced. "Everyone except Ray. He's got a broken arm. Even if we manage to get the harness on him without injuring his arm further, he won't be able to climb one-handed."

"I'll carry him. If we can somehow strap him to my back, I'll get him up and over."

"What are you, Bane or something?" I wasn't more than an amateur climber, but I knew how much strength it took to get up here. I couldn't imagine doing it with a Chihuahua on my back, let alone a person.

Brent looked affronted. "He's a villain. Compare me to the Hulk, or He-Man, but not Bane."

I shook my head. "You could be Samson and you wouldn't be able to get Ray up here. We can't leave him behind alone, and I don't think it's a good idea to split up."

"We need to set up camp closer to a source of water, and

with the trees down there, we'll hopefully have a source of wood for a fire. If we're stuck here long term, we can build shelters, hunt for food. I'll get Ray up here. I'm stronger than I look. I can carry him up."

Stronger than he looked? I didn't think that would be humanly possible, but he didn't seem like the kind of guy who would brag about something he couldn't do. "Okay, Muscles. Let's round up our merry band and get a move-on. With any luck we'll find water before nightfall."

Brent lifted his head and sniffed the air, then turned to me with a smile. "I guarantee we'll find water before nightfall. Guarantee."

I believed him. This whole thing was so weird. If we'd fallen through an interdimensional rift, I guess it wasn't too much of a stretch to think this guy was some combination of the Hulk and a water-whisperer. In fact, I wouldn't complain if he had other superpowers. Conjure a breakfast buffet and a hot shower superpowers, hopefully.

CHAPTER 29

AHIA

I awoke just before dawn to the smell of bacon and coffee. I brushed my teeth and ran a comb through hair that looked like I'd spent the night in a wind tunnel, then decided it was time to face the day.

"Hey Zeph, any news from the wolf watching for the rift?" I asked as I walked into the kitchen.

"Wrong guy." Raphael was shirtless, frying bacon. My heart leapt right out of my chest at the sight of him. As much faith as I had that he'd return, there was a tiny voice inside my head that kept repeating Nisroc's words, that doubted things could possibly work out between this angel and me.

I walked up and wrapped my arms around him, smushing my face against the warm skin of his back. "Did you send Zeph home?"

I felt a bit sorry for my werewolf friend being woken up in the early hours of the morning and having to drive home sleepy in the cold.

"No, he's still asleep on the couch. I didn't have the heart to wake him. Poor guy looks like he had a rough night."

He did. I'm pretty sure this was one of the longest nights of his life. I was glad he was able to finally get some sleep, but surprised that Raphael took the time to notice, that he cared enough to leave Zeph to his slumber — that he cared enough to set three plates and three coffee mugs at my little table.

Rafi turned around, tongs in hand, to wrap his arms around me and plant a kiss on the top of my head. "He's your family. These werewolves are your family, which means they're my family too."

I caught my breath. What had happened last night? I knew he desired me, that we had fun together. I hoped we might have something long-term in our future, but I'd never dreamed of this. My family was his family. Did that mean I'd be meeting a bunch of archangels soon?

"Brent, too?" I teased, instantly feeling a pang of sorrow that Brent might never get a chance to really know Raphael, that this angel might never get to consider my best friend a part of his family.

"Yes, Brent too." His arms tightened. "We'll get him back, Ahia. We'll bring him home."

"Get a room." Zeph's voice was gravely with sleep as he walked in and grabbed a mug. "Actually, don't get a room. These walls are paper thin. I'm not sure I want to hear you guys banging wings or whatever y'all do."

Rafi laughed. "Banging wings? Hmm, we'll need to add that one to our list, Ahia."

Rubbing wings, yes. Banging, no.

"Why are you cooking shirtless?" Zeph asked as he poured coffee in his mug. "Not that I'm complaining about scoring some breakfast. I'm just curious if the half-naked state adds to the dining experience."

Nobody fries bacon without a shirt on, and it wasn't like Rafi had to go to any effort to create one with a snap of his fingers, so the half-naked attire, or lack thereof, was clearly for my benefit. As was the bacon and coffee, although for an angel he seemed to have a fondness for food. And sex. And all sorts of other things I'd always assumed angels were too lofty to enjoy.

"My angel likes me half-dressed. And she likes bacon with her pancakes. Go ahead and get started, folks. We've got a busy day ahead." He gave me a swat on the rear with the hand not holding the tongs and pushed me gently toward the table.

He was cooking breakfast for me, before we embarked on a task that would either end in failure or might result in our deaths. He had welcomed Zeph to the table rather than send him home and have me all to himself. As much as I would have enjoyed him sliding under my sheets for morning sex then a romantic breakfast alone, this warmed my heart. A sexy half-naked angel, cooking bacon and sharing what might be our last morning with one of my pack-mates. It meant he had confidence that this would work out. And that he intended on having an eternity to have sex and romantic breakfasts with me. Sharing me with Zeph, embracing my family with open arms, made me love him even more.

"Milk and two sugars?"

He turned to me, holding the coffee pot, and I saw that in spite of the odds of death, he wasn't afraid. He had the same easy, casually cheerful smile that he always had. I suddenly realized that this was how Raphael dealt with an uncertain future. It wasn't that he was irresponsible, or irreverent, or immature, it was him understanding that even if he did everything in his power to steer his course, there was always an element of chance, of fate, that he couldn't control. Raphael saw that, and instead of working himself into a frenzy trying to control every little thing, he did all he could, then let go. What happened, happened. There was no sense ruining a beautiful morning, or perfectly good bacon, fretting about something that was out of his power to control.

That was the Chaos in him that the other angels didn't understand. That was the part of him I *did* understand. It was one of the many things about him that I loved. And those other angels were fools, every last one of them, for not seeing what an absolutely perfect being they had in their midst.

"That's the way I like it." I took the pot and waved him back to the stove. "I'll get us coffee. You keep frying bacon. That way I can admire your ass as you cook."

"Yep. Eating as fast as I can so I can get out of here before you two start swapping bodily fluids," Zeph announced. "And these pancakes are out of this world. What did you put in them, manna from heaven?"

Rafi set a plate of bacon at the table and took the outstretched coffee cup from my hand. "Oat flour. Ground pecans too."

And real maple syrup. I was going to weigh a million pounds with this angel cooking for me. "Yesterday he made yeast-raised ones and had raspberries and cream."

And the bacon, It was perfectly cooked. Not too crispy, not too fatty, with only a slight wave to otherwise straight strips of meat. They were thick chunks, with the tang of applewood smoke behind the mouth-watering smell of bacon. I had no idea where he'd gotten this stuff, but it hadn't been from my fridge.

"Next time it's pumpkin spice with a sweet cream cheese instead of syrup." Rafi announced as he sat down. "Or maybe the almond vanilla pancakes. Or the coconut and macadamia ones."

Yes. A million pounds. I wasn't going to complain, though. I loved food, and a guy who enjoyed cooking — a guy who cooked half-naked, unafraid of hot grease splattering on bare skin. My dream man...angel.

The three of us ate and joked, Zeph meeting every one of Rafi's wisecracks with one of his own. The whole time, though, a cloud hung over us. Great food. A sense of family. Witty, light conversation. But we all knew what was ahead. And Zeph and I knew in our hearts that the odds of finding Brent and the others alive were slim to none.

All too soon we were done. Rafi refused Zeph's offer to do dishes and the werewolf left, realizing that we needed time to ourselves. We cleaned in silence, the angel's spirit-self touching mine in a way that was more comforting than erotic.

"Let's pour some coffee in to-go cups and get a move on." Rafi said as he put the last dish in the cabinet.

I felt cold, realizing that as desperate as I was to find Brent and the others, to bring them home, I didn't want this morning to end. I didn't want this to be possibly the last of our time together. But I needed to remain positive. I needed to follow Raphael's example. Do my best, then trust in the fates to work in my favor.

I poured the coffee and plopped in the sugar cubes, digging the milk out of the fridge.

"We'll need to drive there," he told me as I popped the lids on our cups. "I need to save all of my energy for this."

I felt horrible, realizing what I'd asked him to do. A powerful archangel was worried that teleporting, that even the slight effort it took to reveal and dismiss his wings, would compromise his ability to open a stable gateway. He was doing so much for me, all to save a group of humans neither of us knew and a werewolf he saw as a rival. "No problem. We can take my Jeep."

I locked up and as we walked to the car, Rafi pulled the keys from my hand.

Seriously? "Do you even know how to drive? I appreciate the offer, but I'm not sure I want an unlicensed angel driving my car."

"I've experienced your driving. I can definitely say that I don't want a certain licensed angel driving me anywhere. I need to be calm and focused this morning. That's not going to happen if I spend a half-hour drive convinced that my immortal existence is about to come to a very bloody and abrupt end."

I pretended to be offended, and probably failed miserably. "I've been driving since the first car came to Alaska. Yeah, I'm not much for obeying the speed limit, but I know by now how fast I can take the corners without going over the side of the mountain. Sheesh."

He stashed my backpack in the rear seat. "I'll drive there, and I'll let you crash us into the side of a mountain on the way back. Deal?"

We'd be coming back. We'd be coming back, and we'd have Brent and those humans with us. "Okay. Just don't kill us."

He snorted, hopping into the driver's seat and starting the car as if he'd been driving for decades. "At least this way we'll arrive in one piece."

We might have arrived in one piece, but by the time we pulled up to the remains of the tourist shop, I was ready to strangle Raphael. He didn't know the roads, so he drove like a three-billion-year-old angel, slowing to half the speed limit at every curve in the road, and riding the brakes down every hill. If the bacon and pancakes this morning hadn't been so darned good, he would totally have been on my shit list.

But, pancakes. And he was doing all of this for me. And I loved him, even though he drove like an old man.

"Where are the remains of the creatures that came through?" Raphael asked, jumping from my Jeep and stepping over chunks of concrete and broken shelving.

I waved at Drake, the werewolf who was guarding the area then turned to point at a blue box. "There. In the cooler."

He stopped shooting me a puzzled look. "In a *cooler*?"

"We could hardly leave dead monsters lying around. People don't need to see that kind of thing, and we didn't know if their remains would pose a biohazard or not. The techs bagged them up and took them to the morgue for storage, but brought one back in case we needed it."

"And they put it in a cooler. With some ice packs and a six-pack of beer?"

Now that would be cool. Although it probably wouldn't be seemly to be drinking beer at sun-up. Nah. I was an angel. I could drink beer anytime I wanted.

The cooler didn't hold beer, and the head within had leaked gray liquid all over the inside. It stank. And it made me want to puke all the pancakes back up.

Raphael sighed. "The things I do for love," he muttered before plunging both hands into the cooler, elbow-deep in goo. The angel closed his eyes, and I saw a golden glow surround him, like an aura.

After about five minutes of this he pulled his hands from the cooler, shaking them and curling his lip at the disgusting mess that still clung to each finger. "You wouldn't happen to have a towel, would you?"

"No." I grabbed a filthy, dusty T-shirt from under a pile of broken glass. "Here. Use this."

He wiped his hands and threw the shirt into a corner.

"You fought these things? I'm impressed. And for the record, I've never felt anything so foul before in my life, and I've read a lot of pretty hideous beings."

"What were you doing?"

"I was reading their energy for clues as to where they might come from, as well as any memories that might have remained in their neural pathways. Of course this will only work if I'm familiar either with their location or somewhere nearby. And with the memories I'm reading comes all sorts of nasty stuff — emotions, flashes of individual experiences, sometimes a very graphic moment that was significant enough to remain imprinted for some time after death."

"Eww."

Rafi wrinkled his nose. "Tell me about it. I won't share with you exactly what this monster's significant life experience was. Suffice it to say that I'm feeling an urge to curl up with a blanket, a puppy, and a bottle of tequila."

"So what's next?"

"Where did the rift appear?" He walked around the ruins, looking around as if there might be a flashing neon sign that said rift was right here. "I didn't recognize the location based on that disgusting cooler of remains. I have some ideas, but I'm hoping there is enough residual energy left from the rift to guide me. Sometimes they close, but don't fully close. Even the ones we angels seal up sometimes have little tags that identify where they went."

I went over to the spot that was between the case of antler jewelry and the leather wallets — or at least where those two displays had once been — and put my hands out, framing where the rift had appeared. Raphael followed my motions, hesitating about three feet off the floor.

"There's a spot here. I'm going to see if, between this and what I got from dead-dude-in-a-cooler, I can open this." He looked at me, his normally lighthearted expression stern. "Stand back. In fact, stand over by the Jeep."

I didn't think that thirty feet was going to make a difference if this thing blew up. Besides, I was an angel. I'd just put the pieces back together and go on with my life. But there was something in Raphael's expression that made me take notice, so I did as he said.

The angel put his hands out then vanished, transformed into white light. I squinted against the brightness, feeling the thrum of power, a sound like wind chimes. Then the white became a swirl of color, coalescing into a line of gold that looked very much like the rift I'd seen.

"You did it!" I ran over, slowing when I saw how exhausted Raphael appeared.

"No I didn't. It's not the right spot." He took my hand and held it to the gateway.

"I don't know. I can't tell the difference. Are you sure?"

"Remember how the rift felt, the energy coming off of it, the sound and color of it and tell me whether this is the same or not. It doesn't feel right to me, but I wasn't here when the original one came into being."

I closed my eyes and felt the edges of the gateway, listening to the music it sang, feeling the pattern that the colors formed. No. The rift was red and orange with a yellow light. This was gold with a white light. The sound was all wrong. It just felt off, somehow. "You're right. This isn't the correct location."

He sighed, then closed it. "I'll try again."

"Can I help? Maybe if we join, you can feel how the rift felt. How it looked."

He smiled. It was that naughty little boy smile of his that made my heart sing. "I'm not sure I can concentrate enough to form a gateway while joined to you. You're very distracting, you know."

I felt my body come to life at his words. How could just the sight of him, just the sound of his voice make me long to touch him, to feel him inside me, to have his spirit-self wrap around mine and hold it tight, to feel myself fly as we became one, body and spirit?

"Well, restrain yourself. You're an angel, you're supposed to be all about patience. Put on a hair shirt or something and let's get this done."

"Sex afterward?" he reached out and put the pad of his thumb against my bottom lip. "Here in the rubble. If I succeed, will you reward me with a quickie?"

"If you succeed, I'll reward you with a blow-job," I promised, kissing his thumb and sucking the tip of it into my mouth, just to tease him a bit. It worked. His violet eyes darkened to a midnight purple, his breathing suddenly ragged.

"Deal."

He yanked me into his arms, kissing me as though he was going off to war. Then we came together, a swirl of color and sound as we joined. I shuddered, the barest part of myself still in my body. Trying to concentrate and not lose myself in the glorious sensation of being one with this angel, I showed him the rift from my memories, transferred to him every-thing I knew.

He pulled away, a portion of his spirit still merged with mine, then with a grin that was purely carnal he turned and put his hands out to the spot where the rift had been. This time I was in the center of it all feeling like I was about to be swept away in a tornado of energy. His spirit-self merged with mine was my anchor, the only thing keeping me from flying apart into a mess of particles.

The gateway opened and I saw it, felt it. The complexity of the construct was amazing, so far beyond anything I could even imagine doing. Then I recognized the pattern, the sound, the odd discordant note of the rift. He'd done it. Raphael had managed to find the location.

And then it all exploded. The angel wrapped himself around me — my physical as well as my incorporeal self. I felt the jagged bits of energy strip my skin, tearing the tiny edge of my spirit-being that Raphael hadn't managed to protect. When it was over and I opened my eyes, I saw the damage he'd taken physically. With a flash of light he'd healed both himself as well as me, but I'd seen beneath his form to the wounds his spirit-self had suffered, wounds his healing energy hadn't seemed to repair.

"I can't do it. I can't." His voice was wooden. "I'm so sorry, Ahia. I know how much this means to you, but I just can't manage this."

"But you *did* do it. You had it. It was there. It just wasn't stable. Maybe if we try again–"

"I can't do it." This time his voice had an edge to it. I looked up and saw the anger, the self-blame in his eyes. "You need a better archangel. I'll ask Gabe to help you. Or Micha. He owes me a favor, and I know he'll be able to open a gateway that doesn't explode. There's a war going on in Aaru, and I'm not sure they'll be able to get away, but maybe if I beg them…"

Before I could protest he walked away, hopping over the rubble, striding past my car and down toward the harbor. I'd seen the wounds on his spirit-self, the wounds in his heart. He'd always been the weakest of his four siblings, hiding his humiliation by acting the carefree clown. He didn't think he was good enough. He didn't think he could do it. I knew better, but I couldn't be the one to give him confidence. That was the sort of thing that needed to come from inside.

He needed his space right now, not me coddling him and being his cheerleader, so instead of following him, I sat down on a pile of shredded sweatshirts, put my head in my hands, and cried. I cried for Brent and the tourists, because by the time another archangel got here, it might be too late for them. It was probably too late for them already. With each passing minute I felt my hope eroding away.

And I cried for Raphael. I cried for the little angel who'd been loved by his siblings, but had grown up thinking he'd never be as powerful, as valued as they were. I cried for the archangel who felt like a fraud leading his choir, knowing most of the angels there were only using him as a stepping stone. I cried for the lonely angel who no one wanted, who suspected every advance was because of his position and status. For the beautiful, powerful, fun, daring, amazing angel that I loved.

I felt a hand on my shoulder and looked up into his violet eyes. He frowned, then wiped away one of my tears with his finger. "Don't cry. We'll find him. I promise, we'll find him. I'll try again. And again and again until I've got nothing left. I've already sent for Micha, but it might take him a few weeks to get here. I won't give up trying until he arrives. I promise."

Silly, adorable angel. I stood and threw my arms around him hugging him tight and nestling my face into the crook of his neck.

He stroked my back and murmured into my ear. "We'll find your werewolf friend. I won't let you down. I can't promise I won't screw it up, but I'll give it my best shot."

It took three more tries, but finally Raphael managed to get the gateway to stay open and hold back the explosion. I threw on the backpack and grabbed the rifle, standing beside him to wait for his signal.

"Ready?"

I hesitated. "You're coming, right?"

His face was grim. "I'm not letting you go in there alone.

I'm just not sure how long I can hold this together and I'm trying to give you a head start."

I nodded, feeling a sudden spike of fear. Raphael wouldn't send me in if he wasn't sure it was stable for travel. He certainly wouldn't send me in first if he didn't have faith that he could get me through safely. It was *him* I was afraid for.

"Go."

Jumping through the gateway, I felt it tear and pull at me. This was different than the others that had seemed more like doorways. This was like a huge tunnel. I flipped around, pushed forward and spun by unseen winds. Everything was red and orange with no substance, a discordant note so loud it hurt my ears. When I came out the other side I felt an explosion at my back, propelling me further forward. I was disoriented and fully expected to stumble and fall onto my face. What I didn't expect was to find myself free-falling through the air.

My wings burst from my back, ripping both my shirt and the straps from my backpack. I grabbed at my waist, and caught one of them before I lost the pack, my other hand clutching the rifle. The ground was far enough away that I managed to right myself and slow my descent somewhat before hitting gritty, metallic sand that thankfully cushioned my landing.

Jumping up I looked around in panic. I'd felt the gateway explode. Had Rafi made it through? Was he still on the other side? Had he been in that tunnel when it had blown up?

I stood up, slung the backpack and the strap of the rifle over my shoulder and debated what I should do. It was blazingly hot, especially for an angel who had lived in Alaska for five thousand years. Should I start walking to see if I could find Rafi? I was worried that he might be hurt and unable to heal himself after expending so much energy on the gateway. But I was afraid that I'd be heading the wrong way, that I'd get completely lost. I was afraid that if I left this spot, Rafi wouldn't be able to find me. After searching as far as my eyes could see for some sort of dark blob that could be my angel, I decided to wait. In an hour or two if he hadn't found me, I'd leave some sort of marker, and head out.

CHAPTER 31

The trip over the mountain had been harder than I'd imagined. We'd needed to use the climbing equipment for everyone except Kennedy and me. I'd stood at the top and basically hauled Renee up, then went down to tie Ray to my back for the climb up. It was impossible to do it any other way except putting him over my shoulder. We'd tried to immobilize his arm as much as we could, but by the time we were down in the valley, his face was gray and covered in cold sweat. Doc was right — this was a bad idea, although it was the better of a whole bunch of worse ideas. We couldn't stay in that cave to starve and die from lack of water. I couldn't run back and forth multiple times per day filling four plastic bottles and trying to hunt or gather food. But now we were faced with the prospect of camping out in the open on the edge of this valley.

"Should we stay here and try to reach the water tomorrow?" I asked Kennedy, nodding toward Ray.

She chewed on her lip. "How far is the water from here?"

I closed my eyes and lifted my head, scenting the breeze. "Five miles, give or take."

"Ray can't walk that far. I'm not sure he can make it more than a mile, and we'd be traveling at a snail's pace."

"I can carry him."

Her lip twitched. "Aren't you tired? You hauled four people up that mountain and fireman-carried Ray. Sure you don't need to run around naked for a while to recharge before you perform any more heroic feats of strength?"

I was tired, but I needed to make sure these humans were safe. "I'll get naked once we get to the water, I promise."

"I'm going to hold you to that." She looked over at Ray once more. "We can't keep bumping his arm around."

"I'll carry him like this." I scooped Kennedy up, one arm under her thighs and the other supporting her back. It was worth it to hear her quick gasp, smell the faint scent of lavender and vanilla from her hair.

"All right, Muscles. If you can carry him like this for five miles, then this doctor gives her approval."

Five miles took much longer than I'd anticipated. Renee was struggling. Crystal and the two boys were clearly not used to long hikes like this, especially thirsty and hungry. Even Kennedy looked like she was ready to collapse. It was beginning to grow dark when we staggered in view of the water. Kennedy insisted on running it through her little filtration system, while I set the boys and Crystal to finding wood both for a fire and for a shelter.

There were much larger mountains about twenty to thirty miles straight ahead. We were in a rocky-sandy area with knee-high blue-green grasses and squat, gnarled trees. The trees were taller, greener, and clustered closer together near the creek, and off to our right I could see what seemed to be thick forest. That might be where we'd want to go eventually, but I didn't want to drag everyone all over the place with our food supply at zero.

The boys started a pile of sticks, then ran off for more while Kennedy passed out the water bottles.

"Can you get a fire going? I'm going to explore a bit around the area while it's still light out," I asked her.

"Does this involve you getting naked again?" she teased.

"Actually it does."

She sighed. "Fine. I'll stay here, make a fire and check everyone's injuries. But the next time I want to run around naked with you too."

"Next time," I promised. Then I headed along the creek bank until I was out of sight to change. Stripping off my clothes, I began to shift. Claws and snout lengthened, fur thickening along my arms and torso. I dropped to all fours, stretching when I finally finished. Then I ran.

The fur shielded my skin from the setting sun, cooling me as I raced toward the forest. My clawed feet dug into the dense sand and dirt, kicking up behind me. It felt glorious. My blood sang with the extension and contraction of each muscle. With the snout, I definitely scented the aroma of plentiful water in the wooded area.

And the smell of something else — cooking meat. While that meant there was something edible, a deer or rabbit or whatever animals they had here, it also meant that there was someone, something, cooking that animal. The fur prickled up on my neck, rising in a ridge along my spine. Something deep inside me growled, warning me that whatever awaited us in the forest, it wasn't something I wanted to meet face-to-face.

CHAPTER 32

RAPHAEL

*E*verything exploded as I exited the gateway. I knew my hold on it was unsteady, but kept it together enough to ensure Ahia got inside before it slipped from my grasp. In all my three billion years never had I known of a place so resistant to connecting to a portal.

I revealed my wings, tried to fly, but couldn't. I was drained, exhausted. I'd given every last bit of myself to keep that gateway from tearing us apart, and being shoved through it, keeping Ahia safe had thrown me completely off balance. I didn't even know which way was up. I spiraled downward, unable to lift a finger to help myself.

When I hit the ground I bounced, feeling bones twist and snap even though I'd landed in something that felt like warm, gritty sand. When I came to rest, I could do nothing but lay there, wings sprawled out, limbs bent in places they shouldn't be bending.

Ahia. I had a moment of panic thinking that she might have been trapped in the gateway, crushed when it closed, but I remembered sending her through ahead of me, feeling her with me when we'd come through the other side. In the disorienting fall, we'd separated, but she was here. Somewhere.

And although I was relieved she'd not been trapped in the gateway, I wasn't sure how much better off she was here. I should have made her wait on the other side while I went on this rescue mission. I shouldn't have sent her through. I knew they were prone to instability. They'd self-destructed three times. What did I think would happen? We were trapped here and I wasn't sure I could manage to get us back home. This was all my fault. I'd screwed up once again, and no shrug and cocky grin would make this one go away.

I healed myself, nearly passing out from the effort, and got to my feet. She had to be close by. Where was she? If she was lying crumpled and injured in the sand, I'd never forgive myself.

"Raphael!"

I nearly dropped to my knees in relief hearing her voice. I turned around and saw her, running as best she could across the sand, using her wings for balance. I staggered toward her, falling backward to the ground as she launched herself at me.

"I waited for you where I landed, but when you didn't come I went to look for you. Thankfully I chose the right direction. When I saw you lying on the ground, I thought you were dead. But then I saw you stand, saw you heal your-self. You're okay. You're okay." Her voice rose in pitch, fear in her eyes as she ran her hands all over me. I won't lie, it felt good. It gave me an excuse to lay there on my back with her on top of me for just a few moments longer.

"Yes, I'm okay. It knocked me sideways when we were thrown through and I couldn't manage to fly, so I crashed pretty hard. Are *you* okay?" I got to feel her up too, just to check for injuries, of course.

"I fell through, but I managed to right myself and get my wings under me. I couldn't see you. I'm fine, but," she bit her lip, looking up at me. "Do you think they fell too? Did the rift come out that far above ground? Because I'm not sure anyone, even Brent, could have survived a fall like that."

Something made me think the rift hadn't opened at quite the altitude that my gateway had. "Those weird monsters came through, and by your description I doubt they could fly. If they were pulled through the rift, it couldn't have been too far above the ground."

She nodded. "Do you think they came out near here? I don't know how big this planet is. I'm hoping we don't have to search it all."

I scanned the horizon. "We'll just have to start looking. I followed what I knew of the rift pattern, so I doubt they came out more than a few miles from here at most."

The breath she let out did nothing to ease her tension. Her head dropped to rest on my chest, her hands fanning out along the side of my ribs. "Oh Rafi, how are we going to get out of here? We might be stuck here as well."

I didn't have the heart to add to her worries. Yes, we were most likely trapped — at least for the time being. It would take me a while to recover enough energy to attempt another gateway, but I'd do it. Even if it killed me, I'd make sure Ahia got home safely, with or without her werewolf and the humans.

"I'll figure out a way," I told her instead. "We'll search for signs of the others. I doubt they stayed here in this heat, so I'm going to assume they'd head toward those mountains off in the distance."

"It's so hot. If they were injured, they'd have died of heat-stroke or dehydration by now." Her voice was defeated.

I cupped her cheeks and kissed her forehead. "Then we'll find their bodies, and you'll know what happened. If we don't find their bodies, then there's a good chance they made it to shelter. Keep positive. We're here. We came for them.

We might as well assume they're alive and waiting some- where out of the heat for rescue."

Her head came up, eyes sparkling. "I can't imagine my life without you. I love you." Then her lips met mine, pouring every bit of feeling and emotion into the kiss.

She loved me. By all that was holy she actually loved me. I'm not sure where I stood in relation to this werewolf-guy, but she felt something for me that she didn't feel for him. When she pulled away, I reached out to touch her hair, stroking her spirit-self as I ran my fingers through the dark strands.

"I love you too." I'd never been one to hide my feelings. Ever. Even if it meant I was vulnerable. Even if it meant I got hurt. Although I got the impression that this was one time I wouldn't walk away with my heart in pieces.

She gave me a quick kiss then pulled back. "Let's go rescue some humans and a werewolf." Her smile turned wicked. "And I believe I owe you a blow-job."

CHAPTER 33

AHIA

*R*afi had to take a raincheck on the blow-job, and as much as I wanted to snuggle up to him and forget about the world, time was most likely running out for Brent and the others. And then there was the sand, which was hot and especially gritty, and managing to work its way into all sorts of areas that sand should not be.

We decided to search on a grid pattern heading toward the mountains in the distance, looping back and forth so we didn't lose track of each other. I was scared. I was scared to be separated from Rafael. The day's activities had taken a visible toll on him, but even with the wounds to his spirit-self and his exhaustion, he was still the most powerful being I'd ever known. What if those raggedy monsters showed up and ambushed me? What if this endless sea of sand disoriented me and I never saw Raphael again? What if I was alone here, trapped for all of eternity?

But Raphael would never leave me. If we somehow lost each other, I had faith that he'd find me. He'd turn this world upside down to find me. And as much as I didn't want to draw attention to our arrival, if I needed to I'd fire the rifle.

That would bring Rafi, and I was hoping bullets would either deter or take down any attackers.

After the third circuit, we met in the middle and eyed the mountains. I thought they were about ten miles off, but they looked to be close — maybe five miles at the most. It was slow going having to weave back and forth on our search and I weighed the possibility that Brent and the others could be in the mountains suffering from exposure and dehydration versus the chance that we might miss them or their bodies if we headed straight there.

"Hey." The angel's fingers caressed my cheek and he pulled me close for a soft kiss. "We'll find them. I'll get us back. And I will kill anything here that so much as looks at you wrong."

I know he was trying to make me feel better, and in a way his words did. As long as I was with Raphael, had him nearby, I'd be fine.

We continued for three more hours, crisscrossing each other's paths multiple times. The sun was touching the horizon, temperature dropping a good twenty degrees before I saw it — something rectangular and reflecting the setting sun in a section of churned-up sand.

It was a cell-phone. I couldn't believe there would be any other reason for a high-end Samsung smart phone to be someplace that I was pretty sure didn't have cell reception. It must have belonged to one of the tourists.

The battery was drained. And about six feet from it was a suspicious mound of sand. With my heart thumping, I knelt down and brushed the grit away, revealing a body.

It wasn't Brent. It was a girl with reddish hair and a nose piercing. She was wearing jeans and a snug blue shirt. Her arms had been folded across her chest, and resting in the spot they made was a gold chain and a packet with one of those tiny freshwater pearls the jewelry stores give away to cruise ship patrons. I recognized her — she was one of the teenagers. And she couldn't have been more than sixteen or seventeen.

Tears stung my eyes as I covered her back up with sand. She'd been buried. They'd taken the time to leave a few mementos and cover this girl's body. That must mean that at least some of them weren't terribly injured. I didn't see any blood in the area or signs of a struggle. I didn't see any other graves in the sand or out-of-place items. This must have been where at least some of them had landed. And the only logical place for them to go from here, the only place promising shelter from this horrible heat, was the mountains.

There was more churned-up sand heading into the distance, but I waited, knowing that Raphael would soon miss me at the crossing point and come to find me. Soon enough I saw the angel, outspread wings casting long shadows on the sand as he approached. I waved the phone in the air and after he ran to meet up with me I told him what I'd found.

"It won't be light for much longer." Raphael looked at the churned up sand leading into the distance. "Let's follow this track as far as we can. Hopefully there's somewhere we can shelter for the night. There's a sandstorm in the distance, and I don't know enough about weather patterns here to tell if it's coming our way or how fast it's moving."

A sandstorm. I began to panic. "We've got to hurry. If this path gets smoothed over, we'll have no way of telling where they went, if they made it to the mountain range or turned off somewhere along the way."

Raphael started walking and I followed. "That's not the only worry. Unless we make it to the mountains we won't have shelter from this storm. I suggest we keep moving even after dark. Your night vision should be just as good as mine, and if not I can create a globe of light. I've no desire to be out here, exposed, during a sandstorm."

Me either. Raphael stepped up the pace until I was nearly jogging alongside him. He stretched one of his wings up and out, pulling me close to his side. Then he curved it around my shoulders, warming me against the rapidly dropping temps.

The sun seemed to vanish within seconds, leaving the landscape black with gray from the light of two moons. It was so cold that each inhalation stung my nose. I shivered and Raphael wrapped me tighter in his wing.

He was hurt, exhausted, and here he was, warming me, practically carrying me as we moved forward. I reached out with my spirit-self to touch the damaged parts of him and felt him wince.

"Sorry." I didn't mean to hurt him. Honestly, he was scaring me. I felt like he was pushing ahead on sheer willpower alone. He was my anchor in all this, and seeing him hurt and tired worried me to the core.

"No, it feels good. I like when you touch me."

I felt his smile and again reached out to brush against him, soothing the hurt, stroking and merging portions of myself, pouring every bit of my feelings for him in each touch.

"Okay, now you better stop it. Unless you intend on doing that blow-job right now. In that case, keep going."

I laughed, then stumbled as my foot caught something. Don't let it be another body. Was it a body? Raphael stopped, pulling his wing away to stoop down at my feet. I immediately began shivering, my teeth chattering in the cold. I'd lived my whole life in Alaska. I was used to cold temperatures. My inability to shrug this off sank in and I realized how low the temperature had dropped. Was it forty degrees? It had been spring back home. The locals were practically in tank tops, but the tourists in the store had been in T-shirts and light jackets. None of that would be enough to be comfortable in this. Brent would be fine in his wolf form. Actually if they found shelter and were able to huddle up against him in his wolf form, the humans might have had a chance of pulling through this with only some minor frostbite.

But this was night two. Two nights of this, hungry and probably dehydrated. Was that a body at my feet? I wouldn't be surprised.

"Is it…someone?" I whispered to Raphael, as if using my quiet voice would make it all go away.

"It's a purse." He stood and handed it to me. "A tiny purse. I guess women use them kind of like wallets?"

I took it from him, squinting at it in the darkness. My night vision was not as good as Raphael's and all I could make out was some kind of leather wristlet. I frowned trying to remember. A woman and two boys. She'd had a bag, but I think it was one of those big, cross-body ones. An older man. Brent. That woman waiting for the bus to go hiking or rock climbing or something. No, she had a backpack. Two girls, late teens or early twenties. They both had wristlets. So possibly one of them.

No woman would have left her purse behind, even if she'd found herself suddenly transported from a tourist shop in Alaska to some interplanetary desert, but a wristlet? I opened it up and squinted to make out the contents. Money. A door pass key. A driver's license. It was too dark to make out the picture, so I stuffed the wristlet in my backpack for later.

"At least we know we're 'on the right track," I told Raphael. A sudden gust of wind whipped my hair to the side and I realized with a sinking heart that we were out of time.

"Come on." Raphael grabbed me so fast that I nearly

dropped the backpack, yanking me up into his arms. Then he sort-of ran-flew, using the wind at our backs to push him forward and slightly upward. The wind picked up, sand whirling around the angel and stinging me in the face. The storm was changing direction, and we'd soon lose our speed-boost. Sure enough Raphael began to struggle, his feet now firmly on the ground as he powered forward against the wind. Since he could no longer use them to propel himself forward, he wrapped his wings around me, sheltering me in a cocoon of warmth that protected me from the sand.

I realized he was going to continue this way until he either found shelter, the storm passed, or he dropped from exhaustion. He'd keep going, carrying me, keeping me warm and safe while he bore the entire brunt of the storm and the cold.

I wasn't used to being the weak one, and I certainly wasn't some princess, some damsel in distress to be saved, but from a practical standpoint there was no alternative. Walking I'd just slow us down, and I doubted I'd be able to withstand the storm as well as he was. So instead I snuggled into his warmth, soothing him the only way I could, by connecting my spirit-self with his. I felt him respond, somehow strengthened by my touch, so I continued. Yeah, I was probably turning him on, but if we were going to freeze or be sand-blasted to death, might as well fool around a bit before we died.

You're a very bad angel, you know that? I heard him in my mind.

Can you hear me? How are you doing? Is the storm any better?

Worse. I'm just walking blind right now, hoping that I'm not going in circles.

I felt tears sting my eyes. We were going to die. He was going to die and it was my fault for insisting he open a gateway, for dragging us into this mess.

Hush. I'm three billion years old. I'm fully capable of saying no, although that's a very difficult word for me to say to you. I made my choice, and I'm here of my own free will. Don't blame yourself.

I wasn't sure that made me feel any better. The storm was worse. How long could he hold out? How long could he keep this up?

I may look like a pretty-boy, but I'm tough. I'll outlast the storm. I do want to warn you that your friend, the humans, they may be in trouble if they've been caught out in this without shelter.

I wouldn't have found the cell phone if there had been a previous storm like this, or the path. I'm sure they've arrived at some shelter by this point.

If one or more of them were hurt, it would reduce their chances of surviving even further. If it were Brent, he might have been able to heal himself, but an injured human wouldn't be so lucky. Hurt, walking miles in the sand, hungry, dehydrated, making it through a subzero temperature night and possibly this sandstorm.

But I'd promised to bring Brent and the others back. I needed to know. And if one or two had somehow managed to make it, then I owed it to them to keep trying.

Although right now I wasn't doing squat. It was Raphael doing all the work, and he didn't even know those humans or have any responsibility for them. He didn't even like Brent.

There's something odd in the storm pattern. I think something is breaking up the velocity, altering the direction of the wind. We might be close to the mountains.

I caught my breath, understanding what he was trying to say. There might be no more than a boulder or two sticking out of the sand, but if they were big enough to cause a shift in the wind, then they would be big enough to shelter us from the storm.

Yes. A definite difference in the wind. There's something ahead.

I felt it too, felt him moving faster, with less resistance, felt him stride forward with renewed energy and hope. I waited, unwilling to break his concentration when it was so important for him to find this shelter. I didn't even realize he'd done it until he shifted his wings aside and set me down on the cold stone of a cave floor.

"The storm is beating against the side of the mountains and bouncing back. It's the weirdest thing I've ever seen, Ahia. This is less like a mountain range and more like huge monoliths of rock just sprouted from the sand. We won't know if there's water or any kind of food until the storm passes and daylight, but at least we're safe."

I shivered. "And we can wrap ourselves in our wings and the emergency blankets to keep warm as we sleep."

"I'm not sleeping, but I will definitely wrap my wings around you to keep you warm. And I might do other things to keep you warm too."

Now that was the Raphael I loved. I turned around the cave, unable to see anything and afraid to move lest I fall down a hole or off a cliff.

"Here." The angel formed a ball of light between his palms and sent it upward, illuminating the ten-foot square space that branched off behind him into an angled tunnel. Bits of sand drifted in from the storm outside, but there was an expression on Raphael's face that made me realize there was something in here other than rock and sand. I turned around, wondering if I'd see one of the raggedy monsters, or some sort of giant cave spider.

Instead I saw a note.

CHAPTER 34

RAPHAEL

At the very back of the small cave was a piece of notebook paper with bold black handwriting on it — Brent's handwriting according to Ahia.

Finding a cave right at the edge of the mountain range like this meant the survivors would most likely have found it, too. The sandstorm had been brutal, but I'd managed to keep to somewhat of a straight line using directional senses that I wasn't completely sure worked here. Whatever I'd done, the werewolf and humans must have done the same.

Went over the mountain, straight to the opposite range. We're heading to where I smell water. Will camp there, then onward hoping to find more water and food.

Ahia threw her arms around me, nearly crying with joy. "They're alive. At least some of them are alive. We'll ride out this storm, then head out in the morning to track them down."

"But in the meantime, you need to get some rest."

I sat her down, wrapped in one of the emergency blankets with a bottle of water and a granola bar from her backpack. She ate, then rested her head against my shoulder. "I know

Brent, and if he's with them, they're in safe hands. He'll take care of them, lead them to safety."

"Tomorrow." I turned to kiss the top of her head. "Right now I want you to get some sleep."

And sleep she did, wrapped in my arms and wings with an emergency blanket around the pair of us. I kept watch, hearing the storm die down and watching as the stars and two moons lit up the sky. I felt her warmth against me, her breath across my neck, her spirit-self curled against mine, and in spite of every effort to stay awake, I couldn't help but doze off, as comforted by her touch as she was by mine.

CHAPTER 35

BRENT

*D*arkness came quickly. It seemed day one moment, then black and gray the next.

The humans shivered, huddled around the fire for warmth. I had mixed feelings about starting the blaze after what I'd smelled only a few miles away from us. We needed the warmth, and the firelight was reassuring a group that had seemed to be losing hope. But if whoever was in the forest saw it… I wasn't sure if they were friendly or not, but I didn't want an encounter in the night.

Please let them be friendly. I'll admit I was starting to lose hope, too. This was our second night here. It would be tough enough to survive here, but if we were attacked, it would seal our fate. Nobody had weapons beyond two pocket knives, Ray would be unable to fight, and I couldn't see Renee, Crystal or the two boys being able to help defend us. That left Kennedy and me. With no weapons. Which left me. I might be the Alpha of our pack, but I wasn't sure how I'd fare solo against what could be multiple opponents. And even if I prevailed once, I wasn't sure I'd be able to continue to defend us against repeated attacks.

Two nights. I was beginning to fear we'd be stranded here for the rest of our lives — our very short lives.

"You feel as tense about this whole thing as I do?" Kennedy asked. She was looking around at the darkness outside the little circle of firelight with a wary eye.

I nodded. "I don't want to scare the others but there's something in the woods over there. I didn't have time to go see what, but I can smell cooking meat."

She caught her breath. "We need to set up a watch. We've got a few stout branches we can cut down into makeshift weapons. I'll put the boys to work on it and at least we'll have a couple of them in case the worst happens."

It was a good idea, but I'd be more use to them on four legs than on two in a fight. And I needed Kennedy to know so she didn't try to brain me in the middle of the night, thinking I was a danger to them.

"Can you come over there with me away from the others?" I asked. "There's something I want to show you."

She eyed me, but still followed. "Seriously? Now? I mean, I've already seen it and as impressive as it is, I think the timing isn't quite right for us to be admiring each other's naughty bits."

I rolled my eyes, but felt a rush of heat at the thought. Great. We were all going to die and my dick wanted some action. "No, not that. I want to show you something else, something about me. I don't want you to think I've disappeared on you all, or whack me in the head with a stick if you see me. It takes me a while to change, so I can't just pop back and forth."

"What in the world are you talking about?" She folded her arms across her chest and frowned at me. "Watch you do what, gymnastics? Meditate naked? And how long is 'a while'? I'm freezing out here away from the fire."

I decided to answer her last question first. "If I rush it,

five minutes. Normally it takes me ten." I pulled my shirt over my head and unbuttoned my pants. "I'm a werewolf. I can smell and hear any intruders better in my wolf form and my night vision is better. Plus, I'm better able to defend you all as a wolf than I am as a weaponless human — or a human with a stick."

"A werewolf." Kennedy stared at me. "I'm very sorry, but I don't have anti-psychotic drugs in my first-aid kit."

"A werewolf. I'm not having a mental breakdown, I'm really a werewolf." I removed my pants and her eyes roamed over my body. I stirred in response, going half-mast. Great. If I didn't shift soon, I'd be standing in front of her sporting a massive woody.

She raised an eyebrow at my obvious response. "Either you're having a psychotic break or I am. Maybe I'm in a morphine-induced coma. I've fallen through an interdimensional rift to a place with two moons and am traveling with five people and a werewolf. Morphine-induced hallucinations, because this can't possibly be real."

"I'm going to show you. Just don't freak out or scream or anything. I don't want the others to panic."

"I don't scream," Kennedy muttered. "I'm not a screamer. And I don't freak out."

First time for everything, I thought. Then I began to change, bones and muscles rearranging, twisting, contorting. I heard Kennedy gasp, saw her back away wide-eyed. I rushed the change, knowing how horrific it looked. When I was done I faced her, panting from the effort, then waited for her to come to terms with my appearance.

I knew what she saw. I was dark gray, about double the size of a timber wolf with golden eyes. Slowly she approached, her hand outstretched. I could scent her fear mixed in with the lavender-vanilla scent of her hair and skin.

"Brent?"

Carefully, so as to not scare her, I lay down, resting my muzzle on the ground and wagging my tail. She put her hand on my head, running her fingers through my fur, tickling my ears, then smoothing her palm down my neck. "I'm in a narcotic dream, but I might as well go with it. Land of the Lost with a hot dude who's a werewolf. At least there aren't clowns, because that would really put me over the edge."

I nudged her hand in agreement and she continued to pet me a while. It was nice. It was more than nice. It made me wonder how her fingers would feel stroking their way across my skin. As if she read my mind, she smiled, brushing the fur along my nose before standing.

"Okay Muscles, you take first watch. I'll stay with the humans and carve some sticks. Come get me when it's my turn. Wake me when it's my turn." She looked at me, her expression stern. I nodded, although I had no intention of waking her unless absolutely necessary. Let her get her sleep. Let everyone get their sleep. It was fitting that I keep guard, that I be the one to worry, while they had what could be their last night of peaceful rest.

* * *

THE NIGHT TURNED out to be less than peaceful. Our fire was nearly down to coals when I first smelled it. The scent drifted in on the occasional breeze from the mountain we'd left behind, I'd thought the danger would come from within the forest, from the place where the smell of cooked meat had emanated. That place still worried me, but there was something out beyond the forest line that worried me more. I'd chosen to turn my back on the threat in the forest, to stare unblinking at the scruffy grass and sparse trees. That's when I saw them — dark shapes that shambled from rock to rock. They were man-sized, lumpy, their movements slow and careful. Most alarming was the fact that they gave off no scent whatsoever. If I hadn't been in wolf form, with my superior night vision, I would have never noticed them.

Back by the light of the fire, Renee was asleep, her two boys curled up next to her. Ray lay on his back, arm carefully cushioned by a pile of twigs. Crystal sat with her back against a rock, her long hair covering her face as she slept. Only Kennedy remained awake, watchful as she sharpened a stick with a knife. I approached quietly, jerking my head toward the tree line with a soft growl.

Kennedy caught her breath, then squinted as if trying to see what was out there. "What's out there? How many do you see?" she whispered.

I pawed the ground five times.

"Bigger than us?"

I shook my head.

"My size? What are the chances the two of us can take down five of them?"

I didn't need to answer that one. She knew as I did that our chance of surviving an attack was slim. Even in my werewolf form, five against two wasn't good odds. Especially since we had no idea what these things were.

"Think you can get close enough to get a look at them without them seeing you?" she asked, putting away the pocket knife and fingering the sharp edge of her stick.

I shrugged, not sure if the gesture was coming through accurately in my wolf form. Then I left, staying close to the ground and trying to hide among the shadows. The creatures had moved closer, but I still couldn't smell them, and their heat signature was faint, meaning their body temperature was almost that of the surrounding air.

Either way, I was unsure what to do. They didn't seem to be aggressive or attacking, just cautiously approaching. I tried to put myself in their shoes, or feet, or whatever. If I were out on a night hike or hunt, and saw or smelled something unusual, I'd investigate, too. And I'd be just as careful in my approach. *We* were the intruders in this world. It would be wrong of me to assume these creatures at the edge of the forest mean us harm.

And it would be stupid of me to assume otherwise. My senses screamed a warning, but I wasn't sure if I was just hyper-sensitive from being out of my territory and the care-taker of injured humans, or if these creatures were truly a threat. Either way, I'd need to be just as cautious as they were.

They'd be upon our little campsite soon. If they were hostile, I wanted them to reveal their intentions away from the humans I was trying to protect. It was time to make my presence known. Just in case the five figures hadn't realized I was here, I stomped on a twig, and watched as all five snapped to attention facing my direction. Breaking a few more twigs, I shuffled my way out into a clearing, pausing a few feet from the tree line.

Out in the open, light from the two moons gave greater visibility than in the forest. I was very aware that the creatures twenty feet from me could see my shape as well as the fur that covered my body. I was also well aware that my eyes reflected the light, glowing gold. But I could also see these creatures, covered in raggedy cloth with huge google-shaped eyes. Their snouts extended out not as far as mine did, but far enough to make it clear they were not human. And the grill of narrow pointed teeth at the end of their snout confirmed it.

One pointed a stick at me and I instinctively jumped to the side, not quick enough to avoid the flash of light that shot from the end of the stick. The light hit my front shoulder, searing through fur and flesh. I snarled, my eyes watering with the pain.

Had that been an attack, or just a panicked shot from a scared local? The wolf in me insisted it was the former, but I wanted to wait and see what they would do next. Still, I crouched at the ready, just in case another shot came my way.

The one with the stick shuffled forward, the others spreading out to the sides. I kept the camp at my back, vowing to run to the left and lead these monsters away if things went badly — well, more badly than they'd gone so far.

The creatures made a clicking noise, gesturing with their arms — all five of them. Were they waving me away, shooing me like they would a troublesome pest? Another flash of light came my way, and I successfully jumped to the side this time. No, they were clearly attacking.

So I did the same. Light stuttered like machine gun fire from the stick, but I moved faster than the creature could aim. The others scattered, but I pivoted, leaping forward onto one of them and clamping my teeth into the raggedy clothing. Only it wasn't clothing. The boiled leather-like surface gave way with a crunch, and foul liquid filled my mouth. Spitting and shaking my head, I switched to claws, scratching at their hard flaps of skin. Hands scraped against me, digging into my fur as the others tried to get me off their friend. The clicking increased in frequency and volume.

"Get away from him!"

The hands left me at Kennedy's shout. I once again saw flashes of light and abandoned the creature I was clawing to rush the one with the stick. Kennedy was grappling with him, trying to hit the creature with a burning stick as he kicked and pushed. The fire on the stick was dying, and as it did the others approached. Five against two.

I tackled the creature, knocking the stick from his hand. Kennedy jumped away, grabbing the laser stick and swinging the burning branch with the other hand. There was a flurry of clicks, and a scurry of sandy dirt as four of the creatures fled.

"How do I fire this thing?" Kennedy flicked the stick at the retreating figures, trying to shoot it.

I ignored her beyond hoping that she didn't manage to fire it in my direction. The creature beneath me seemed to be insect-like, with a hard exoskeleton under the flappy leathery bits. My claws had barely scratched the other one, but when I'd hit this one, I'd managed to dig one set of claws into the space where two body segments joined, sinking deep into soft, gooey flesh.

"You okay?" Kennedy asked touching my injured shoulder.

I nodded, wiggling my claws to free them from the creature. Hopping off, I carefully nosed the thing over, remaining alert just in case it sprang into action.

There was no springing into action anymore for this insect thing. Its eyes were smashed into glassy bits, teeth jagged chunks on the ground. Along the front, the leathery flaps were dotted with burns. It was dead, but what the heck killed it? I wasn't sure if it had been the eye injury, the fall, the burns, my claws in the back joint, or a combination of them all. Either way, I was betting that my claws must have hit something vital.

"Ugh." Kennedy extinguished her stick, and looked around. "Let's get back to the others. I've got a feeling those things will return, and although they seemed wary of the fire, I'm not sure how much of a deterrent it will be next time."

I agreed. If only we could figure out how their laser weapon worked, we'd have an advantage. There were probably more than five of those things in this world, and figuring out how to use their weapon against them would help if, or when, our paths crossed again.

Kennedy had gone back to comfort the others who had awakened at her shouts. It gave me time to change back into my human form and dress. I'd talk to the humans, reassure them that the intruders wouldn't be back. Then I'd change back into a wolf and spend the rest of the night ensuring that the monsters didn't return.

CHAPTER 36

AHIA

I woke with my head in Rafi's lap, his wing covering my legs. I could tell by his breathing that he slept, although from what little nighttime experience I'd had with this angel, I knew he was a light sleeper — when he actually *did* sleep.

Parts of his anatomy were not asleep. I smiled, seeing the bulge in his jeans right in front of my lips. Sexy, even if we were who-knows-where. I lifted my head trying not to wake him and slid my hand up his leg. Carefully I unbuttoned his jeans, the soft rip of the zipper sounding loud in the cave.

"Just what do you think you're doing, Hot-stuff?"

His voice was soft and raspy. I felt his hand in my hair.

"I seem to remember promising you a blow-job."

"Oh, well then by all means, proceed." There was a sexy little smirk in his voice. I was pretty sure if I turned my head and looked up, I'd see those dimples that never failed to slay me, but there was something else calling for my attention.

I ran my fingers along the teeth of his zipper, feeling him jump in anticipation. Then I paused.

He pushed his hips upward. "I know we're immortals, but I'm begging you to hurry things along a little bit."

"Struggling with those virtues again?" I fingered the pull of his zipper.

"Darling, lust has won the war this morning. I'm afraid all the virtues have fled the field of battle."

Taking pity on the angel, I reached into his pants and slid him free, skating my fingers along his base, then up his shaft to sweep my thumb across the tip. He jerked his hips again, this time with an involuntary movement. I continued to play, light touches here and there countered with a firm slide. I wanted to lay here all day in this cave, touching him, tasting him, but from the lightening sky I knew we didn't have much time before we'd need to set out. Taking him in my hand, I pumped three times, rewarded by a bead of moisture at the tip.

"Can I touch you?"

I reached out my tongue and licked the white pearl. "Spirit or body?"

He hissed. "Both?"

I'd need to scoot around for him to reach between my legs, but in spite of my reluctance to move from my warm spot I wanted this encounter to be physical only. There was something so naughty about getting an angel off like this, dragging one of the archangels down into the very belly of sinful ecstasy.

I made a quick decision. "Body only. And only what you can reach without me moving."

He made a grumbling disappointed noise and I felt his hand feel along my ass. "I can reach this."

Blowing a warm breath across the head of his cock, I smiled. "Then go for it."

Then I took him in my mouth, scooting more upright for a better angle. Tasting him with the flat of my tongue, I slid my mouth halfway down, then back up and off with a pop of suction.

"You're killing me," Rafi said, his voice strained. I wasn't sure if he meant what I was doing or that he was desperately trying to get my pants undone and reach between my legs — and having very little success.

I laughed and wiggled my butt, once again taking him in my mouth and this time dropping down until he hit the back of my throat and my nose brushed the soft curls of his pelvis. He let out a soft curse, and abandoned his futile efforts to get in my pants in favor of stroking my hair. Encircling his base with my hand, I pulled off once again, proceeding to lick and taste every inch of him.

His one hand tightened in my hair, the other stroking my neck. Once again I took him in my mouth, setting up a rhythm of shallow and deep bobs. Each time I pulled back I countered with a firm stroke. His hand in my hair gently pushed, encouraging me. I felt the tautness in his legs, felt him tense and swell, and I pushed down deep taking every bit of his release, then gently easing my mouth upward and off.

The sky was gray, light enough to travel. Rafi's hand stroked my hair, fingers tracing along my ear and cheek. "I wanted you to come too," he complained.

"And I wanted to concentrate on you without the distraction of your very talented fingers." I leaned my face against his waist and smiled up at him. "Raincheck. Next time I'll just lay back and let you have your way with me. Deal?"

That naughty glint shined in his eyes. "Deal."

CHAPTER 37

We flew up to the top of the small mountain, looking down into the valley below. It stretched out for what I estimated to be fifty miles, with a much larger mountain range hemming it in on the other side. To the right, the meadow-and-tree valley became thick forest. To the left, the trees spread farther apart until it seemed the landscape was solely rock and grass. I knew Brent would take the humans to the water, but where *was* the water?

"You know this werewolf best. Where do you think he'd head?" Rafi asked.

We could spot them best from an aerial view and cover distance better everywhere except that forest. But the presence of that many trees pretty much guaranteed food and water. "I don't know. I don't have his sense of smell, oddly enough. I'm thinking he might head toward the forest over there."

Rafi squinted. "Is that smoke? Maybe they started a fire?"

I hoped so. Otherwise someone else had started a fire. Was I a bad angel that I wanted the smoke to be from a naturally occurring forest fire as opposed to those raggedy-guys having a camp-out?

"Let's fly down to that forest and check it out." I launched myself off the mountain, holding the backpack in one hand and the rifle in the other. Rafi passed me to take the lead, sweeping down low.

"Wait. There's a creek or something down there. Let's fly along it before we go into the forest."

It was a good idea since we'd need to walk through the forest. Might as well rule out the banks of this creek. That's when I saw them — walking along the creek bank toward the forest. We swooped low, landing far enough away that we didn't startle them.

Brent ran, grabbing me in a crushing hug. I threw my arms around him, tears stinging my eyes.

"Ahia. I'm so relieved you're here. And I never thought I'd say this, but I'm glad that angel is with you."

We pulled apart and I saw the humans behind him, staring wide-eyed.

"Mom, they have wings," one of the boys whispered.

Crap. I'd gotten so used to the folks in Alaska knowing about the supernatural that I'd forgotten these tourists wouldn't.

"They're angels," Brent announced. "And they're here to save us."

Whatever alarm they might have felt at seeing two people with wings sprouting from their backs was obviously alleviated by Brent's words. Their relief was palpable.

"There are injuries," Rafi said to me. "We need to discuss a course of action. Privately."

What course of action? Heal the injured. Create a gateway. Hold it stable long enough to get out of here. If we needed to do it in shifts, then the humans would go first, Brent and us last.

"Okay, but we need to include Brent. He knows these people, and he's had a day longer than us to get a feel for this place."

Rafi didn't look pleased, but he nodded.

"And Kennedy, too," Brent added. He pointed at a woman with a backpack who was muttering something about narcotic-induced hallucinations. She came forward and we stood in a tight circle, with the others watching.

"I can't open a gateway right now. Well, I could, but we'd all die. I need time to rest. And if I heal the injured humans, I need even more time to rest and recharge." Raphael looked exhausted, and defeated.

"But you're an archangel," I said. "I thought…"

"I'm not God." He looked at the other two before turning back to face me. "Yes, I'm an archangel, but I have my limits and I've been running flat-out since I got to Alaska. At first I was trying to impress you, then I didn't want to let you down or disappoint you, but I'm pretty close to being useless right now. I barely got the two of us here. If I try to establish a gateway now, it will kill everyone. It might even kill me."

I was such an idiot. He'd seemed pretty God-like to me with all that power rolling off him. I didn't stop to think about all the things he'd been doing — teleporting, closing rifts, opening that gateway. Had I once shown appreciation for the huge effort he was making on my behalf? No. I might have thanked him, but I'd never realized the extent to which he'd gone to please me, to make me happy. His wooing wasn't just pancakes and sex, it was nearly killing himself to rescue my friend and seven humans. Had I ever given that much for someone?

"I'm sorry." I put a hand on his shoulder and brushed my spirit-self against his. "I didn't know. I'm so sorry."

He put his hand over mine and smiled. "I didn't want you to know. I wanted to be invincible, and I figured I'd have time to recharge, but everything kept happening. I made a choice, but now we need to figure out how to survive long enough that I can safely get us home."

"How long do you need to rest?" The woman asked. Kennedy. That's what Brent had called her.

"If I heal the injured, a week, give or take. If I don't, probably three days."

The woman's face fell and Brent put his arm around her. "We have no food or shelter, and we were attacked last night. We were on the move because I was worried they'd come back tonight. If we're going to stay here, we need to find a food source, plus a defensible area."

I exchanged glances with Rafi. Great. If we had to fight to defend them, it might take him even longer to recharge. "I've brought emergency blankets and vacuum-packed meals, but I've only got enough food for a couple days. I've also got my pistol and the rifle, but not many bullets."

"I've got some laser stick that the attackers used last night. Maybe you can figure out how it works," Kennedy said.

"Maybe…" Rafi frowned in thought. "If we go back to our original entry point, it should be easier for me to establish a gateway. The tracings of the last one should still be there. I'll need less energy if I don't have to start from scratch."

"But that one blew apart. Is it safe to use that framework again?" I asked.

Both Brent and Kennedy looked unnerved at my words. "It blew apart?" the werewolf asked. "Like blew apart after you were through, or when you were in the middle of it?"

"If it had exploded when we were in transit, we wouldn't be here," Rafi commented dryly. "But I was barely able to hold it together for the two of us to travel. It's going to be tough to hold it for the nine of us. Still, I think we're better off going back so I can reestablish what I did before. Judging from what Ahia told me and my efforts to get us here, I think any passageway is going to be somewhat unstable. I just need to do better; to modify what I did last time so it holds for us all to get through."

Was he pushing himself too far once again? I got the feeling that even rested and recharged, a stable gateway from here to home would take everything he had. But what was our alternative? We could hardly live out our lives here. None of the humans would want that, Brent and I wouldn't want that, and I'm pretty sure Rafi didn't either.

"What do you think?" Brent asked Kennedy. I blinked, wondering who this woman was that she'd made such an impression on my Alpha for him to ask her counsel.

"Ray needs healing. He's in such pain, and we can't keep asking him to keep going like this. Renee might be able to hold off, but having her ankle injured slows us down. I'd rather take the extra time and face whatever with a healthy group. We can ration the food. We've got water. We've got weaponry, two angels and a werewolf." She smiled at Brent and reached out to take his hand. "For the first time in two days, I actually think we're going to be all right."

CHAPTER 38

I healed everyone. The older guy had the broken arm and nose, but he also had a heart issue I took care of along with some arthritis and scar tissue in his knee from an old injury. The mother had a bad sprain, but also a spot of cancer that I'm sure she was completely unaware of. The boys were just cuts and bruises, as was the teenage girl. The other woman — Kennedy —was missing her leg. I stared at her prosthetic, baffled. I'd recreated my own limbs or those of angels more times than I could count, but I'd never 'healed' this traumatic an injury in a human.

She laughed. "Oh, the expression on your face!"

"What happened? It happened prior to your travel through the rift, obviously, or you wouldn't have an artificial leg."

"Car accident. I survived three tours in the Army only to nearly be taken out by a drunk driver. I'm lucky it was just my leg and not my life." Her expression turned serious. "I'm fine. I'd far rather we get out of here than have my leg back. I can get around just fine. Save your energy for the gateway."

"You don't believe any of this is real, do you?" I asked. The boys had been fascinated by my wings, following me around and peppering me with questions. Renee and Ray believed I was proof of the divine. I'm pretty sure Crystal wanted to date me. Actually, I think she wanted to do more than date me, which was a bit alarming.

Kennedy sighed. "I don't know what to think. This is all so unbelievable, like the plot of a big-budget fantasy movie. Rifts, and other worlds, werewolves and angels, raggedy bug-men with laser sticks. I might be in that weird twilight spot between life and death. I might be having drug-induced dreams or psychosis and I'll wake up in the hospital in a body cast. I'm just gonna go with it and act like it's all real because that's the only thing I *can* do right now."

I liked this woman. And Brent clearly did too. It's the only reason I wasn't punching his face in for running off with Ahia to fill the collapsible plastic jug she'd brought in her backpack. They were down by the creek, kneeling down, their shoulders touching.

"Are they together?" Kennedy waved toward the pair.

"Over my dead body," I muttered.

She chuckled. "Good. And if it's any consolation, I think angel beats werewolf in her eyes."

"And in your eyes?" I knew the answer, but just wanted to see if she'd admit it.

She looked down at Brent, her gaze soft. "Werewolf beats angel. Werewolf beats everyone."

Ahia and Brent came back from the creek with her five-gallon jug full, as well as four smaller bottles. We passed around the vacuum-packed meals and Ahia realized that she hadn't packed any silverware. Lunch was a messy affair, everyone laughing as they sucked cold stew and chicken dumplings through the metallic bags. Laughed. Joked. I could feel the relief coming off the humans, the renewed hope that they'd soon be home with their loved ones.

I'd done a good thing. I never would have bothered to go after them if Ahia hadn't been so adamant. I'm not heartless, I just was sure they were dead, that it would be impossible for me to recreate a passageway. It seemed that with Ahia, the impossible was achievable. Saving these people did something to me — it made me proud to be an angel. It made every exhausting effort worthwhile. It made risking my life to get them home worthwhile. I wasn't just doing this to impress Ahia or out of love for her anymore, I was doing it because these people's lives justified the risks I'd taken.

All too soon lunch was over and we were heading back toward the smaller mountains. Brent had the large water jug. Renee was carrying Ahia's backpack so the pair of us could take to the sky and scout ahead. The news that they'd been attacked last night sat heavy on me. Waving for Ahia to stay behind and fly closer to the rest of our party, I flew ahead, angling along the small mountain range to the highest point, about five miles from where the cave was. That's when I saw them. The figures were on the desert side moving toward the small mountains. We wouldn't meet up with them if they kept on their current heading, but we'd need to be quiet and forego a fire. With any luck, we could camp in the cave for a few days and give me a chance to recover my strength.

I folded my wings behind me and sat out of sight, watching the group as they approached. When they came near enough to count I saw they matched the description of the raggedy, bug things that both Ahia and the others had encountered. Brent said he'd fought five at the camp. This was eight of them.

I climbed down a bit so I wouldn't be visible as I took flight, then I headed back to the others. We'd need to keep low, and we'd need to hurry. I wanted us to be up and over the mountains before these guys were close enough to see us. And I wanted us out of here as soon as I was able.

CHAPTER 39

AHIA

We huddled together under the emergency blankets while Brent and Kennedy took turns keeping watch. He'd insisted that Rafi needed his sleep, that the pair of us were their best defense in case of attack as well as their ticket out of here. They needed us well-rested. I didn't argue, and I was glad to be cuddled up with Rafi, his wings wrapped around me as I dozed.

Kennedy stayed near the mouth of the cave, even when Brent was guarding us. I knew he'd taken his wolf form and was surprised not just that he'd revealed that side of himself to a tourist, but that he treated a human absolutely like an equal. He'd dated human women before, but they'd always been like China dolls to him — fragile objects to be pampered and protected. He treated Kennedy like a wolf, which made me wonder what exactly had happened those days they'd been here alone for him to recognize her not just as a bad-ass, but as an Alpha female.

In the morning, Renee and I sorted through the food I'd brought, rationing it in case we needed to be here a whole week. I figured by day five, if we thought we'd need to stretch our supplies, we could cut our meals even further. Thus breakfast was a protein bar each and water. I was dying for a cup of coffee. And a shower. And Rafi's pancakes. But I was sure the rest of the crew was wanting those things even more than I was. We spent our morning drawing a makeshift checkers board on the stone floor and using the kids' change as game pieces.

While everyone passed the time, cheerful and full of hope, I flew out on a scouting mission. Rafi had told me what he'd seen five miles down the range, and I wanted to check and see where the troop of raggedy-men were now. Raphael had a fit at me going alone, but we needed him to rest, and I'd promised him I'd come right back if there was any trouble.

I climbed to the top of the ridge above our cave, then flew with short, low hops along it, keeping alert for anything that moved, anything that looked out of place. I made it to the point where Rafi had seen the raggedy guys yesterday without seeing anything that made me pause. There were signs that the rock had been disturbed down below, where a logical pass through the mountains would be. I knew where they were most likely going, so I swooped down into the valley and flew close to the ground, weaving in and out of the trees. There was a trail of disturbed grasses. The body was gone from where Brent had skewered it with his claws. They'd been here, and they hadn't found our group at the campsite. I dropped to the ground and walked around the edges of the place where Brent and the others had bedded down for the night, seeing the spot of red where Brent had bled before he'd healed, the blackened remains of their fire.

Brent's blood. Any shifter worth their salt would have gotten enough of a scent from that to track the group. Actually any decent shifter would have gotten enough scent from the campsite to track us. We weren't particularly stealthy, and after a couple of days without bathing, we were a pretty fragrant group. A human could have probably tracked us at this point.

The thought was chilling. I knew exactly the route we'd taken, but hesitated, knowing Rafi would kill me if he found out I'd followed these guys and put myself at risk.

Oh well. I hadn't seen them when I'd climbed up to the ridge above our cave, but that didn't mean they weren't somehow camouflaged in the valley, or that they hadn't been camping for the day under the trees. I didn't know if these guys were nocturnal or if they traveled during the day, but I sure as heck didn't want them surprising our group and trapping us in the cave to pick off like fish in a barrel.

But I could hardy fly around looking for them, and walking in a human form was inefficient, plus I'd clearly look out of place here. I had only seen the raggedy-men the one time, but that had been enough to grab their basic appearance. That might not be the best idea, though. If they caught me wandering around and spoke to me, they'd know right away I was an imposter. I didn't know their language or culture. I'd be better off with a different form.

Not sure what would work best, I shifted into a sparrow and took off, trying to keep to the tree canopy as best as I could. Tracing Brent's route along the creek to where we'd met up, I headed along the route we'd taken yesterday and found the raggedy guys disturbingly close to the mountains, less than half a mile as the sparrow flies from our cave.

I hovered out of sight, unable to understand anything they were saying or planning. They'd tracked us this far. It wasn't a stretch to think they'd be able to find us in our cave. Would they wait for nightfall to attack? Would they call for reinforcements? Either way I needed to alert Rafi and the others. We needed to move, to stay one step ahead of these guys. Either that, or we needed to fight, and if we fought, we needed to make sure none of them survived to tell the tale of our presence.

CHAPTER 40

$\mathcal{I}$ had to fly a circuitous route to get over the mountain and back to the cave without being seen. Once there, I ran straight to Raphael.

"We need to leave."

The pair of us had said the words at the same time. Rafi took my arm to the cave entrance and pointed. At first all I saw was the red sands of the desert, then I realized some of those sands appeared to be moving. It was the raggedy-men, their leathery skin blending in with their surroundings.

More alarming, this meant we'd soon be trapped in between this group and the one just over the small mountain. Brent and Kennedy joined us and I told them all what I'd seen.

"Where do we go?" We'd be clearly visible on the sand. It would be impossible for most of our group to climb along the mountain to further down the ridge. Going over the top had been tough enough, and now we'd be dropping down right into a camp of raggedy-men.

"We'll have to head down into the sand, then hug the edge of the rocks." Brent said.

"They're tracking us," Kennedy argued. "We can't keep running and expect to stay ahead of them. They know this place better than we do, and they're close to trapping us."

"I agree," Rafi said. "We need to go. I need to open a gateway now and get us out of here."

I caught my breath. "You're not ready."

His eyes met mine. "I'll have to be ready. If I can hold it long enough to get the most vulnerable of our party through, then maybe we can fight these guys off and I can try again in a few days."

I didn't like the sound of that, but I was coming to realize that this was the only solution where the humans had a chance of surviving. "What can we do to help you?"

Rafi looked out into the desert. "I want to get as close to where we came in as possible. I know that will put us close to those raggedy guys, but I'll have a better shot at getting the gateway right if we're down there."

"We can hold them off," Brent said. "Ahia can blast them with lightning. Kennedy can take the rifle, and I'll take the pistol."

"That will work." Rafi turned around to head back into the cave. "We need to leave now. Right now. Grab everything you can because we're heading out."

There was a flurry of activity, and within minutes, we were climbing down onto the sand and running. If we'd been able to keep up the pace, we would have made it to where we'd found the purse before the raggedy-men were within shooting distance, but in less than a thousand feet we had to slow to a fast walk. Ray couldn't handle the pace. Crystal didn't have shoes for running any distance. We moved as quickly as we could, then halted at Rafi's signal.

"We're not close enough," I told him. I was worried — worried that he was going to kill himself trying to save everyone.

"I'm worried if we go any further I'll be dodging lasers as I'm trying to open the gateway," he replied. "Put everyone on guard so I can concentrate. Have the humans ready to run through on my word."

The angel began to concentrate while I conveyed his orders. Kennedy loaded my rifle, while I took the pistol. Brent pulled the laser weapon he'd retrieved from the raggedy-man he'd killed, and tried to see if he could figure out how it worked.

They'd seen us and they were running. I got ready. Rafi blurred into an aura of white and a gateway opened, red-orange with gold light. Then it winked out with a pop. With a deep breath, he tried again, and again, and again, each time unable to hold the gateway steady enough for travel.

Laser shots filled the air. I positioned myself to cover Rafi and ensure nothing hit him and broke his concentration, then I opened fire. Kennedy had swapped with Brent and he knelt beside me, shooting with the rifle while she banged the laser stick on her palm and shook it in the air.

The bullets were slowing the raggedy-men down, but not killing them. I heard Rafi's muffled curse, and looked over to see another gate pop and fizzle. He looked like he was ready to fall over. His hands shook, his face was ghostly pale. And through his exhaustion, he kept trying.

The raggedy-men were almost on us. I started aiming for their google-eyes, and was thrilled to see two go down. Brent's shots felled two more. We were finally killing them, but it was taking too long. There were too many.

Kennedy screamed and I saw a burst of laser-light coming from the opposite direction of the rest. It sliced one of the raggedy guys in half and I cheered. Between the three of us we were slowly holding our line steady.

"Got it!" I looked over at Rafi's shout and saw a flash of silver light. The gateway opened, orange and gold with a harmony it hadn't had the other times. I shot Rafi a questioning glance, not wanting to doubt that he'd got the end location right, but worried about the difference in sound. I needed to concentrate on keeping these guys away from us. He knew what he was doing. And besides, pretty much anywhere he took us would be better than here. Heck, I'd take Hel at this point.

"Go!" Kennedy shouted at Rafi's signal. Out of the corner of my eye I saw Ray vanish into the gateway, then Crystal, then Renee and the two boys. Brent motioned for Kennedy to leave, shooting as he backed toward the gateway. The woman waited for him, then with one last shot they were gone.

I unloaded the last few bullets then ran for the gateway, only to stop when I saw Rafi's face. He was struggling, and knew from one look that he was holding it open for me, that he'd not have the strength to hold it open once he got inside. He'd either die in there, or be left behind.

And neither of those two scenarios was acceptable to me.

"Ahia, go. Now. I'll be right behind you," he told me through clenched teeth. A laser shot ripped through my backpack. We were going to die here, or die in the rift, but I wasn't leaving him behind.

Another shot hit my leg and I stumbled. I felt Rafi's hold slip and dove for him, slamming my spirit-self into his and abandoning my physical form.

Together we can do this, I told him.

Lasers seared across his back and I felt him merge completely with me, leaving his body behind. Just as we came together as one, we jumped, soaring through the tunnel. I saw a bright light, felt the slam of an explosion, felt an excruciating tearing at the edge of our joined selves. I screamed in pain and Rafi launched me forward and away from him.

I was unraveling, then suddenly everything came together

— particles, atoms, molecules — and I found myself rolling across the sidewalk outside of an all-night convenience store just down the street from where the tourist shop had been, naked. The sidewalk was horrible, with old gum and dried ketchup, and smears of grease, but I wanted to kiss it. Home. I was home. My spirit-being hurt like I'd been bounced around a rock-tumbler, but I was alive.

I jumped to my feet, frantically looking around, and nearly collapsed when I saw him.

"We made it." He grinned at me, my very own angel. I reached out to him and felt the same wounds on his spirit-self as I had. We were hurt, but we were alive.

He came to me, crushing me and covering my face with kisses. "We made it. We made it. And I am so going to make you some pancakes tonight. Lots and lots of pancakes."

"And sex?" I asked hopefully.

"Definitely." He kissed me, hard and deep, only to pull away when someone nearby coughed.

Spinning around I saw Crystal and Ray, open-mouthed, Renee covering the eyes of her two boys, Kennedy with a huge grin on her face, and Brent, shaking his head and rolling his eyes. Behind them were people pumping their gas and slurping fountain drinks, staring. Drivers going by were slowing down to gawk.

"Ahia, think you might want to create some clothing before you get arrested?" Brent said.

I looked down at my naked body then laughed. After everything we'd faced in the last few days, indecent exposure was the least of my worries.

"Shall we go home, where you can be naked without fear of arrest and I can feed you pancakes while you lounge on your sofa?" Rafi whispered in my ear. He revealed his wings, and mine also burst into view.

Home. Our home, not just my home. "I'm all about naked dinners, Pretty-boy. Let's go home."

IMP WORLD NOVELS

The Imp Series
A Demon Bound

Satan's Sword

Elven Blood

Devil's Paw

Imp Forsaken

Angel of Chaos

Kingdom of Lies

Exodus

Queen of the Damned

The Morning Star

* * *

Half-breed Series
Demons of Desire

Sins of the Flesh

Cornucopia

Unholy Pleasures

City of Lust

* * *

Imp World Novels
No Man's Land

Stolen Souls

Three Wishes

Northern Lights

Far From Center

Penance

* * *

<u>Northern Wolves</u>

Juneau to Kenai

Rogue

Winter Fae

Bad Seed

ACKNOWLEDGMENTS

A huge thanks to my copyeditors Kimberly Cannon and Jennifer Cosham whose eagle eyes catch all my typos and keep my comma problem in line, and to Damonza, for cover design.

Most of all, thanks to my children, who have suffered many nights of microwaved chicken nuggets and take-out pizza so that Mommy can follow her dream.

ABOUT THE AUTHOR

Debra lives in a little house in the woods of Maryland with her sons and two slobbery bloodhounds. On a good day, she jogs and horseback rides, hopefully managing to keep the horse between herself and the ground. Her only known super power is 'Identify Roadkill'.

debradunbar.com